From The Wom
34 Great Sutton St

C000004512

Ravinder Randhawa is a founder member of the Asian Women Writers' Collective. She has published in the anthologies *More to Life than Mr Right* (Piccadilly Press, 1986) and *A Girl's Best Friend* (The Women's Press, 1987); *A Wicked Old Woman* is her first novel. She has worked for an Asian women's organisation which set up refuges and resources centres for Asian women, and has been involved over the years with the Black/Asian Women's Movement and in anti-racist campaigns. She is currently researching an idea for her next novel.

RAVINDER RANDHAWA

A Wicked Old Woman

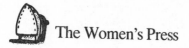 The Women's Press

First published by The Women's Press Ltd 1987
A member of the Namara Group
34 Great Sutton Street, London EC1V 0DX

British Library Cataloguing in Publication Data

Randhawa, Ravinder
  A wicked old woman
  I. Title
  823'.914[F]   PR6068.A5/
  ISBN 0-7043-5032-7
  ISBN 0-7043-4078-X Pbk

Typeset by MC Typeset Ltd, Chatham, Kent.
Printed and bound by Hazell Watson & Viney Ltd, Aylesbury, Bucks.

To Ramesh

Red teardrops on a Russian doll. More real than the salt-tasting water running down her face: transient, impermanent couriers of grief. One wipe of the tissue and erased for ever, leaving the face unmarked and clear like newly washed sand. A false front to the pain that still lay coiled within. Rubbing the tissue over the doll's face: the dust removed, they glinted a new greeting. Fingering their solidity, she is reassured by their permanence.

Kulwant hadn't known then that playing with nail polish would be a playing with fire and that in trying to give her doll a bindi the scarlet blob would slip from the loaded brush and landing on the cheek run a red streak all the way down to the chin and there, come to a quivering full stop. Tears come in couples. Load the brush again and carefully drop a scarlet blob on the other side. It lands by the eye and sticks and stays. A pretty dysjunction.

Kuli's Cover-up

Stick-leg-shuffle-leg-shuffle. Stick-leg-shuffle-leg-shuffle.

Walking on the stick was still an experience; its staccato ringing on pavements an out of tune accompaniment to her experimental walking. She'd tried the slow quick step, setting herself a prancing pace on thin high heels, simulating a non-existent busyness; till the day when the mind quarrelled with this mincing and tangled the stick with the inch stepping feet. The bruises weren't many and the indignity there wasn't any but she was bored and agreed with the mind the need for a change. Trying out a basketful full, a variety of walking, culled from the endless watching of those on the streets; if they had known what entertainment they provided each would have charged a fee for every cackle from her lips. Resisting the temptation to prolong her studies into the territory of human perambulations, she decided waddling was the best and that's what she did.

Seen from above, she was a strange three-legged insect, head waving on a thin neck, the neck resting on a thick bulbous body whose sides waved and swayed as it manoeuvred in its travelling.

'You don't need it, Mrs Singh. There's nothing wrong with your back. Your back's all right,' shaking the yellow hair around her nurse's cap, sending out a little spray of dandruff and raising her voice another notch. 'What shaking? You've walked up and down this room Mrs Singh. I've watched you. The doctor's watched you. There's nothing wrong with the legs or your back,' voice now lowering itself into the file in front. 'Not so sure about the HQ. If anything needs investigating that does.' Closing the file in a gesture of finality designed to signal Mrs Singh the futility of her efforts, hoping she'd understand the sign language if not the Anglo-lingo. Mrs Singh was too far gone to give up and muttered another list of reasons. 'The outside is different? We all live in the same world, Mrs Singh. You've been here long enough to know that.'

'Long enough to know that's a lie.'

'What was that, Mrs Singh?' Voice jumping another notch on the noise-o-meter. 'You want to have a lie down? Now you know you can't do that, and you don't need to anyway. Yes I know this is a hospital. I should know. I work here. But it's not a hotel, Mrs Singh. A-l-l r-i-g-h-t?' Nurse speaking slowly and carefully wanting Mrs Singh to understand and go away.

Persistence (sometimes) does turn a wish into a fact and finally flung into her hands this badge of old age she wanted so bad; one thing leads to another and making friends with the new walking accomplice necessitated procurement of the right accessories which were only to be acquired at the local Oxfam boutique.

The sweet-smile ladies thought it strange and said so loud to see an Asian lady trying and choosing cast-offs and rejects of who knows who for it was said they were particular about second-hand skins. 'Oh dear,' she said. 'I meant second-hand things, how my daughter muddles me up till I don't know what, mixing my standards with my slangs, but that's not the usage these days too. I can't keep up. Can you? Oh, thank you,' taking the old delapidated coat, with a headscarf of matching degradation and wanting to suggest to the lady that she could have one of the better coats and with a wink and a nod the price could be adjusted but wary of wading into waters unknown for these Asians were particular about their pride; for losing face was a social calamity as anyone who'd read John Masters should know.

Going out, and making her way to the public loos; casting a cautious look to check that no one she knew would know that she'd gone into the Ladies Convenience for a character change

3

for the she that emerged up the urine stairs could be an old bag or a smelly hag whose address was a patch under the Charing Cross bridge.

Kuli's Double-Up

Waking up on a dark English morning, rain pitting against the windows of her emptied house, widowing her of all enthusiasm and adventure. Ignoring the reproaches of the hard-won stick, leaning lonesome in the corner, she pulls the quilt over her head and burrowing into the darkness closes her eyes waiting for the shifting shades of darkness to take her back to sleep. Instead of slumberland her mind travels backwards to unlock a segment in the past where she's a teenager in pig-tails, running wildly down a flight of stairs; school satchel flying out behind her, pushing through the crowded corridors, dodging furtively across the dividing strip of green and through the doors, into the silence and secrecy of the gym.

He was living up to the lie, notebook in hand checking off the equipment that remained and calculating that which had gone AWOL. His blue eyes lifted as she entered and giving her a list he told her to start on the cricket section. Taking her cue and keeping her face straight she obediently turned to follow his instructions, but a hand on her plaits pulled her back and two arms came sneaking round to hold her tight.

Running down the school drive, heart and feet thudding, mustn't miss the bus, must be home at the right time, must maintain the outward pattern, mustn't let suspicion get a toe in, mustn't blow apart her salvaged bits of freedom.

Believing the messages that came with the jam, spreading the golliwog's smile on hot buttery toast, biting it, and crunching it and swallowing it whole as the eyes read avidly of Kipling's Kim, or latched like leeches on to Stewart Granger in *Bhowani Junction*. What the food and fiction missed out the history and geography books filled in: Clive coming out shining like a saviour and Wilkes got his gain, by gaining the ear of the whole nation. Freedom become an English patent and to be free was to imitate an Englishness and in those early days of immigration, when she was the only Asian among a sea of whites, she was so continually and constantly different to yearn to be the same and being the same meant having a boyfriend.

Being her she went one better and got the one that everyone wanted and listened in delight to catty barbs that wondered how he could fancy a plain and dumpy dowd like her. She'd caught the school status symbol and gained the status to be bitched about. He being with her erased for ever her given position as that old-fashioned, traditional Indian girl in pig-tails.

He turned her differentness inside out, creaming her as his 'Indian Princess', 'the mysterious oriental woman', and the 'Mata Hari of his heart'. She feigned nonchalance though every pore of her loved every syllable and not till later did the memory cringe at these borrowings from schoolboy comics.

Michael the Archangel, she called him though never told him, reserve reining in her tongue, come down to earth just for her, all finished off with golden hair and bright blue eyes.

She was avid with hunger to learn, experience and experiment, to step out from her insulated, closed-off home life and dip her feet into the world's whirlpool; feel the swirl of the waves knocking through her skin, telling her of the ways and whys of how things are: to discover whether the fire in the flesh was only a story printed in the fiction books and if this life was clay for her to mould or a viscous substance, resistent and tacky, so sticky on her fingers that they'd be changed for ever.

Michael the Archangel was the first shake of a kaleidoscope and she a newly emergent Machiavelli; soon skilled in circumventing the protective barriers of parents and community: lying with ease to cover her tracks, lying with ease to clear her path. Aghast at the monster within her, overpowering sense and reason, flicking aside respect and duty. Was this truly her who set up strategic stratagems through smiling lips and eyes that shone as clear as honesty?

Those were the days when the Indian community was small enough to know each and every one of its number; when the families had hardly started arriving and men lived in the camaraderie of an enforced bachelorhood; still believing that soon they would have earned enough/saved enough to go back and rejoin the fabric and tapestry of a life left behind, they talked as if they'd merely stepped out of a picture and left a blank outline of themselves waiting for the day when they could step back into the frame.

Many criticised her father for bringing them over. What necessity when the money he sent back could keep them comfortable? And who knows what would happen to women and children under the English influence? Her father countered by asking what they would achieve with their money after having paid for the family expenses? Very little for there was little left over. True his expenses would increase and he wouldn't be able to give them anything much in abundance, but he could give them something much more important, a good education and with that the chance of a life better than he had ever had. The father's hopes were not only for the son but the daughters as well. And that was why and how the daughter got away with what she did; though not scot-free for a penalty is attached to every foul and in her rushing and her running she was forever looking over her shoulder, anxiety ridden with guilt and fear. Did anyone guess? Had anyone seen? Had they already told tales of her to her parents?

All Indians believed that the children of anyone were the children of everyone and everyone else's business was their business too and no keeping quiet about what was going on. Silence may be golden but who knows what nightmares it will spawn to wreck the tranquillity of a peaceful home. Children were a pleasure that was taxed by duty, the duty to bring them up Right according to the rules, of whatever pond you swam in.

Having snatched a fraction of freedom she'd smile and laugh with the others and seem to agree as they applauded her courage in defying her backward and traditional society, in trying to escape her primitive background; the smile sticking to her lips like painted plastic while her insides folded in around an agitation that said this is treachery.

'What are you grinning at?' he asked looking up from the record player, golden strands of hair falling over one eye. Not getting a reply, crawled pleading-like on all fours to her side as she sat on the floor by the door. 'Oh great goddess of the East grant this infidel the merest crumbs, the slightest morsel of your thoughts.'

'I was thinking,' she said, resisting the impulse to rearrange his hair, 'of colours. And that it's time I went home. Can't be studying with Caroline the whole night.'

'I'm going to call you Hello-goodbye. 'Cos there's not much that happens in between. Have you realised you always sit there, right next to the door?'

'I'll get into trouble if I'm late.'

'Family bloody family,' he groaned, lying back and staring at the moon and stars on his ceiling. 'My mother did those. Thinks she's artistic.' She didn't like this swearing but didn't want to say so. Being prudish as well as primitive would be more than enough to make him drop her like a hot brick. 'I've got an idea. Caroline's brother will run you home,' and he smiled thinking he'd made a joke about a joke. 'Have another cup of coffee.' That bitter, dark stuff she was forcing herself to drink because anyone who wanted to be anyone drank coffee.

'No thanks,' but bent forward and gave him a kiss, the first unsolicited kiss from her to him, 'and no thanks. You can't drive me home.'

'In case your Dad's waiting with a loaded gun?'

'Kirpan more likely. We ain't your Wild-West Red Indians.' Pulling away from him and pulling on her coat, 'We're the sub-continent ones. Remember?'

His hands to his mouth doing whooping war cries and running around her in best Hollywood tradition, 'Great God of the skies, grant that we never mix our sub-continent with our incontinence or we will be forever in the shithouse. Great God grant . . .' Satchel on her shoulder she opened the door, cutting short his TV dramatics. 'I'll walk you to the bus stop.'

'You might meet a bloodthirsty war party on the way.'

'No matter, I will sacrifice my all for you, my Turkish Delight.'

'Geographical confusion. Poor boy,' shaking her head in sympathy, 'got lost.' But she let him kiss her before she left.

8

She sat in the front seat behind the driver's cab, wanting as hidden a seat as the bus could give, in case someone who might know someone who knew her family, saw her and then saw fit to ask the parents what she was doing travelling around at this time of night. She turned to get a book from her satchel and froze as she saw the advice on the panel in front: 'Smoke Signals only. Indian Driver.' Heart pounding she searched everywhere for her handkerchief, in her pockets, in the sleeve of her jumper and among her books. Nowhere to be found, but she found her pencil case and extracting a crayon started to scribble over the graffiti.

''Ere what do you think you're doing?' It was the ticket inspector, hat pulled back over a frowning forehead. She thought it was pretty obvious but his compressed lips told her different. 'You kids are all the same. No respect for property, particularly other people's. But I'm surprised at you, must say I am. A nice Indian girl like you! Who would have thought it. Hey Sing-Sing what do you think of this 'ere lark?' Kulwant followed his gaze as the Indian conductor came down towards them. It would have to be one of her father's friends!

'Hello Uncleji,' and then indignation welling up inside her she asked them to look and read.

'Look love,' said the inspector, 'it's only a joke and we pay an army of cleaners to keep our buses clean and tidy. Now be a good girl and leave it alone. After your efforts it'll be twice as much work. Now let's have a look at your ticket.'

'Haven't bought it yet.' His look of disbelief made her feel like a thief. The conductor intervened and she looked away feeling embarrassed for him as he tried to explain in his heavy accented English that he'd been upstairs and hadn't yet taken her fare.

'Well you'd better do it now, hadn't you? Where did you get on love?'

She told them and knew that if Uncleji mentioned it to her Dad, her Dad would know it was nowhere near Caroline's house.

The inspector went upstairs and Uncleji gave her a ticket, telling her there was no need for the money.

'But you'll get into trouble,' she protested in her rusty

9

Punjabi. Now if he was as nasty as her he'd look away in embarrassment.

'No, no,' Uncleji would put in his own money and then Uncleji commented that she was out very late.

'Oh I've been studying with a friend,' wondering if her tongue would rot apart in her mouth, as each lie seemed to corrode it like acid, 'I've got some very important exams coming up.'

Uncleji looked pleased and said she must work hard and with a paternal pat on her head went off to click out more tickets.

Turning the handle she let herself in through their orange door which was only locked at night. Cold and curry smells hit her as she entered. Hanging up her coat and exchanging a silent greeting with the flower lady in the picture she went off to find her mother.

Everyone was busy doing their own thing as long as their own thing didn't collide with those things that were forbidden. Her father was upstairs changing into his dirty workclothes. She'd forgotten he was on night-shift this week. Murmuring a quick hello she dashed back down. In the front room her brother Pauli was sitting curled up on the sofa, eyes glued to the TV. Her older sister busy twirling hands and arms around the old sewing machine.

'Who's this for?' asked Kulwant fingering the pink silky material. Her sister looked up, glaring for answer.

'It's for whatsit, the new bride down the road,' put in Pauli, without turning. 'Can't have her wearing the same clothes twice in one month, can we. And she never even says thank you.'

'Thankyouthankyouthankyou,' her mother said coming in, her Indian accent rendering the mimicking far funnier than it was and they all gurgled into giggles.

'Indian people are always asking you for favours. Oh lend us this, do that for us, come with us to speak English. And they don't say thank you,' repeated Pauli, folding his arms for emphasis.

Half teasing, half serious her mother cuffed his head. 'English people can't tell you the time of day without expecting a thousand thank yous,' reverting back to her Punjabi. 'And if you don't lend, you can't borrow, and if you don't give help you can't ask for it.'

'It's the Indians who are always giving a thousand thank yous,' said Kulwant still sitting by the sewing machine. 'Uncleji with the long beard always does. It's embarrassing.'

Her mother looked at her sharply. 'You children can laugh. We don't know the English ways but we do our best. How do you think I feel when I hear your terrible Punjabi? It's not just embarrassing, it's shameful. Your sister's the only one who speaks it properly.'

'Goody two-shoes,' Kulwant almost said but bit it back. No knowing when her sister would take revenge.

'Indian people are funny,' younger brother Pauli again (his teacher had found Parminder too difficult, and Pauli had insisted the family adopt his school nickname). 'You remember when you met the other women in that posh store. You lot talked for hours and hours and at the tops of your voices. The Sales Ladies were whispering about you. Said you should find some other place to hold your mothers' meetings. I had to duck behind the net curtains to hide from Robert Grieves. He and his mother stared and stared at you all as they went by.'

'Find yourself an English mother,' their mother snapped, and flounced off to the kitchen. As soon as her steps had receded her voice shouted back to Kulwant to come and eat.

'Spoilt. That's what you are,' hissed her sister Gurinder as Kulwant went out. 'And close the door behind you. It's cold.'

Warmth, steam, and all the masala smells of an Indian kitchen. Back turned to the door, her mother was standing at the cooker slapping pieces of dough between her hands, making hot, fresh rotis for her daughter and in between stirring the dal and sabji in the frying pans.

Mother works too hard, thought Kulwant, taking over the stirring but not with the conviction that would make her give up her time to help her. 'I don't need fresh rotis Mum. You should just make a whole lot in one go.'

'You can eat stale rotis when you don't have a mother. I saved some dhahi for you. Parminder would have eaten it all if I'd let him. Sit down and eat.'

The table was squeezed into a corner of the kitchen. She twisted the chair sideways so she could still look at her mother. 'You shouldn't work so hard,' her mother was saying, pausing in her bustling to rest a hand on Kulwant's shoulder, 'we want you to do well but not to make yourself ill. Have some achar.' Grandmother's special achar sent all the way over from India with the last arrival; one of the many packages he'd carried for other people from the village, each one a cipher of goodwill for he would need all the goodwill he could get in carving out a new life for himself in alien England.

'Has achar-uncle got a job yet?' asked Kulwant through a mouthful of roti and sabji.

'No. Your father and his friends are still trying. These Goras won't do anything unless you put something between their fingers.'

Kulwant said she couldn't believe it and her mother retorted she had a lot to learn about the world.

Pig-tails Goes to a Party

Stick-leg-shuffle-leg-shuffle. Stick-leg-shuffle-leg-shuffle.

Banging the door closed behind her, her shoes scraping the pavement as if doing overtime in carrying the body above them. She'd stepped out of her memories for a shopping trip to buy milk and bread for her empty fridge. Stopping at a zebra crossing, stretching her neck out like a bony bird she peered up and down the road. A pair of NHS specs was what she needed. The final authentic touch. She who could get stick, could get specs too!

A briefcase came and stood next to her. Sliding her gaze upwards from hand to pin-striped arm, to shoulder, to eyes, she met up with a cold speculative stare.

'Would you help me across the road?' quavering her voice.

'It's empty. In fact it's a morgue of a road,' and so saying he loped across, briefcase swinging forward like a hatchet.

What a brute! Requiring dramatic denunciation. Lifting her stick she waved it at his retreating back, 'Ain't got Aids you know mate. Not like you City Gents. Riddled with disease you are. Inside and out. Look what a mess you've made of this country. Stashing away your loot and leaving us to starve . . .'

'That's enough madam.' The local bloke in blue doing his community bit. 'You've had your say and you're holding up the traffic.'

One lonely car, stopping to see the fun, the driver winding down the window. 'Right you are lady. Say it again,' a left-over hippy, face invisible behind flowing hair. Revving up and shooting off as a warning glance flew his way from the boy in blue.

'Now let me help you across the road,' his hand firmly under her elbow, indicating the futility of resistance. She didn't.

Delivered across she didn't look back at him either, concentrating on scuttling away. He might decide on a closer examination and decide that she wasn't all that she was making out to be. Make-up! She'd overlooked the make-up. Get some today and start practising. Crumbling undercoat on a podgy nose, bright red lipstick over wrinkled lips, glaring rouge on sagging cheeks! She'd gather together all the paraphernalia of the feminine mystique and time warp back to the days of her youthful flings. Not that they lasted long for she had soon given up make-up and making up stories. No more lies that twisted her tongue, no more rifts in real-time reality.

Michael the Archangel thought love was a lift to a heaven of bliss. Couldn't understand her ifs and buts. Thought she should break out of her chains and leap into the light of freedom. Not that he said it in exactly those words, but he pushed and nudged and waged a war on her reserve and reluctance. Though her nerves were frayed and her control fragile she couldn't yet say no and end it all. So she gave inch by inch: meeting him for longer and taking greater risks, till it fractured, beyond repair, at Caroline's party no less. In later years she would refer to parties as the 'witches' cauldron' because those who partook became the ingredients of the bubbling, emotional concoctions that displaced and rearranged, binding some into a passionate beginning and cleaving others into a bitter ending.

It didn't terminate because her family found out or other people snitched; would have been easier if things had happened that way. Her illusions, her first love remaining intact and pure, aureoled in gold-dust memory. 'But for how long?' she'd often asked herself over the years; she couldn't have kept her eyes closed and her mind locked and mute for ever; wouldn't there have been a day when resentment and acrimony spilled out like angry lava? when her integration became insufficient for him and her disintegration too great for her?

A party to celebrate Caroline's birthday, or Caroline's

birthday an excuse for a party. And for once she was legitimate, able to tell the truth without a twinge. Even so, Mum and Dad and carping sister in the background had needed to be persuaded that their precious Kulwant was not being enticed into a party that would be full of vice. Caroline had come round and done her 'I'm a charming English girl, and won't be refused' act. Her mother had relented, unfreezing the opposition of her father and fuelling the spite of her sister. Her mother had always liked Caroline, because Caroline was polite, well dressed and you could see she came from a good family. Background being all important to the Indian mind.

'Now if Pauline had come to invite you to a birthday party, I could never have said yes. Her clothes are always messy or torn, or with a button missing. They look as if they came from the second-hand shop.' This last with a shudder of disgust.

'Probably did,' Kulwant almost said and bit it back but contented herself by saying that Pauline's mother was poor.

'Why?' came back the snap question.

'Because – because,' Kulwant stammered, stalling for time to think and in the end blurting it out, 'because her parents are divorced.'

'Ah.' Nothing else could have damned Pauline more.

She had told her mother that Caroline's Mum would bring her back and not to wait up. She could see from her mother's unhearing concentration on the cooking the uselessness of saying more. Of course she would wait up till she came back. The tyranny of love.

Walking to Caroline's house: walking from one world to another; the shopping centre a buffer zone of plate glass alluring the lascivious consumer: lovingly laid displays of urges. Tea cosies to TVs, sofas to shirts, and towels to trowels: from scraps of cloth to coiled wires, illusions were converted into dire necessities. All was allurement and procurement and she thought with a sick shock that's what we are. England allured and England procured and like tadpoles to a shark we swam right in deep into its pink mouth; and not only us, we're only part of the endless stream from grain to tea to art to ideas, and thinking thus the church bells struck, startling her back into what she was looking at: low cut summer dresses, lit like warm

15

sunshine, though they would never seem low cut to her friends, only to her who'd had modesty drummed into her like a catholic catechism. As she turned to go her sparkly shalwar/kameez flickered on the glass against the dresses, quickly fading to nothingness as she walked out of sight.

Caroline lived in the posh part of town, where the streets were as wide as they were pretty, where each house stood in its own individuality, surrounded by a ring of space for the air to flow and freshen each brick and leaf. A long driveway embellished with rose bushes led to the front door and looking back she thought, 'Phew, what a trek from the pavement to here. For my house you only have to step off the pavement to step inside. Ours is a real labour-saving entrance.'

Music thumped from inside as she rang the bell and as if she'd been standing waiting for the signal Caroline swung open the door just as Kulwant's finger lifted from the button. Her eyes did a quick flick over (it was the pre-time to Beatle-time and not yet chic to be ethnic) and she said, 'Are you comfortable? Else I've got lots of things upstairs.'

'Why shouldn't I be?'

'No need to be so prickly. What time do you have to get back? Follow me,' Caroline sailing through the throng of her guests like a queen and Kulwant following behind like a puppy on a string, raising her voice to lob it over Caroline's shoulder.

'You know my mother. She'd have made Cinderella come in hours before midnight.'

Stepping into the kitchen and latching the door behind them, Caroline turned eagerly, ears wide open to receive: 'The thirsties will have to wait. Now fill me in on the latest with Romeo. What do you want to drink? He got here early and has been hanging around like a spare part, mooning and moaning for you. Red or white? What have you done to him?'

'What?' She'd never had wine before.

'No orange juice or Babycham. I've banned them for the night. A dictatorship would suit me. Told my Dad and he said Directorships are hard to come by these days but I'll keep my eyes open for you. He does think he's witty. Try the white?'

'Can't go home drunk. Else you'll find me in the river tomorrow morning, and it won't be for a morning swim neither.'

16

'This stuff will do you. Not very different from lemonade. Say when?'

When? When what? 'That's enough,' as it frothed to the rim, 'can't drink more than that.'

'You haven't told me the latest on you and Him-him.' Him-him from the early days when everything had to be Top Secret, till she was sure of him, till she was certain he wasn't just giving her the once over. 'Oh God. There goes the bell. The trials of being a hostess. I'll catch up with you later.' Ushering her back out through the door and pointing to her left, 'That door leads to the garden. That's where I saw Him-him last. Staring stupid like at the flowers.' Caroline rushed off and she eased herself into a corner. Him-him could wait. She wanted to look in on her first English party; be a fly on the wall and absorb not only what her eyes could see but feel all that which was happening beneath the surface. Not knowing when she'd be allowed out for another such experiment.

Square-paned windows filtered in the dying evening, lighting faces that changed ripple-like from stony laughter, to a listening pose, to a girding up for a plunge into the talking pool; a constant ripple of movement, shifting people into changing configurations. Sure in themselves and of their stake in the future they moved with an ease of belonging that acted like floodlights on her internal landscape of broken desolation, where no one scene fitted into another; where fragments of scenes faced each other in alienation; and those chunks that were childhood memory could never be trusted as true reality for they could so easily be spun fantasy and, like flotsam, her inner world floated in space without history to anchor the location or a future to give it a guiding assurance.

Dancers dancing with arms entwined and bodies locked, a slow scraping of the feet, one set of lips coming down on another; she wondered what was happening in their minds. Was this ecstasy? this shutting off of the world and mingling of the salivas? Nothing like anything she had ever felt with Michael. Were they truly drowning into each other as they seemed to be? But she knew the couple. Had known Joanie since junior school and Patrick since the fourth form. Joanie had built her reputation on the number of boys she could string along but

Patrick had been steady with Sally and now Sally was nowhere to be seen. Had these two found instant love? or was it a transferable commodity, able to be taken from anyone and given to anyone? Processed since birth through the framework of Indian puritanism she felt a recoiling from such emotional liberality.

'It's not a film, you know, where you can just sit back and watch.' He had thick glasses and an intellectual air. 'You have to join in, that's the idea of a party.'

She didn't like his interruption, hadn't yet finished thinking her thoughts but she also felt ridiculously pleased that an unknown bloke had wanted to talk to her. Despite being Michael's (part-time) girlfriend she was still unsure of herself, always feeling herself to be a gauche fuddy-duddy, unable to compete with the flirtatious scintillation of a Caroline or Joanie. Not having any boys of her own age in the family and unused to meeting them socially she always became painfully self-conscious, as if she'd suddenly sprouted two heads and elephant ears; manifested in a horrible tendency to blush every other second ('I didn't know Indians could blush,' Michael had said to her once, confirming her suspicion that she was weird).

'Where are you from?' asked intellectual glasses.

'Up Birmingham way,' she hoped with the right Brummie accent, imitating her cousins who actually lived up that way.

'I mean where are you really from?'

If he wanted it let him have it, he was merely looking for an excuse to recount his father's adventures in the imperial army: 'Village Gianpur, P.O. Jullunder Cantt. Punjab. India.'

'Jullunder? Can't say I recognise it.'

'Well it's not exactly the jet-setting centre of the world.'

'My father's lived in India, and travelled all over.'

'In the army I suppose.'

'Daddy was born there. Family lived in India for generations. We go and visit every year. Although I haven't been able to go for the last couple of years because of exams, but I'm determined not to miss my trip this year. I suppose you must go as often as you can also.'

How she hated him. She was consumed with envy, jealousy and malice. Her parents could hardly afford to go themselves,

18

let alone take the children. Intellectual glasses had probably seen more of India than she ever had. 'And how do you get on with the local people?'

'You know how it is with ex-patriot communities . . . but I've managed to pick up a few words of Hindi from the servants. They're very exploited . . .'

'Sure. Must go and say hello to Caroline's Mum. Should have done it earlier,' side-stepping, sidling away, 'Been terribly rude. Bye.'

Unthinkingly she ploughed her way to the other side of the room, wanting to hide herself before intellectual glasses followed to regale her with his egalitarianism, which no doubt began and ended in India. Stepping back and nearly tripping over a pile of records.

'You don't like the music. Say so. I'll change it. But just don't step all over my blue soul records.' He spoke out of one corner of his mouth, a cigarette clamped tight in the other, legs crossed on the floor. She bent down to sit beside him and turning round to say sorry saw herself doubled on his dark glasses.

'You want your scarf wine coloured?' he asked reaching behind her and picking up the end of her dupatta. 'It's like a thirsty plant sucking up blood.' His fingers spreading it out on the carpet, they watched the red stain creeping upwards. She should be rushing off to the sink to wash it out. One of her mother's most expensive dupattas and she calmly sat and watched it being ruined.

'Sorry about your records. Didn't mean to step on them.'

'No necessity to worry. Mostly possessions of Madam Pompadour Caroline. You really should wash this out.'

Get up and push her way through this throng? Holding a dupatta dripping drops like blood! Ghastly. 'Doesn't matter. It'll wash out later.' Lying again.

'You must be Caroline's Indian friend with the secret boyfriend.'

Ghastlier and ghastlier. 'Doesn't seem to be much of a secret.'

'Why aren't you with him?'

'Do I have to be?'

'Of course my dear. Dear me, it's not love if you're not constantly telling each other how madly you love each other and rushing to each other whenever you meet. Doesn't it hurt, that you're in the same house, probably only yards apart and yet not together, not gazing into each other's eyes?'

'Where's your girlfriend?'

'I observe. I do not participate. And the longer you stay away from him the more chance he has of fancying someone else. You don't want some other woman stepping into your shoes do you? Nothing is constant in love or war as they say. If you must rust, I mean trust, put your trust in the English weather, never the human heart, for nothing so fickle has or ever will be invented; look through history, think of wars and tragedy, and like as not what's the spanner in the works?'

'Yes. We all know about Helen of Troy.'

'And Troilus and Cressida. I'm a student of human nature, and I can see you're a genuine sheep under that sheep's clothing and don't know that you teeter on the brink of losing all and everything. Find him, pour words of love into his ear (declarations made under the delusion of love are never binding), make sure his eyes never stray to other pastures, where the grass is always greener as they say, or temptation cross his path. His spirit may be noble and dedicated to you but the flesh, as you should know Oh Lady of the Land of the Kama Sutra is forever weak and vulnerable. Especially male flesh. Cigarette?'

'No thank you.' What was the Kama Sutra?

'Against your religion I suppose.'

Time to move. 'I'd better take your advice. Goodbye.'

'Didn't mean a word of it you know – verbiage on verbiage – don't take me seriously – I can do a different version – Made to Order Philosophy – everything for everyone . . .' his voice faded away into the party hum.

'You've still got a glassful?' Caroline accosting, eyes accusingly on the wine glass.

'Oh, I forgot.'

'Forgot! I don't believe this. You need someone to teach you the ways of civilised debauchery. What's Michael been up to? making you daisy chains?' Kulwant confessed that Michael had not yet been met. 'Oh boy, you're in trouble. So who've you been chatting up all this time? Didn't think I'd invited a single interesting person to my party. You're a dark horse.'

20

'Dark is right.'

'You know what I mean,' giving her a sly nudge. 'Ready to move on are we? Oops here comes Him-him. Tell me tomorrow. If there's anyone even half interesting I want a share. Hi. Michael. Want a refill? Let's have your glass. Look after our Inscrutible Eastern Beauty for me.' Caroline twirled away on the wings of wit. That's how Caroline would have written this if she'd been writing this.

Michael was sour. 'I've been waiting for you all evening. I thought you were going to get here early so we could have lots of time together. I suppose you have to leave in the next five minutes.'

'I had to help my mother. And I wanted to see what the party was like.'

'Getting bored with me?' Not waiting for an answer, Michael counter-attacked, 'You don't usually bother helping your mother. Guilty conscience?' She didn't answer, hoping her silence would calm him down. 'You don't have to do what they say. It's a free country.'

'But Michael, my parents let me do a lot of things other people wouldn't. Not everyone's the same. My sister hates me because she thinks I get my own way all the time.'

'She's jealous.'

'Well, she wasn't allowed to do half the things I am.'

'I would think she never even wanted to. With a face like hers it's a good thing she doesn't have to hunt for a husband herself. She's probably the one who invented arranged marriages.'

'She's all right. You've never even met her.' No matter how much she and her sister sniped at each other he didn't have the right to criticise.

'I've seen her and if anyone's going to take the lid off your secret life, it'll be her.'

'She thinks I'm going to rack and ruin anyway.'

'That's a rotten place,' he grinned at his joke coming nearer, and put his arms around her, 'wouldn't want you to go there.'

She was panicking. How could he put his arms around her in public? 'Caroline hasn't brought your drink. I'll go and find her.'

'Having an attack of the Indian scruples?' She replied that she was feeling claustrophobic, meaning his arms. He turned it around for himself, 'Let's get some fresh air, works wonders for attacks of outdated morality.'

Why did she always jump from the frying pan into the fire? Why jump into the frying pan in the first place? What was wrong with living a nice, ordinary, Indian-girl-type life? Millions did. Why couldn't she? 'Everyone will see us going into the garden.'

'Too busy doing their own thing.'

'You're joking. Some of these people have eyes in the backs of their heads. MI5 is nothing on them. I mean, you don't know what kind of gossip does the rounds – so blistering it peels the paint off the walls. Why do you think they're always having to redecorate the girl's loos?'

'You're always worrying. You've never seen Caroline's garden in the dark, have you?'

She was too agitated to pick up on seeing in the dark. 'I thought you understood. I explained. About everything.'

'Don't understand stupidity.'

She turned away so as not to show her hurt. She didn't know what more to say to him: conflicting thoughts bubbled in her mind, spiralling her into confusion, while the colour in her skin somersaulted into a new awareness, heightening her self-consciousness and showing herself to herself as a stranger among a confederacy of friends and acquaintances. She pulled her falling dupatta tight around herself, the flimsy material drawing the line of demarcation between them. What was she doing trying to swim in these strange waters? The red stained end wrapped around her hand, its wetness cool to her conflicts. Why hang on? Surely it was time to go.

'Won't you dance with me? Please.' Michael disentangled her hand from her dupatta and lifting it to his lips kissed it. 'And I don't care who saw me doing that.'

'Can't. Never danced before.'

The music was a slow swirling silver stream, inducing journeys towards the borders of sensuality, as body swayed on body – but she held herself away and he said, 'I'm not contaminated.'

Caroline opened her eyes and lifting her head from her partner's shoulder gave her a huge, big wink. She couldn't respond and looked away and he said, 'It'll be ever so much nicer if you rest your head on my shoulder.'

'It's so smoky in here,' she complained, attempting to cover up for her reserve.

Michael didn't need to be told twice. Taking her hand he pushed their way through to the coolness of the garden. Running her hand along a hedge, leaves bending under her palm, feet sinking into springy ground, grass overlapping the thin sandals, tickling her toes; the dark shapes of flower beds and the denser filigree and smudginess of flowers: they walked the leisurely walk of nowhere to go, his arm around her and the garden stretching out in front of them. His arm was a loving around her, its pressure joining them together, making her feel the preciousness of being wanted and desired. She'd stepped across the line that separated spectators from participants, she was at one with the murals of experience: taking and giving and growing and learning.

They were still softly walking and the garden still stretched out in front and she thought this is the luxury of the rich, owning enough greenness to give you space to breathe, being able to stroll without hitting your foot against a wall every three yards. No wonder romance was for the rich, they could afford the ambience.

'Stop,' said the Archangel, 'turn towards me, put your arms around my neck, like this, oh one hand I need . . .'

'Any more instructions?' she teased looking up at him.

'Yes. Close your eyes and kiss me.' She did as she was told, wondering why he was fumbling around with her hand.

'D'you like it?' Lifting her hand for her to see: a glint of something bright against her finger.

'What's this? Not my birthday yet.'

'Ye Olde English Tradition. Rather a good fit, don't you think. You're not supposed to take it off.'

'Think you can fob me off with your plastic Woolworth's stuff,' she didn't know what was happening, but instinct said to make light of it, keep it frothy or they both might sink. 'Now if it had been real you wouldn't have been able to tear it away from me.'

'It is.' She held it out to him. 'Olde English Tradition say when ring on girl's finger, girl say yes and marry boy.'

A tingling through her body and a stepping back from him. 'Oh I get it. April Fool. I must be using the wrong calendar. You know us Indians. Always behind the times.' Artificial giggles hitting the grass with stony thuds.

'Don't be a dope. Say yes. Yes thank you and Yes I will.'

'My mother says it's not necessary to say thank you all the time. If you get it enlarged it'll fit you. It'll look ever so nice.' Taking his hand and trying to uncurl the fingers from the fist.

'What's wrong with me? Not good enough for you.'

'I've got to study and work and see the world and do lots and lots of other things. So have you. Look, let's talk about this in ten years time,' false jollity buoying up her voice.

'You're a dream come true. I mean you're living in a dream. Come the time, you'll get arranged off to some village boy from India, who'll only marry you to get into England. And you people like to marry young. Start early and get in lots of practice. That must be the motto.'

'I'm not "you people". And my parents would never force me. Don't believe everything you hear about the heathens.'

'Just like they never "force" you to lie to them, hide things from them, make you feel perpetually guilty?' a new harshness lining his voice. 'They should realise they haven't transported a bit of their village here you know . . . "a corner of England that shall forever be India" . . .' That was almost what they had done, but she wasn't about to tell him that. 'If they're going to stay here they'll have to change.'

'You lot didn't when you came to our country.'

'That was different. We ruled it.'

'Just as you want to rule me.'

'Very funny. Ha ha ha. Don't over-use that joke, it'll get worn out.'

Caroline's voice cut across his forced laughter: 'Kuli . . . Cooeee . . . Kulwantiii . . . Mummyyy wants you.' Caroline was trying to float across the grass in her high heels. 'Hi you lovers. Did I interrupt something interesting?'

'Go away. We haven't finished yet,' Michael taking her arm and trying to walk her further into the garden, Kulwant

24

protesting, saying that they didn't have anything more to talk about; Michael not listening and telling Caroline over his shoulder to give her mother a glass of something strong: 'Indian custom before driving young bride home.'

Caroline plumped up on wings of excitement: 'What? Did I hear right? How exciting!'

'It's not true.' Kulwant tried shouting back, her voice strangled as Michael hurried her away and anyhow Caroline was already tripping back towards the house. 'Now look what you've done. She'll go and tell everyone.'

'You're always worrying about gossip. Once we're married you can forget all that.'

She twisted her arm away. 'Why do you have to talk about marriage?'

'I see I'll have to explain it to you. It's like this: if you're going out with someone and you love them, it's normal to marry them.' What trap had she walked into all unwary? Had her experimental venturing into the forbidden turned the page on to the dark and painful?

'But I didn't go out with you to marry you. I didn't think that . . .'

'What did you think? You thought you'd find out about the weird customs of the English . . . we're not animals in a zoo. And I thought you were the shy and innocent one. You were just holding back . . . watching me. You never took us seriously. Not for a minute.' Understood and misunderstood. Could she find the words to separate the truth from the false? Words congealing in her throat she remained silent. 'Not cricket old chap . . . that's what we English would say . . . write it down in your notebook . . . unfair . . . that's another English idea for you.'

'But, not everyone marries their boyfriend,' there must be some way of reasoning this through.

'But they might marry them, it's a possibility as soon as you start going out. For those who play fair. But I forget. I forget, you wouldn't know about playing fair, would you? And all this time you had me feeling sorry for you, wanting to help you, rescue you . . .'

'Rescue me! How dare you. You're the dream come true,

aren't you. Galahad on his white horse! Is that what this ring's for?'

'It was for love.' Taking it from her, lifting his arm and throwing it high and far away from them, 'not any more.'

His face blurred as her tears splashed out 'I do care for you. This is crazy, mad. You're English, I'm . . . Why do you have to talk about marriage?'

'Save yourself for the Indian husband. And I thought it was your parents who were traditional, old-fashioned and us English who were prejudiced. Boy, have I learnt a lot from you . . . the funny thing is . . . you thought it would be the other way round.'

'Kuli . . . Cooeee,' Caroline's voice floating towards them again, 'Mummy's getting anxious. Kiss him goodbye and come along. Look, I'll turn my back so's you two can have your privacy . . . just don't be too long about it.' Kulwant stared at Caroline's primly held back; what could be said to make it come right?

The Archangel clasped both her hands in his, 'Say yes. Prove I was wrong.'

'How can I?' Exasperation drying her tears, 'You're being . . .'

He didn't let her finish, 'She's all yours Caroline,' dropping her hands and moving away, 'take this Indian to her wig-wam.'

Pig-tails Weeps Over a Wimpy

That was that. And it was all over. She felt as if she'd been turned inside out and forced into an eclipse. No more experimentation. Eyes down to the nitty gritty of reality, no matter that it seemed like walking backwards into a narrowing cave.

School became an endurance test. All their previous arrangements to maximise togetherness now turned to taunt them with their disintegration; their backs peppered by whispers that recounted, in mounting voltages of fiction, how the great split had come about.

She wanted to be friends and tried to be so, but he would look through her as though she was transparent glass or ask her what research she was engaged on now.

'If you've split up, you've split,' said Caroline in answer to her bewilderment. She couldn't reconcile the present with the past; how could there be such a cleavage between two people who had shared closeness and intimacy, had given a part of themselves to the other, focused on each to make the other precious. Surely there should be a residue that survived beyond the ending, changed but containing a permanent connection. 'How untidy,' and Caroline flicked her hair back from her shoulders, 'You want to forget and move on. Not have a string of ex-boyfriends messing up your chances.'

How many times do you move on? How many stop-starts, stop-starts? Why go through this game over and over again?

Why end up with battered emotions and a past that was constantly being amputated?

'Love is horrible,' she said to Caroline as they truanted at the local Wimpy. 'I didn't realise how much I cared when I was with him. Didn't know it would hurt like this. What a thing to invent. I mean why couldn't you lot go off and invent artificial gold or something? Something useful. Instead of Cupid and his stupid arrows. Never seem to hit the mark and if they do, it doesn't last long. And then there's nothing but enmity afterwards. Why can't he be friends with me? I mean I haven't become a two-headed monster have I? Now I know why England went out and conquered. Everybody wanted to get away from love gone sour. The best way to forget your enemies at home is to fight the enemies overseas. Does anybody know what it's all about? This thing called love. Do you?' she asked the waitress as two cups of frothy coffee plonked down in front of them.

'Here's your bill. It's a bomb m'dears,' she said, folding her arms and looking down at them. 'Guaranteed to explode in your face. But that's only my opinion and others will tell you different. Not to say it's always the other person's fault.' She shook her head and slid into the seat next to Kulwant. 'Meself, I think we could do without it. What you don't know you'll never miss. Isn't that right. Now the problem is, we do know, and we reckon we should have our share. Sad. But we can't go out and buy it at the grocer's. You know what would help, Love Courses! Like them exams things, you know, O's and A's. If we knew more about it with our heads . . .' A shout from the bar pulled her to her feet. 'It's warfare my dears. Look at it that way, and you'll have your defences up, all the time. You'll be protected. Let him be the casualty for a change. Shout if you want anything else. But I tell you one thing,' coming back to add a postscript, 'when it happens, it beats bingo, bingeing, champagne and caviar any day.'

'Do you think every woman is a philosopher on love?' asked Kulwant, sipping her coffee and gaining a frothy moustache on her lip.

Caroline turned away in despair. 'If I'd known you were going to go on like this I'd have stayed in school, and,' she turned to wag a finger at Kulwant, 'I'd never have helped you fix it up with Him-him. Oh,' suddenly seeing Kulwant's face go frozen, 'how about a Rum-Baba?'

She felt as if she'd been turned inside out and forced to choose. No more trying to walk in the middle. There were too many pot-holes and she was like a blind woman without a stick. Safer to stay in territory that she knew. If she'd stuck to her Indian way Michael wouldn't have been so hurt, wouldn't have chucked in his studies and left school, and she would have been free of the pain that she lugged around like a cross. She'd messed it all up because she had wanted everything, wanted to be Indian and English, wanted to choose for herself what she wanted out of both. Couldn't be done. Thinking of all that, she rubbed the colour on her skin, which wasn't ever going to rub off, and made her decision.

'Frankly Frankenstein'

Stick-leg-shuffle-leg-shuffle, Stick-leg-shuffle-leg-shuffle.

Eyes back to today, back on the pavement playing childhood games: Counting the flagstones, walking ritually over every grating, pulling the stick backwards and forwards in a chain of sound. Making it more complicated: adding half a point for the number of fag-ends squashed flat by the stick, one point for a newspaper kicked aside, two points for chewing gum, gathering in a dirty wodge at the bottom of the faithful stick. The streets weren't as clean as they used to be, for that matter, nothing was as it used to be. Carry on . . . and damn! she'd lost count. She'd have to start all over again.

Bright spots glinting on the pavement like coins thrown in front of a bridal party, jumping on to her stick as she moves it through, flickering on to her hand: A dalmatian Asian!

Rajasthani mirrorwork on a wall hanging, suspended in front of draped saris cradling a fan-spread of multi-lingual leaflets giving the know-how from rickets to racism. She'd landed up in front of the Asian Centre. How convenient. Pushing open the door and stepping into simulation Sub-Continent. Misbegotten child of a guilty conscience, Frankenstein patched together with the flotsam of travel posters, batik work, examples of traditional embroidery, cow bells and last but not least woven baskets that you knew were from Oxfam. It was supposed to be inviting, user friendly: a home from home for the Asian woman trapped in the isolation of her house; a helping hand for the Asian man shell-shocked from dealing with the revolving door racism and vagaries of white bureaucracy.

Searching for something more authentic than the approximation in front of her, her eyes roved the room – trying to categorise what she saw: were they souvenirs? reminders? exotic bric-à-brac from a country that for some was home, for others nothing more than a distant childhood memory, and for those born here a patchwork land transmitted through parents' stories of places, people, happenings: an infrastructure kept alive with letters, imbibed with baby milk, mixed with rotis and savoured with the mature taste of chillies. Throwing up some who strived to be more Indian than the Indians over there, though born in England as they were. Was it a testimony to the power of transference from generation to generation, or a testimony to the force of the hostile world outside.

Here in the Asian Centre, there should be no doubt of who or what you are and of your value. Yet no one, not by any stretch of fantasy, could make any such categorical claim. This was no haven of calm in the middle of a storm, buffeted as it was by the pull of many an opposing demand, staffed by workers who in themselves are uncertain crucibles in search of a self.

Making a profession out of one's nationality had its shades of coolie-ism, but who could deny anyone their daily bread. All good arts graduates can gravitate to the buffer zone; the middle-person jobs between them and us and us and us, hybrids trying to serve the community while they tried to change it while trying to protect it from external attacks.

Many living away from home, away from the restrictions that would cramp their style. Revolution doesn't always begin at home; easier to run it in the neighbour's yard; not that she believed living 'a proper Indian life', any kind of pre-requisite; having plunged into it herself on the premise that if England is so rotten then India must be so much purer, only to rapidly loose her footing on such groundless idealism.

However her jaundiced eye would not be kept at bay: for a regular income and a job in 'comfort politics' is more than enough to cool the revolutionary fervour of most, and those who funded such jobs and centres were no fools; a few pounds now could save a whole bundle in the future. And those pounds enabled the workers to increase their collection of Indian clothes and purchase tickets for every Indian 'arty' event going. Security has its compensations.

She sidled towards a chair and plumped down, resting her chin on her stick and chiding herself for the cruel eye within. How was she any better? She had been through the mangle and what had she done with it except lock it up inside her, as if it was something valuable needing a safe deposit box. Waiting for someone to notice her she half closed her eyes and eavesdropped on the conversations in progress:

— A denim-clad body tilting on the back legs of a chair, one hand ploughing through hair in exhausted world weariness, the other cradling the phone to the ear: '. . . nothing doing, why should he get away with it . . . what about him hurting you . . . telling him what you want isn't being nasty . . . if you decide to be aggressive you will be, there's no magic, you just have to be clear about what you want . . . all men are oppressive, don't matter what colour pigment they got ∿ . look, why're you listening to his bullshit, white people can't be anti-racist just by saying so . . . what if he is doing more campaigning work, about time they recognised it's their problem . . . we'll have to meet up, I can't spend the whole day on the phone . . . well of course you go back, you live there, don't you . . . yes, yes. I'll be there . . .' —

— Two other heads were engrossed over a sheet of paper: 'have they any idea what we do? . . . they sling a few pounds our way and demand blood for every penny . . . they forget our community's paid rates and taxes for decades . . . we should sling these statistics sheets back at them . . . they'll only ask what we're hiding . . . it may prove useful having someone from the council sitting in on the management committee, we could subvert the situation to our ends, use them as a resource . . . that's not the point, the fact is we're the only voluntary group being asked to accommodate a spy . . . they're afraid we'll run off with the money and have glamorous holidays in Goa . . . let's refer it to the management committee . . . Hello Auntiji' —

Good God! Asha had seen through her without a moment's

ado! So much for her efforts at projecting a new persona. A dejected Kuli sank into a fit of the sulks. Asha abandoned her deliberations on the council's demands, and came over, her dupatta trailing behind her.

'Can I help you? Is it a housing problem? Social Security?' speaking a mixture of elementary Punjabi, and half-way through trying out her equally elementary Hindi.

Saved! Run while you can.

'Cold,' she muttered, getting up, 'outside.'

Asha was all concern. 'Have a cup of tea. Warm you up.' Hands on Kuli's shoulders gently pushing her back down. Kuli shook her head but sank back, keeping her eyes lowered.

Asha pulled up a chair, suspecting deep depression or something worse. 'We're having a cutting in two weeks' time. Would you like to come?'

She was certainly going deaf, another step into the mechanics of old age. Cupping her hand around her ear she shouted, 'What?'

The community worker recoiled, but recovered and rallied to the task. 'Outing. Trip to the seaside.'

Kulwant leaned towards her, almost colliding with Asha's short cropped hair, 'Why seaside? Cold.' Why repatriate, give the oldies pneumonia.

She'd leaned far too near, for Asha's eyes opened wide, telling clear what she'd guessed, though her words hid all indication except that she gave up on her pidgin Hindi, English tumbling out in a rush, 'The old people never get to go out anywhere, they hardly fit into pensioners' link. They end up being stuck inside all day. It won't cost very much because we'll pay for the coach hire.'

What an unexpected bonus! Pretend and thou might receive according to thine pretences. Kulwant was shamed into assent, they tried hard and all she did was play games with them. She nodded, Asha smiled and rushed off to get the booking form.

She returned with an overflowing mug of tea, her shoulders now bare of the troublesome dupatta. 'We had thought of having two coaches, one for the men and one for the women . . .'

'Why?' Was all her conversation a questioning here?

'Because . . . we had thought everyone would feel more comfortable.'

'Not much fun.'

'It'll be mixed now. Mrs Desai said it wasn't necessary.' Poor children. Old age was the one thing that freed the sexes from their lifelong restrictions; she herself had been surprised at the amount of teasing and flirting that went on between the older generation. She grinned inwardly; half those older women considered her far too disreputable to be associating with.

'The coach will leave early in the morning and pick up people from various points. If you bring a lunch we'll provide the drinks.'

Typical, thought Kulwant. Last time the workers hadn't taken any food for themselves and were setting off to go to a restaurant; of course the women who'd brought up a host of children between them wouldn't hear of it. What restaurant could offer food as good as home cooking. They were plied with shares of food and drinks from every bulging package, the scene slipping into a delightful parody of every Indian dinner party:

'. . . have some more.' '. . . what will you eat off an empty plate?'

'No, no, this is enough.'

'. . . just a little portion . . .' deftly spooning it on to the plate.

'Very full already,' through mouths attempting to eat and speak at once.

'Ranjana's speciality, you can't say no to this,' more dollops of food landing on their plates.

'Couldn't eat any more,' hands over plates, clumsy defences against further attacks of generosity.

'You don't have to diet, so thin already . . .' '. . . one whiff of wind and you girls will blow away . . .' something else landing on the already full plates. The workers becoming covered in confusion, the women sharply amused, watching to see how adept these youngsters were at this age-old Indian game of seducing the coy stomach. Not very, came the verdict. They didn't have the right phrases, the social graces with which to parry the onslaught.

Not fair, Kulwant had felt at the time, although enjoying their

34

discomfiture. She was hardly much better and her own children worse.

'I'm just praying it won't rain on the day,' said Asha, finishing off her mug of tea. Are you really Asha? wondered Kulwant. Which God do you pray to?

'I will come to the centre. No. No. Stick is very good. I will be punctual. On time.' The projected trip promised to be entertaining. She would drag Caroline along. Dress her up in an old sari, fix her up with an Indian biography, and they'd have fun together, fitting in and being with the Asian Oldies: wandering on the beach, kicking up sand, teasing each other to go into the water, and amazed (with a forever amazement that had lasted all their years in England, not unmixed with moral censure) at the brazen display of flesh by white women.

'We, the workers were wondering if you would like to be a volunteer here?' Asha was hesitant, Kulwant astounded.

'I don't think I would fit in,' that was a good cop out, but an admission of identity.

'You have a lot of experience. Mrs Desai was telling me . . .'

'Gossiping!'

'No Auntiji. Of course not.'

Kulwant gritted her teeth; if you call me Auntiji one more time I'll wrap it round your tongue and tie a knot in it. So the past was being raked up, stirred and aired? 'I don't think I could do anything here,' standing up, shaking the stick ready for action.

'Oh, don't rush off,' Asha was persistent, 'there's an . . .'

'Too busy, too busy,' Kulwant muttered, turning away, 'find patch for sleeping.'

The look of consternation on Asha's face gave Kuli a long-lasting glow of perverse delight.

Maya the Myopic

Maya, Maya go slow, go careful, don't wear mountain boots on frozen water, else Ammi will catch you in her nightmares, and neither will know who is dreaming. Don't give your dreams into others' keeping, their world is not yours. Guard yourself against invasion, weave your words into a shield around you, others' nails are sharp and wounding; head pregnant by others' stories, when yours was taken from you with a suction pump. Why empty your inside at the say so of another.

Why buy a vacuum cleaner, your home is hardly big enough, gadgets have their fascination, long cylinders and floppy hose-pipes, or a self-contained upright, arrogant in its independence.

You must buy one and will buy one, for possessions are self-affirmation. Carrying it home is a burden and many the bus passengers who feel its corner on their bodies. Happiness is tearing the sellotape, ripping open cardboard, pulling out the insulating stuffing, arranging the different pieces in a display on the floor. She'd forgotten the plug. Tidy it away in a cupboard. Having it didn't mean it had to be used.

Shopping basket loaded with bleach, cleaners and scouring pads. The check-out lady won't let you through for your bag is empty of your purse. Another gap between intention and action. You wander away into a park, cramming into a bench corner, staring at monkey children on slides and roundabouts, fantasising what could have been. Internal slide-show rudely shattered as a slap lands on a demanding face and the pretty little girl kicks her mother, the two caught into a knot as the boys come and take sides; punches fly, howls shriek agony, till they tumble to the ground in a tangle of hate. A smile lights Maya's face, chuckling she walks away.

Eyes closed, Shanti opens the door, the folds of a red embroidered dupatta framing her face. Standing aside for Maya to enter she follows her into the lounge. With a gesture Shanti invites her to a seat. Maya feels like a queen upon a throne as the wings of the wickerwork chair fan out around her, and the velvet cushions curve around her body.

Poonum looks in, her eyes alive with laughter, and can be heard in the kitchen, running the tap, tinkling cups and saucers. Shanti settles cross-legged behind a charkha, its mirrors and bells tinkling and twinkling as the wheel spins. Eyelids never opening, Shanti's hand rises and falls feeding the cotton wool, the other turning the wheel, halting occasionally to disentangle a knot or straighten the thread. Maya watches and waits, hypnotised into a waking somnolence. Poonum enters carrying a loaded tray of food and drinks; placing it on the floor she fills a plate and hands it to Maya. Shanti has stopped her spinning and waits as Poonum pours tea into a glass. Moving out from behind the charkha Shanti picks up the glass and comes to sit on a stool next to Maya, one wrinkled hand on the chair rest.

Maya had seen Shanti at the meeting she had attended with Big Sis, and her eyes had fixated on Shanti's closed ones. Eyes whose eyelids never lifted, not even quivering into a peep. As the evening ended and they were leaving Poonum had approached, inviting Maya to visit, saying Shanti would like to meet her.

Staring at Shanti's blue-veined, rounded eyelids, contoured like a gentle hill, a black river of lashes ringing the base; Maya feels uncomfortably voyeuristic, for a face that retires behind the eyes is private to itself, and to gaze at it with unrelenting curiosity is to assault it. But Maya cannot turn away, her own eyes caught among the wrinkles and creases, exploring the shadows and stains; lifting her gaze an inch away from the surface and the rest of the face jumps into relief, its terrain a page showing the years that have tramped over it. Smooth away the folds and lines and the young Shanti will step out of the old:

skin burnished brown, glowing over beautifully arranged bones, tantalised by full and luscious lips. Though the skin is now patchworked and discoloured it pulls more compulsively than the original, the lips may have lost their old sensuality but are no less alluring in a resolution that brooks no faltering.

'Youth is for giving to the children,' says Shanti, speaking for the first time, 'and who would begrudge it.' Maya is entranced by the bell-like voice, each Hindi word modulated into a rounded fullness. 'The English with their fears have made a deity of youth and degraded experience and age into the dustbin. And like lemmings we are rushing into their horrors. Of course we are not perfect but our children believe that by rushing into the English life they will leave behind all the Asian problems. When will they realise it's only an exchange. An English set of problems for an Asian set. Look at Rani.' Shanti points to the wall where a gallery of photographs capture Rani from infancy to adulthood. 'Sixteen,' said Shanti. 'One for each year. She always wanted to be older than she was.' Detaching the last one from the wall she brings it over and places it in Maya's lap, while all the while Maya wonders how Shanti can move with such precision and direction. 'You are as fragmented as she; our children have shattered into pieces. Look at Rani.' Guiltily Maya moves her gaze to the picture in her lap. How did Shanti know that she was still staring in fascination at her.

Rani was her mother's daughter, the full lips and high cheekbones overshadowed by brilliant almond eyes. 'Sixteen. She looks older, does she not. She couldn't wait. Each photograph was taken on her birthday. On her sixteenth birthday we had a little party for her and her friends, all girls of course. My husband would not allow a mixed party which Rani wanted, with boys and drink, late in the night. In the evening her friends Sarah and Tessa wanted to take Rani to see a film. We said yes. After all you cannot say no all the time. We gave them more than enough money for tickets and a taxi to bring them home. It was after midnight. We thought she had gone home with one of the friends. We waited for a telephone call. She will surely phone to tell us. Half-past twelve. We did not know where the girls lived. Did not even know their surnames. One o'clock in the morning, my son telephoned the police. They said these youngsters are always playing pranks. She'll turn up in the morning. Half-past one my son and husband went out. To look. They went to the cinema, walked around the town. You'll probably ask what for. It's better than waiting at home. I had to wait at home.' The voice paused, her hand comes over and lifts the photograph from Maya's lap. Held between the hands like a prayer book, she continues. 'They came back, two hours later, three hours later. I can't remember. Again Arjun phoned the police. They took down the details. I do not think they did anything else. And you know what kind of people we are. We did not ask for help from our friends and relations. We also thought, we hoped, it is a joke, she is angry with us, she will come back in the morning. Why stir up gossip about her. Again they went out, looking, searching. They were stopped by the police.

'I was waiting. I waited in her room. Her pop posters, dolls, clothes around me. Holding on to my stomach, where she had grown for nine months. We had a son and wanted a daughter. I think now she was too much loved. The light was coming and the birds were singing outside. I looked through her books, her schoolbooks, covered with her writing, and the red ink of the teachers. Many ticks. She is an intelligent child. She was twenty-one on the last birthday. We bought a cake and I made Indian sweets. Every birthday I do it. You're not shocked.' Said as a statement, because Maya wasn't. How can she guess behind those closed eyes? How much more does she see?

'I looked through her clothes. Some of them still had her smell. So many clothes she has. Some smelled of her perfume. Here girls start using these things so early. Her dressing table was covered with creams, and eyeshadow and powder. I used to say to her these things hide beauty, not make it. The young do not understand till they are old. She has a jewellery box. It is an Indian one, with enamel work on it. It was empty. Every birthday her father had given her something made in gold. Small pieces. Not very expensive. Sixteen things. I suppose they would fetch some money. It is bad I did not cry. Have not cried since that day. A police car brought Arjun and his father home. Arjun was extremely angry, at the police, at Rani, threatening terrible punishments for when she came back. I stopped him. If something is said. It lives on.

'I didn't care any more about gossip. We went to the school, talked to her friends. They all said she had talked so many times about leaving home. It is like entering a different world, when you find that your child is a stranger. A door shuts on the past. They did not tell immediately. Not till the police questioned them. Tessa and Sarah said she had left them at a tube station. I was worried. She did not have enough clothes, she did not have enough money. Then Sarah told. Rani had been taking clothes out one by one, money also she had been saving.

'Tubes. I travel on them many times. I have been on every station on every line. They are like the arteries in a body. And I have walked, miles and miles in London. London is not the same. Every street is different. At that time the police made many enquiries. And they said do you know how many runaway Asian girls there are? But you know they say it with delight, as if she has done a wonderful thing. The papers also. If they could, they would encourage every Asian girl to leave home. For what? A bed-sitter? A strange man's bed? Social security? Freedom? How happy are they with their freedom? How happy are you?'

Maya started as if waking out of a dream, the silence alive between them. 'Perhaps happier than if I had stayed at home.'

Shanti nodded. 'Perhaps. It is a very thin word. An oblique between two paths. But you are not as brave as my daughter. You had your degree before you made a move. You play chess?' Maya shakes her head. What had happened to Shanti's eyes? 'Chess is a game for living by. It would be good for you. Rani did not claim social security. That way we may have been able to find her. What did she do for money? Where did she live? What is she doing now? I cannot open my eyes until she comes back. I search for her through her voice, her smell, her walk. These things cannot be changed. Hair, face, make-up, clothes? They are borrowed skins. If someone changed you, you would not recognise yourself, but you will recognise yourself in Rani. I no longer care what she has been doing, who she has been with. If she is happy she will have been right. You live with perhaps, I live with if. If she is unhappy, ill, badly treated . . . her father died of a heart attack, he is at peace. I cannot sleep for waking up is re-remembering, from the beginning to this day, and all the days in between.

'Arjun said he would get married, a young girl in the house would replace Rani. Poonum came. The heart does not swop so easily, it will grow to take in more, it cannot forget and Ranis are not so easily replaced. As your mother cannot replace you.'

'My mother had no place for me.'

Shanti returns Rani's photograph to Maya. 'Keep it. It will keep her in your mind.'

Shanti walks Maya to the bus stop, the red embroidered dupatta incongruous with her coat. 'It's Rani's marriage dupatta. I had it made even when she was little. In these flimsy things we lay foundations for the future. You must leave the past, it is dead leaves.'

'I'm all right.' Maya mutters. Now knowing Shanti sees too much. Does she see Maya opening the paper over the breakfast coffee? The coffee spilling as Maya sees his photograph, sees him collecting a prize?

At least they spelled his name wrong. A bitter bubble of satisfaction within her. It would have been enough to have seen it for that if not for the trails of imagining that cut through her fragile peace, yet again; imaginings of him with the other, talking with the other as he had talked with her, eyes alive and glittering, talking non-stop, one idea tumbling out after another, mimicking the bus conductor, shop keeper or any one of their friends, turning any ordinary story into a fun trip. And the bed-times! Day-time or night-time, making love with love.

Dangerous territory. Maya go slow, go careful, the jagged edge will slice you off and you'll be lost in Shanti's darkness, trapped behind lashes that will never open.

The bus arrives, and Shanti says, 'No matter how you change you're still the same.' Maya sits at a window seat, her reflection on Shanti's closed face.

Rani is now Rosalind of mythological fame. She wrote the home address on an envelope, the telephone number inside. Sealing it well, she stood on the Embankment and posted it into the River Thames.

Tea for Two *Chez* Caroline

Friendships are peculiar creatures, half here, half there, half imagined, half understood, half misunderstood, half fact, half fiction, half something, half nothing, half a story, half a truth, half of this person and half of the other. A hybrid with four legs, or two tails or two heads; looking neither like the one nor the other. Almost like having a child, she thought. You give birth to it and, like the paper boats we used to make in the floods, you set it on the water and watch it finding its own path through the eddies and currents.

Stick-leg-shuffle-leg-shuffle. Stick-leg-shuffle-leg-shuffle.

Asha and the Asian Centre had re-awoken the old tug-of-war inside her. She thought she'd done with groups, political parties, the revolution that's always coming tomorrow or the day after tomorrow; the excitement of adrenalin pumping on an idea, the chimera of possibilities coming true!

Tired of words and endless talking she'd found some peace in being an onlooker, and had little belief left in those gyrating on the floor, except that she was often troubled by a doubt suggesting that cynicism isn't always the final solution. However tea was always the British panacea and she stick-shuffled her way through the streets to tea and Caroline.

'Caroline's Café' had gone all pine, plants and chintzy curtains. It took Caroline about ten years to work through a phase, each representing the essence of the decade, as Kulwant had once told her; the observation turning into an unintended compliment bathing Caroline's face in a rosy flush.

42

Hair in a bun, granny spectacles, huge-loose-woolly jumper, a lacy-layered calf-length skirt, suede boots falling gracefully round her ankles, a pair of knitting needles clacking between her hands. Caroline glanced up as the door opened and lifted her eyebrows in resignation. 'Darling,' standing up and kissing her, 'next time you want to go to Oxfam give me a tinkle first. You may as well have your pick before I take them round.'

'Your clothes wouldn't look Oxfamy.'

'I'll have "Oxfam Supplied" sewn on to the front of them, though I can't guarantee the old decaying aroma. Now what can I offer you? Decaffeinated coffee? Herb tea? Sugarless cakes? What would you like?'

'Indian tea, you old bag, with as much tannin as you can boil in,' Kuli said in a sing-song doing a dancing twirl round her stick.

Caroline became alarmed, 'You'll frighten off the customers. Here, sit down,' pushing Kulwant into the sofa adorning 'Caroline's Corner'. 'Are you becoming a latter-day degenerate or are you degenerating? However I shall pander to your vice, your tannin tea you shall have. Darling, have I told you about the fortune I've made out of that tea?' Kulwant nodded wearily. Many a time had Caroline talked of it as though it was a miracle that profit could be made out of a commodity.

Depositing her knitting, Caroline's boots tapped her over to the other end of the room, her plump figure cutting a swathe through the customers. The food counter ran along one whole end, displaying salads, fruit, fresh juices and cooked, wholesome food. Kuli loved the feel of crispy freshness, the colours and lingering aromas. Caroline had refused to go totally vegetarian. 'I like sinking my teeth into a morsel of flesh occasionally,' she'd said, saying more than the sum of the words.

'Especially if it's young and tender,' Kulwant had added, lifting an eyebrow to underline the unsaid.

'And who encouraged me into paths of temptation, you wicked old woman. Now, by rights I should be doing penance for the sins of my past, not embarking on new ones. All your fault,' a satisfied smile shining on Caroline's lips.

Making herself comfortable on the sofa, Kulwant picked up

the first magazine that came to hand from the pile spilling over the table. *New Labour Review*. Kulwant hadn't seen it before. Must have come out after her retreat, though that did not stop her being impressed by Caroline's steadfast commitment to the Labour party; it was Caroline who had persuaded her to join all those years ago, bright-eyed and eager, wanting her friend to step out of the sidelines, to do something for herself and others, to add to the numbers working for a common purpose. Ah, the fervour of youth! Kuli suppressed her briny smile. She had given up, but Caroline had continued. Books, magazines and newspapers lay invitingly on the shelves by the other window. Caroline believed in spreading the word. Whoever wished to, could come and do their reading in the comfort of her café. Accessibility and warmth in a cold climate. Cynics would say one newspaper is worth twenty cups of tea.

'Sid will bring it over,' said Caroline returning, flopping into the deep, cushioned chair, 'He's better at it than I am. Remember when your mother first made it for me?'

Caroline had been ill after the birth of Rachel, unable to look after herself or the child. The doctors couldn't diagnose anything specifically wrong and whispered postnatal depression outside her hearing. The wind in the house carried the words to her and she sat up and screamed a stream of negatives, 'No, N Noo. Noooo No N Noooo . . .' missiles thrown into the house, like bats released in daylight. They pushed sedatives down her throat and all the while she was saying, 'It's no use, why did I do it, it won't do any good, it's all my fault, I should have said no, no, no, the first time and all the time.'

Months later she talked to Kulwant about her nightmare time, sipping another cup of the mother's Indian tea. 'God knows what your mother put in it. It wasn't just the mixture of all those "oriental"' (this last with a smile of complicity) 'thingys, the cardomoms, cloves, fennel. Takes you out of yourself merely rolling those names round on your tongue. Cardomoms! Say it, and you can almost taste them. The tea warmed where I was coldest, fed me where I'd never known I was hungry. You've never had that, have you, the bottom falling out of your world?'

'Perhaps my world never had a bottom.'

'No. How could you have. You came over the sea. Cradled in

44

water, day and night, just like a baby in a womb.'

'And starting a new life.'

'And hating it as much as a baby hates leaving the womb.'

That came later, Kuli wanted to say, but kept quiet, not wanting to interrupt Caroline's thoughts.

'Do you know what it's like, when the truth suddenly hits you? You could be having a cup of tea, or arranging the next dinner party or sitting in the pottery class . . . it can hit you anywhere, at any ordinary moment, and you can decide to hear it and accept it, and take the pain that goes with looking at its ugly, nasty face. Or do what I did, tell yourself you imagined it, hide it, sweep it under your skull where no one will see it. The trouble with doing that is that it's the same as if you'd given it a gilt-edged invitation to come and live in your home, share your bed, share your food, share your body. Part of me couldn't believe it. Not me, it kept saying. Can't happen to me. May happen to other women, not to me. I'm special. I'm Caroline.

'He doesn't love me. Won't love me tomorrow, next year. Didn't love me. Doesn't mean a thing said out like that. Words like any other words. Coming out of one's mouth. Like "do come and visit" – "lovely party" – "brandy or port". To me they were like the button that sets off the nuclear bomb, they were going to explode my world. Not nuclear. Neutron. I gathered them up and locked them away, except they corrode the lock, and their poison seeps everywhere, till you live it and breathe it and think that life is like this anyway. That's why I got pregnant. A woman's eternal gambit. I used to think I was so strong, invulnerable.

'He doesn't love me, and it was like the acid that dissolves. I dissolved, disappeared. Because if no one loves you, you aren't anything.'

'I didn't love my husband.'

'Different between you. Wasn't it. You weren't expected to do that. And I thought you were starting off with a handicap. What a laugh. Remember the hours I spent trying to persuade you not to. And for once your mother and I were agreed. What was his name – Himmler? Golden boy . . .'

Kulwant laughed, 'Michael, the Archangel, Him-him to you.'

'I said, it's not worth diverting your life on account of one man, you do it for one, you'll end up doing if for all of them. Ha. Me, giving advice! Strange. He did love me. And then he stopped loving me. As if someone had turned off the tap, switched off the supply and sliced away half of me, but the half that was left wasn't worth anything, because he didn't love it. What did your mother put into that tea? Some of "that old Indian magic"? You'd bring that huge thermos and I'd drink half cups out of it, all day long. Smelling it, tasting it, feeling it go all the way inside me.

'I went bonkers, or I decided to go bonkers. Can't remember. If I'd had a son – a man-child as they say – maybe I wouldn't have. I wouldn't have been horrified that I'd brought another woman into this world. To do for me what I couldn't do for myself. To grow up and fall in love with one of those bastards. Talk about child abuse. It's the loneliest thing in the world, unloved and living with the loved. It's not just the gap where passion used to be, or the silence where excitement used to be; it's that respect goes out the window, consideration becomes a chore and the you-ness of you evaporates. The functions remain: the housewifely, the social, the secrecy: "mustn't let on there's anything wrong," as if everybody else isn't busy trying to hide their own disasters.'

Bruce Springsteen thumping out 'Hungry Heart' and Sid lowering a tray on to the cane table, Caroline trying to give the gentle brush-off to a regular admirer.

'Only comes here to goggle at you,' Sid complained.

'Nothing wrong with his money.'

'If you were as mercenary as you make out, you'd be worth a million and I wouldn't have to slave over the kitchen stove . . .'

'You'd get bored dear,' soothed Caroline, lighting up a cigarette. He grumped off back to the food counter as they both laughed, 'Wish they'd made them like that in our time.'

'Feminism was still in the womb.'

Kulwant leaned forward to pour out the tea, 'Cheers. To us. Who'd have thought we'd grow old together.'

'Not so much of the old,' objected Caroline, 'haven't done our half centuries yet.'

'Not far off.'

'Right old misery guts today, aren't you darling. You should

46

come round more often. Must be lonely since your old bloke went off. Now don't get sensitive and don't give me one of your lectures about his golden heart, and how it hurt him to leave you and how you never did right by him. Not the point. Point is that you both contracted, morally and legally speaking, contracted to enter an arranged marriage. That's got one set of rules. He goes off and falls in love with some eyelash twirler, that's got another set of rules. You can't Mix 'n Match. One or the other. Which reminds me, I've got two tickets, complimentaries my dear, to the latest local fringe venture. I've heard very good reports of this latest thing. And don't look away, it's not the Asian group you love to hate. It's Roger Lodger and don't judge the writing by the man. The poor dear is *en route* to becoming famous. One day we'll have to pay to see his plays. Have some more.' Topping up her cup. 'Why so hard on your Asian brethren?'

'You think I should applaud them for making their careers on the backs of Asian women?'

'White men do it all the time.'

'Asian women?'

'When they can. Otherwise it's us lot, the natives, the female part . . . we're nothing but their stepping-stones, useful when we're fashionable, displayable and adorable; practical around the house when we need to be kept in the background. Not a bad bargain by any means, and they don't even have to queue up at the sales, in fact we queue up for the customers. Consumers' paradise. Why should Asian men be any different? Rachel's had a daughter,' the voice changing and altering. 'I telephoned you to give the glad tidings. But are you ever in? Gadding around eh?'

'Gladding around. Catching up on the wild oats I didn't sow.'

Caroline looked exasperated, 'I don't know if it's such a good year for new crops. She's going to be called Sarah. Cooeee . . . Kuli, I'm talking about Rachel's baby. Mummy is going to bring her up all by herself. Family history repeating itself. Granny will have her every third weekend. Daddy? I can see it on your lips. She's not decided whether he's going to get shares yet. He'll have to wait and see how the market forces develop.'

He hadn't wanted children but Rachel had chosen to get pregnant, 'Because,' as she had said, 'he and I have the basic ingredients to produce healthy kids with good bodies and probably good brains.' Having made her decision for a DIY baby she was fanatical in sticking to it. No help from anyone. He'd served his function and she could manage the rest on her own. And he'd gone.

'Scared silly,' said Caroline. 'It's her revenge on me. She's going to show me how I should have done it.'

Caroline picked up her knitting and shaking out the wool started looping it round the needles. Another woman become a mother, another baby to become a woman, another woman to go through it all again. Though it was Rachel's choice Kulwant felt a coldness in her heart. Good that she didn't have a daughter. Sons could be sent out into the world and you knew that they'd fend for themselves. Women usually ended up fending for someone else; always giving out from their store of tenderness and love. If it wasn't a man, it was a child. The constant attunement to the needs of the other, like half a brain, one ear and one eye always with the other, anticipating the other, watching over the other, giving spiritual nourishment, advising, cajoling, persuading; the beginnings of an endless list. Who looked after her? Who replenished her needs?

Looking at Caroline's lowered eyelids she saw again the bruised skin, the hot sleepless nights, the emptiness; they never regained that first sparkle, although over the years they'd learnt to smile a different smile. We've been through the mangle but they didn't squeeze all the juice out of us. Asian or English, did it make a difference to the amount of pain you carried through your lifetime? 'We may be sailing in different boats but the sea is the same.' Who had said that?

Caroline looked up, untangling more wool. 'Choose a pattern darling, I'll knit you something.'

Sid came with his coffee and cigarette to take his break; Caroline rushed off to replace him, talking and chatting as she took the orders and served out the food, a lovely, loving Englishwoman, happy and at home with other English people. The quotation was wrong. We're in different boats, on different seas, and they see monsters and nightmares in our sea and they get frightened and want to pull the plug. Women weren't women only, they were also their colours and their national fears.

She had known it, of course. But each time she met Caroline she had to work it out all over again, not so with Maya. Maya whom she'd known only for a miniscule of time, as compared to her lifelong entanglement with Caroline. As long as long with Caroline as long as long with England. As long as she didn't confuse Caroline with England or the English with Caroline; differentiating and separating the individual traits that were uniquely Caroline and the Caroline traits that were General English. In school, elegant Caroline would always be behind her, ready to pop out and defend whenever necessary. 'Some people are just plain stupid,' would be her comment. It took her more years than Kulwant cared to remember to acknowledge that a whole society could be 'just plain stupid', not merely some of the people, some of the time.

Caroline had adopted the newcomer in junior school. Kulwant had probably been the first Indian girl they'd ever seen, and for many years the only one in the class. She was an interesting curiosity and for the first few months the centre of attention. As her self-appointed guardian, Caroline determined which of the others would be privileged to help Kulwant with her numbers, vocabulary, and who was to be her partner in the playground games. Caroline relished her power, particularly when Kulwant got the highest marks anyone had ever had in a maths exam. She was dubbed the 'brain box', the 'eastern genius' or 'eastern genie' as that became more popular. Kulwant wondered what all the fuss was about, she'd been relieved to find one subject that made sense, despite her lack of English. In India, maths had been drilled into her from the day she'd started school, maths being considered one of the foundation stones of education; if you weren't much good at maths you weren't much good at anything, was the general belief. Caroline was as pleased as Punch. The protégée who'd appeared to be helpless and dependent had, with one leap, joined the intellectual toffs of the class. Caroline basked in reflected glory.

The café is filling up, as the lunchtime crowd filters in for midday sustenance: some lingering over a long meal, others dashing in, gulping down and dashing out. Kulwant wondered what lunchtime assignations so accelerated their feet? She had travelled that madness too. Compressing work, rushing chores, short-cutting conversations, walking faster, sometimes running, always in a hurry, stretching time to fit him in. She'd travel half an hour for the pleasure of five minutes with him; attend meetings that bored her to tears because he would be there; a chance to see him, talk to him through the medium of the meeting, savouring the complicity of a private conversation conducted as public debate; the making of complicated arrangements to provide a cover while they sneaked away for a few precious hours. Karm had become an addictive craving.

She stooped down to pick up the stick as it fell on the floor and surreptitiously wiped the water misting her eyes. She wouldn't call them tears, wouldn't give Karm's memory another iota of emotion. If she could she would siphon away the substance of all that she had given and been with him, bleaching that time blank.

Caroline looked up from her serving and came over. 'How's the employment situation?' Kulwant shrugged her shoulders and Caroline stared severely across at her over her glasses. 'Idleness makes mischief. You need something to occupy you.'

Kulwant lifted her stick and prodded Caroline's knee with it. 'I'm having fun, something I haven't had since I don't know when. You want to put my nose to the grindstone again?'

'There's a research job going, friend of mine, works for TV, very highly paid. Let's forget I mentioned it.'

'Your lucky day. I know someone who might be interested.'

She stood up to leave and Caroline gave her a hug and a lingering kiss on the cheek. Placed an envelope in Kulwant's hand and with a smile that admitted her manipulation asked her to drop it into the office, on the excuse that it was urgent and she wouldn't be able to take it round till far too late.

Pig-tails Dives off the Deep End

Stick-leg-shuffle-leg-shuffle. Stick-leg-shuffle-leg-shuffle.

Shoving Caroline's letter away into the bottom of her bag. If it was that urgent Caroline would have taken it round herself. She would go and see Maya and tell her of this televisual opportunity, but first she must stand in front of a posh stainless steel office building, mosaicked with tinted windows; she must stare at the distorted shadow reflected on the shiny polished metal. Smudged outline seeping out in different directions as she waggled, head, foot or hand, stuck out her tongue, made funny faces, twirled her stick in imitation of many a silver screen dancer. Giggles behind interrupted her choreography.

Two nice ladies in silken saris, hands genteelly covering their mouths, eyes looking down at being discovered; they move on as she stares after them and hears a sentence from one to the other about how the English old folk go funny in the head.

She followed behind all moody and sulky, though she'd gotten what she wanted because they hadn't seen through her. But it didn't feel nice for them to think she was one of the others, not when she'd decided how she stood on the divide at a time when others were only thinking of perms and passion.

She was the same as that girl who came home, handed her empty satchel to Pauli and announced that she had left school. Amid shocked gasps and thunderous looks, further declared that marriage was next on the agenda and they'd better ship someone over from India for Indian was what she wanted to be.

She'd dived off the deep end, into the eye of the whirlpool; still wanting to know what makes the world go round. The parents reasoned and argued and refused. She was adamant but they did not believe. They retreated into half promises, vague possibilities, trailed strings to tug her, unaware, towards their ruse. Like a ship on a pre-determined course she ploughed straight ahead, cutting through their schemings and turning them into a swathe of froth behind her.

'We're supposed to force you, not you us,' they complained, perplexed and angry.

'You couldn't. I wouldn't be. I'd not toe the line. I'll bend the rules and make you do what I want.'

The father gave in first, saying it had to happen later, so why not give in to it sooner; but the mother saw the sooner as the sooner loss of glittering opportunities and her anger at this wilful self-destruction never abated through the years ahead; and with gritted teeth lived through the times when she could have flung 'I told you so' in her daughter's face.

The mother would set food out for her as usual, and sit and watch while she ate; she in turn would keep her eyes down and never look up, for how to meet those devouring eyes – eyes of a beggar at a rich man's dustbin. The mother has a litany circling around her head: with each mouthful child I give you nourishment – what nourishment can the illiterate mother give for the mind? Wished – for you to know all that I can never know – to see in all the ways in which I am blind – wished you to go beyond the confines of my living – give life to your dreams for life to change – wished you never to have my workworn and calloused hands – wished I had never brought you here.

He was finishing medicine in India and his brothers here gave full recommendation and she said, 'Yes. You say yes too,' handing herself over to every ritual, hoping the significance of each would seep in, making her what she wanted to be for the world doesn't happen outside, it happens inside here, inside the mind and body, and change takes place where earthquakes were.

Time crouched on the starting-line, coiled like a spring for the pistol shot, released into the race with the setting of the date:

and she became the lens of a camera, wanting to preserve and record every moment, every motion; to say to herself so this is what it is to be an Indian bride. To have the cornucopia of clothes, jewels, and consumer durables emptied at your feet. To be at once the subject of sorrow and celebration as the house filled with guests and an ever-increasing pool of women came to stay from days beforehand; throwing up natural leaders who took command of her and the proceedings: plastered her with turmeric to clean her skin, mixed henna for the intricate designs on feet, hands and face and ensured that all proprieties were observed. This was a marriage whose ceremonies began days before the 'actual' event and if she had not been schizoided by her English growing-up this psychological preparation would have laid the foundations for the changes to come.

She became the catalyst for reminiscences as each woman re-lived her own wedding, remembered families left behind, shed tears for daughters 'given away', unfolded the woes of womanhood for each to share, then with the suddenness of a magician the tempo/temperature would change and they would let loose with ribaldry, sexual innuendoes, crude and vulgar jokes aimed at men, at each other, and take the greatest delight in discomfiting any man who happened to stumble in on such a moment, not that any of the men ever lingered, turning tail faster than a rabbit.

The kitchen turned into a canteen for a perpetual tea service and food service for whoever arrived, whenever they arrived. Underneath this activity and talk ran a rivulet of music which surfaced, erupted, as the stages of the pre-ceremony occurred or after a day's work was done and the women came together to sing and dance; old songs arrived at today through generations of use, sung without musical accompaniment. Funny, plaintive or bitter-sweet, poignant in their bareness, sharp and cutting in their sarcasm. This is how you pass on immortality, she thought, while someone said to keep the noise down in case the English neighbours complained and someone else said let them come and join in, they might learn something about enjoying themselves.

The disorientation of suddenly awakening in a house full of sleeping bodies; tiptoeing over those slumbering on the floor.

heart thudding in case anyone awakens to see and wonders why this bride-to-be is stealing stealthily out of the house.

Freshness, cooling tightened cheek. Dark, murky night, hardly a star in the sky, shreds of the moon occasionally peeping among the bars of heavy clouds. What is Michael the Archangel doing now, this very minute? What is he whom she'll meet tomorrow thinking now? Is he awake like her? Eyes open, unfocused. Tonight is the last night of this life, tomorrow the steps round the holy book that will hurl her into the future.

Back into the camera, wide-lensed sweeping the garden, noting each object in its place, thinking this is all sliding into my past, must imprint, must remember for the remembering in the future.

One shape among the others shifts and moves and its darkness glides towards her. Tiredness playing tricks!

Aren't you cold? asks her mother's voice.

Why are you out here mother? Why is your voice whispering pain? You have other children.

I gave you birth but can't arrange your happiness.

Is it so necessary?

Life is too long a road without it.

You haven't had much and you've survived.

I've known what I am, that has guided me to what I should be. I have never lost my anchor of certainty, this country has put you in one of its mixers and whirled you round till you can't tell your inside from your outside, your duty from your rights, your needs from your responsibilities.

You brought me here.

We were tired of bartering with hunger.

A few more years and I could have ended up marrying an Englishman.

A few more years and you could have been the equal of any man.

Can't live your life for you mother – this is mine and it'll be me who'll live it.

That's the pity.

54

Maya Maybe

Stick-leg-shuffle-leg-shuffle. Stick-leg-shuffle-leg-shuffle.

Landing up at Maya's tiny two-roomed flat, watching her bum sticking out as she bends into the refrigerator.

'I can do you a cheese sandwich, or a cheese on toast, or a toasted cheese sandwich, or a cheese-as-you-like-it with garam masala. Homemade. The masala that is. If nothing else my mother keeps me supplied with genuine G-M.'

'*Quelle* variety!'

'I'll slice the bread in fancy shapes. Then I'll mend that tear in your coat.' Kuli shakes her head. 'Mustn't spoil granny's punk image?'

Maya's hands do battle with the heat of the grill and Kuli removes the cover off the unused typewriter. Hearing the rustle of Kuli's unspoken pressure Maya turns and says, 'I will not write for all is Maya, TV its technological vehicle.'

'Research?'

'Why not? Because tomorrow we will all disappear and there should be something of how it was for us for those who're coming after, and after those noble words the truth to tell is that I'll no longer let grass grow under my opportunities.'

Maya had been met at a performance of *Laying the Blame*. Huddling by the doors as the rain slashed outside and Kulwant came tapping down the stairs, from the stalls, irritation marking each step. Neither spoke to the other as Kulwant sat on the step and time passed, till intermission came and they drowned among the audience who came flooding out seeking drinks and ice-cream; To be left stranded again as the bell emptied the foyer for the second act. Maya turned and asked why she wasn't in there. Kulwant lobbed the question back to her.

'An Asian farce. Not meant to be one. And if he had to, couldn't write one to save his life. Drama tells what life is about if you can read between the scenes.'

They took a taxi to Maya's flat and Maya asked, 'Am I goddess or temptress? Typing drudge was what it came to. And he declined to buy the Tipp-Ex though there was always money for his durex. Harems are always there as they say, it's only the faces that change. Self-protection at any cost. Even if she says it's hers she may make him pay.'

Maya the Myopic was what she called herself: 'I wanted to be one of the Great Explorers, Intrepid, Fearless, Going where no man, note man, has gone before, charting regions unknown. Not for me this sordid world of materialism. The circularity of this globe is but a ball in my hand, one squeeze and puff – dust and ashes. My journeys were to be inward, paddling my canoe into the psyche, a submarine into the imagination. And what happens to these glorious aspirations? What do I end up doing? Bending down for a shitty man to use my back as launching pad to his glittering career.'

Who is this unknown man imprisoned in her tongue?

'I erased all signs. Doesn't it show?' asked Maya. 'You can riffle through the bathroom cupboard, you'll not find a single shaving stick. The deodorant neither, he always used mine. Now I never bother to buy.

'Joint efforts, like children, can be kidnapped, and how do you make a play a ward of court. Get rich and famous double quick! Didn't read the warning signs that would have told me what he really wanted: he'd read reviews yet-to-be written, given interviews yet-to-be requested.

'He says one day: "We don't seem to be getting on well these days. We don't seem to have the same feelings for each other."

'Pride prevents personal petitioning: "Everything changes," she says, blasé as can be.

'"Oh God it's so painful," he cries.

'"Come the monsoon and you find out who's got clay feet," she says.

56

'"If we carry on like this we'll destroy each other," he says. "It hurts like hell. But I'll leave."

'He left. Straight into the wide and open arms of his white woman. You may have noticed him around the circuit: Khadi Kurtas bought at great expense, Achkans for those glamorous, amorous Asian nights, tastefully set off by a shawl slung casually around one shoulder. Someone's doing a roaring trade in essential accoutrements for the Asian Arteeste Arriviste.
'Gripe. Gripe. Gripe. The ones left behind always do.

'Do you reckon it's too late for an arranged marriage? My Dad imagines he could still pull it off. Not that I have the choice I did. Dad gets the blame. Daddy's spoilt daughter spoilt for life. My mother's like that. Arranging endless sightings of the eligible and respected. Now she laments with a tear in her eye and a smirk in her voice. Thing is I used to think I'd won the war. People are more devious than I ever give them credit for. Now she gets sympathy and I get bad blood and early ulcers. Is there time to back-track. Pick someone from the DEAD bunch: The Doctor-Engineer-Accountant-Dentist.

'Here I am, moneyless, manless. Maya the Myopic. Getting tired of my sob story?'

Kulwant is at the door, nibbling the top of her stick. 'Ask not what freedom can do for you – rather ask what you can do with freedom.' The door closes and her goodbyes tip-tap away down the stairs.

Maya reaches for the phone and speaks to the man who's in the TV. Arranges an appointment for a meeting to be.

His office is the attic of a house in Battersea and he thinks he'll make a packet out of his novel idea, though the remuneration he's offering will only keep her in the style to which she's accustomed. Good thing, she thinks, I always liked peanuts.

'Madness,' he says, 'in the Asian Community. A working title.' He or she must be mad to take this on, she thinks.

Imagination she protests is Maya. Of course he replies, extracting a carefully preserved copy of *Siddhartha* from his desk, but it charts the rivers of Kubla Khan, Coleridge you know could never take it easy. Who would sleep with his nightmares in bed. She asks if he can get her a canoe for she's burnt her bridges and sunk her boats. He laughs and says he couldn't have hoped for anyone better, handing her a cracked paddle.

'Let's dissect the Asian terrain,' he says. 'Where does culture turn the screws? How does imagination hallucinate the logic and the rational. Is Asian madness the same as English?'

She agrees to preliminary research, telling herself something has to pay her bills, never imagining this will ever go even half-way serious.

She goes home, draws him and is about to file him away among the others, when she stops for a second look. Why did she draw his hair as a spider spilling over? Sitting neat in a too elegant house, only authentic paintings allowed on the walls. He is neatly scrubbed, expensively dressed. Why is she assailed by a sense of seedy decomposition?

Pencil pictures of all the people who have ever come her way. For all those remembered there must be double forgotten for ever. Flipping through the pages is her history passing, the earliest memories to this morning's encounters, and he is the last, a full stop finishing the sentence.

Spread out on the floor her pictures form a carpet, arranged in rows of years. The remembered shadows of infanthood, that turned into parents, aunts and uncles; friends of early childhood, some who now lived as phone numbers in her diary, others who had gone missing years ago. And in the present a pentacle, the core of her life. After all these years was this the sum total of her relationships. She picked them up and arranged them in alphabetical order. Sunil-rakhee brother at the top, always a calm constant, moderation in everything: moderately happy, moderately successful, moderately boring. Sunil's boat would never leave the shore; her harbour for when she got shipwrecked. He had asked her to share a slice of his life, right at the beginning when neither knew the depth of the sea. Unthinking, she had swum out; mindful of the sharks, he had stayed back. Sunil was pinned with blue tack to the wall. Richard and his big goggle eyes, never invited, merely arrived, met at university, never shaken off, a pet dog pleading to be let in, promising to fetch the papers and not chew the rug. She could marry him. Why not. Let everyone think it an unsuitable alliance, many who had done worse for themselves. How long wait for the perfect Indian mate? Extant only in imagination. Richard was folded and wedged under the typewriter. Ooh. A moan escaped. Why had she drawn this? Foetus floating in space.

Quickly gather up the faces in case they see. For no one knew. Only her and him. And he had gone taking their precious past. Fear thumped within! How much would he tell as he relaxed in satiation with the other; there's not much that remains private in pillow talk canoodling; would he bring out their past, bite by bite, food for their vicarious pleasure, flavoured and seasoned for her particular delight?

It's only paper, throw them away, this is no way to X-ray the hidden chains of bondage and love. Open the old school atlas, place them in the middle. Big Sister's face arrests her gaze.

K → K

Stick-leg-shuffle-leg-shuffle. Stick-leg-shuffle-leg-shuffle.

Endless women, thinks Kuli, singing endless dirges for the departed. Maya would only start forgetting when the remembering refused to refuel with pain, though a tenacious and stubborn memory will hold on even after the last iota of emotion is exhausted. She, Kuli herself, had never felt that passion. At least not for the one that she had married, but his going had left craters of emptiness and might-have-beens.

She hadn't done him no favours by marrying' him. England and its financial rewards were no compensation for a wife who couldn't return love. Such a yawning gap between them, as if they were two people looking across each other never able to look at each other. He was a decent, hardworking man, wanting to provide a good home for his family, a good start for his kids; the kind of honest, ordinary man that most women would be more than happy to be married to.

'. . . making us into a goddamned one-parent family,' Anup the oldest had raged at her, feeling himself to be in the middle of calamity, 'sending father off to some sordid affair with a schoolgirl.'

For his part Anup restricted himself to playing tantalus with the white women who came his way but never strayed from the arms of his upper-class Indian wife. Kulwant had seen him in action and knew he got a far greater thrill from dangling himself

60

in front of them as forbidden fruit than he ever would from actually going to bed with them.

Of them all he had blamed her the most for his father's departure; she had upset his family scenario: no more the united couple standing at the door of the family home, forever welcoming, forever the greeting card parents and grandparents, hair turning grey, benevolent, sentimental, and together.

It had taken three years for Kurshid to 'get' him. He'd been dragging his heels and saying 'yes', 'no', 'I don't know', often in the same breath. Kurshid couldn't wait any longer, she felt her life slipping away and her chances fading into nothing. She'd worked too hard to get him to lose him to his indecision. So she got pregnant and phoned Kulwant. 'He looked unloved. That's why I went for him. I was unloved too. You've had it easy. Haven't you. I can tell. Probably had the typical Indian parents who couldn't do enough for their darling daughter. Well my Dad ran off with a white woman, and she didn't even have to get pregnant. I haven't had a proper home. I want one. And he can give it to me. And I'll be good to him. Not like you.'

'Wouldn't it be better to have someone more your age.'

'Ever tried to get together a dowry for three daughters on social security? And if you haven't got a dowry you need yer high-falutin' degrees and what-nots. I ain't got none of those. But I got him and I'm going to keep him.'

'You don't care,' he'd said. 'Can you care?' stopping in the middle of packing. 'All this time I've waited, not wanting to hurt you, thinking things would get better. But where there's no love there's no hurt is there?' She was sitting on the chair, by the window, arms wrapped around herself, ropes to bind the turmoil inside, let not anything seep out. The suitcase lid clangs down as he drops heavily on to the bed, face drawn, legs turned to water. 'I never thought my life would be split like this. I didn't marry in order to separate.'

'Another one of England's gifts.'

'It's not England. It's what's wrong between us.'

'How can you tell the difference?' He wouldn't go. He couldn't pick up his bags and step outside the door.

'The last time I packed this suitcase was when I came from

India. Remember I was going to give it away, but I didn't. When you don't have much you conserve for the future. People told me not to come to England. They said you'll become a gypsy. A nomad? A no man! I was ambitious.'

He refused to take the car so she called a taxi; he wanted to torture himself for having done what he had, for doing what he was going to do.

The storm broke over her head, the accusations came to her, it was all her fault, she'd practically thrown him out of the house, pushed him into this girl's arms. Arvind/Arnold, the youngest, had kept out of it, though he had come with his brothers and left with them. Seemingly united for once.

'Make him come back.'

'No.'

'What kind of an Indian wife are you?'

'Like any kind I guess. They come in a million varieties, individually packed.'

'Very funny.'

D for Division

Pleasure.

Pleasure in soft warm flesh, face nuzzling every precious inch, fingers on fingers unfolding, the miracle of face and limbs, eyes fluttering with recognition. Where have you come from? Were you waiting for me? Oops here we go again. Who would have said nappy changing could be such fun.

Kurshid blows bubbles on his stomach, his gurgles fluttering butterflies in hers. No more being alone; no more time for thinking and worrying. No more stepping in between the splinters of a family fallen apart, no more being in the middle of being ignored. Big Sister looked after them all while mother racked herself to illness and lifelong recrimination. How could the mother have held on to him when the rules had changed and no one came to give induction training on how to play the new game. Arranged marriages don't equip you to cope with lust and loss. Not that these things don't happen there, but when they do it's in and around the old weatherbeaten framework of family, friends and social pressure.

Her father's friend had written to her grandfather; the grandfather had written to village friends here in England. They organised a deputation which pressurised till her father had agreed to forget the one he was living with and bring over the ones he had forgotten. How long had he been living with this white woman? How many others had there been before? Kurshid never got the story in full, driblets gathered through the years and pieced together.

One day in the pub, tongue turned liquid with too much beer, he had talked of marrying his Diana. Dominoes of panic triggered the chain of events that deposited mother and daughters at Heathrow's Arrivals terminal. Strangers to each other, he had been shocked at their peasant appearance, recoiling from this segment of India deposited in his home. Diana was out and they were in, and he was back living in the past of his first arrival. They couldn't speak English, they didn't know how to cook on gas, they didn't know how to behave the English way, they didn't know how to shop, they talked too loudly, they wore their bright embroidered Indian clothes and got looks in the street, and they cried for their home.

How could he send the mother out shopping when she'd come back with a tin of peaches instead of carrots? How live with daughters who fought in the street, shouting Punjabi curses at the tops of their voices: Kurshid had got angry because the oldest was bought a bar of chocolate and she would only give the other two a small piece, hogging the rest for herself. Pleadings gave way to anger, anger resorted to kicking, kicking demanded hair-pulling and then all reciprocity disappeared as nails and fists took over. Mayhem, as their mother shouted at them, the youngest bawled at the top of her voice, the father struggled to pull them apart, finally slam-slapping them into awareness. Painfully aware of being the centre of attention, he shoved them into order, handed them the shopping bags, and was pushing the whole family pack back home when he came face to face with Diana.

Diana stopped him to speak and asked if they yet understood English, and seeing his embarrassed look carried on in oblique manner inviting him to reconnoitre her abode. He didn't answer and hurried his family home. His wife looked back and saw the woman standing where they had left her, looking back at them. The wife pushed her hands tight into her coat pockets. The next day she practised with lipstick and rouge and when her husband came home from work he told her she looked like a clown. Tears were shed in the arms of the daughters. Those tears became a rivulet and grew into a river between the father and the daughters; living on opposite banks none wanted to cross over to the other. Specially when Diana came, bringing fruit, and trying to talk sweet. Had it been India, the mother would not have allowed her near the threshold; being England she had lost her bearings and didn't have the confidence to guard her home.

Diana came to have a peep inside, wondering how these barbarians were keeping him hooked. This had been her home, her kitchen and, eyes upward, wondering how the bedroom now looked. Telling the wife she loved him, if they'd stayed in India wouldn't it have been so much better. He'd sent money regularly that she knew, and would have carried on till he died. Was it worth uprooting yourself for the sake of one man, travelling thousands of miles to a country whose language you don't speak, leaving everything familiar and cosy behind.

What do you do, she said to the wife, when he's at work and the girls are at school? Stand at your window for hours on end, watching other people on the roundabout of their lives. Many times she'd passed this way, hoping to catch a glimpse of what goes on, and seen the shadow against the net, a head muffled in a shawl, arms crossed to preserve the body heat. He told me you don't light the fire till the girls come home. Stingy. Have you no care for yourself. Your face is drawing in like a wrinkled apple. England's too cold for foreign fruit. I want my home. You've got yours back there, doesn't it make sense to go back. We women have to fight for our hearths, our beds and our men. We're not living unless we've got one to make a living for us. And you think I can go back and get some white man now. My name's muck, don't you know. Not everyone takes kindly to a cosmopolitan life. And your men know how to treat a woman good, make her feel the queen of the hive. When him and his friends, we all went out drinking, they'd be falling over themselves to fetch me booze, food and flowers. I didn't care for the looks I got. You got to take the best you can get. I've been around, I'm not an innocent. If you could see my heart you'd see the bruises, each one a love-token from boyfriends of the *gorai* race (I know what words you have for us). Gory don't begin to tell the story.

Diana talked and smoked and asked for a drink. Blank looks. She stopped talking. They heaved a sigh thinking she must be about to leave. She asked again, making the motion of pouring and lifting a glass to her lips. Now they understood and looked

65

at the mother, their Ammi, for a lead. Ammi wasn't present. She was trapped somewhere where pestles pounded in her head. Where was Anwar, with her jokes and songs, singing to the rhythm of lifting and hitting, lifting and hitting.

The eldest got up and went out and came back with a glass of dripping water. Diana sighed and thought she would make do and then decided to show them whose house this was. Actions speak louder than words as they say. The whiskey and brandy was always kept in the cabinet under the television; and so it was and so it is. She wanted another glass. Didn't fancy water diluted with brandy. Marching into the kitchen and marching back established a thrill of ownership that no words could have given. Coming back into the room she felt as if she could almost shoo them away like so many troublesome flies.

Diana had drawn him away and he had said go back to India; the bharadari 'posse' wore out the pavements toing and froing between the family and the father. His will and pride won out against their persistence. Having made his move the father didn't want to be seen as a pendulum forever swinging between the family and her. Diana was happy, her home was concrete.

Having given up, the 'posse' turned inwards and echoing the father said wouldn't it be better if they all went home, back to India. The father had promised to supply enough money to keep them well, and of course in India it would go further than here. Ammi said no because there was no one left to help her pound the chillies and the masalas; the girls said no because they would have to wear their rejection like badges on their clothes.

Necessity is a powerful incentive to progress and their English improved by leaps and bounds as the visits to the social security office became a regular part of their lives, as they had to accompany Ammi on her regular visits to the doctor, for the body rebelled against the mind and sprouted aches, pains, illnesses that no doctor could locate or cure. It fell upon the elder two to accompany her, and at first they did it rota fashion, but as it became an embarrassing chore, there'd be a constant tussle to cop out, till they decided to decide by the flip of a coin. It can be peace to put yourself in the hands of fate.

Poverty. Arguments. No one to look after you. So you look after yourself. Others will come and visit. Fulfilling their social responsibility; their lips saying we are here to help you, the eyes warning not to ask for help too often: our lives are busy with our families and work. Kurshid hated them and would escape upstairs. Can't make friends at school, you can't match their stories of Daddies and presents and future plans; they might invite you to their homes, you don't want to invite them to yours. Winter's here and you need a coat, but pretend your hands aren't ice-like lumps, the school blazer will suffice, turn up its collar and hurry home. Don't want to go to the school Christmas party, Cinderella has no godmother, not even any mice in the house, no crumbs of food for them to nibble in the dark, they've migrated to better pastures. Father comes with Christmas presents, and you don't want to see him because all you see is Diana at his back. Mother comes upstairs to haul you down, for if he sees flesh of his flesh he might repent and return, and life might switch back to normality. You refuse his conciliatory caress and sit huddled in a corner. What's the use of his presents when he's taken all of himself away. Not that you ever knew him. He left when you were young in infancy, and as you grew older you waited for mention of yourself in the letters from England. Pyar was sent to all, but you wanted a gift-wrapped portion that was just for you, just from him. Grandfather gave special attention and the chachas in the house took you over as their own, but you always wondered what a father was? What is it to have a father who belongs only to you and no one else.

Delight and joy, we're going to England. After years of waiting you didn't question the hurry and hustle; didn't hear the whispered conferences; whirled into shopping visits, fittings for new clothes, visits from far-off relations to say farewell, village friends pleading don't forget us, don't become a memsahib when you get there. The streets may be paved with gold, but our hearts will cherish you; you will live in India for as long as we remember you, and if you remember us then you will live our whole lives long. Which way to England? ask the children playing in the sandy road, is it the road that goes round by the temple? or the road that goes over the railway track? They all laugh throwing sand into the air, England is across the water, through the air, where everyone is rich and they have cities of glass and Kurshid will become rich and speak English and you say I'll come back with presents for you all, wanting to be modest, enjoying being the centre of so much attention and speculation.

The television's broken. Who's going to ask him to repair it. Pride means boring evenings. Amarjeet's father has left some free tickets for the Indian film show on Sunday. Not going to go because everyone dresses up to rival the silver screen stars, and they come out talking of what the heroine was wearing, making plans to make exact copies, ready in time for next Saturday. Shopping trips are a fashion parade, taking time over choosing potatoes, give everyone time to view the style and cut, linger over the tinned fruit 'cos the local heart-throb is stacking the shelves.

Big Sister is leaving school for a job in the local factory. Money coming in at last. What luxury to buy chocolate and cakes. Mrs Khan comes with a proposal for Big Sis. Her younger brother is in Pakistan, a nice well-behaved boy, would it not be good to see them both well settled? The mother grieves over the lack of dowry and Mrs Khan assures that her family are not concerned with such old-fashioned customs, after all what gift can be greater than the gifting of a daughter. The mother says that she will consider it and Mrs Khan goes off secure in the knowledge that where there are few options, few will let such opportunities slip. Big Sis did. Curling her lips in disdain and shaking her head. The mother persuaded, pleaded, wept, accused in anger that she was as unfaithful to the family as her father, and Big Sister looked surprised and said that wasn't the way she would have put it, but it could amount to the same thing.

'You could get out of all this,' Kurshid said to her when they were alone, unable to understand her sister's lunatic refusal. 'You can leave our miserable lives behind. Have a man earning for you.'

Big Sister had looked at her in scorn. 'What do I do when he leaves me?'

If you decide you don't want something then not having it will never bother you, was Big Sister's philosophy; marriage was the same as the clothes, food, household articles that they could never afford. Knowing what she knew of marriage, she couldn't afford it. Mrs Khan sniffed and warned that many people spend their lives in regret.

'Yes. Regrets for those that do.' Big Sister was not to be moved. The mother saw the chance for her daughter's happiness slipping away, and endlessly repeated her repertoire of tactics. Availing nothing.

'You can't live your whole life without a man,' Kurshid's voice was wide-eyed in wonder and warning. Could a woman mean what she said? Could she live merely on conviction? Would there not be a day for wavering and compromise? Would there not come the dark day of regret?

'They're making me forewoman at the factory. That'll mean a few more pounds. We could wallpaper the front room.' Kurshid stamped her foot in anger, and Big Sister looked up unsmiling, 'You'll have to wait and see.'

Mrs Khan was peeved. She'd have to look for another match for her younger brother. Sourness creeps out in conversations half said, words dropped in seeming carelessness, taking the long way round to loop back: this girl must have a boyfriend hidden away, went the gossip grapevine. God knows what happens when you send your daughters out to work; who can control the people they mix with? They get a pay-packet in their hands and think they're 'independent'. If you're with English people all the time, it's not long before you pick up their ways. Like father, like daughter. Once a family goes to the bad it never gets right.

Not enough O levels for Kurshid to carry on, but good enough at English to do a secretarial course. Two pay-packets coming into the family, who would have believed it! Mother can stop denying herself and buy a new outfit of clothes. 'After the bills are paid,' says Big Sister feeding Kurshid's pay-packet into the family purse. Big Sister was getting too big for her boots, at home and at work: at work she was complaining to the union about not being promoted and at home no penny could be spent without her permission. Tapping her head she'd say, 'I keep it all here. I don't need shopping lists or budgets written down.' So much for working. Extra pocket-money was all she got, not that she'd ever had much pocket-money anyway.

Working for the doctor was her second job, taken for the sake of more money. At first she was full of awe and deference, surprised to see an Asian man in so important a job, determined to do her work as well as he did his. Staying till each day's work was done, anticipating his needs, forestalling problems, glowing with pride when they got nicknamed the 'dynamic duo'. He was only human after all and work-life can't be hermetically sealed off from the private: stay around long enough and you get the smell of what happens after hours, stay alert and little clues start etching pictures of what happens elsewhere; talk about yourself and those who want to unburden will see the open invitation. Not that he ever did so, not in words, not even when intimacy erased the lines of demarcation. Call me Napoleon, she wanted to say to the world, I fought a long, lonely campaign: enticing but never leading, hinting but never inciting. It takes guts of iron and a starving need to keep your goal so clear in mind. Her constant justification that if he hadn't been available, her efforts would have rebounded like a ball off a wall; if he hadn't been in need, he wouldn't have been cotton wool, soaking up what she had to offer.

Home was very upset. Big Sister more than most, and started calling her Diana. Big Sister now had a job in the union and talked politics and workers' exploitation. Little sister Shazia's teenage puritanism was outraged, and Ammi took refuge in religion. Kurshid went to work with headaches and red eyes, and talked wistfully of moving out, into a place of her own. He was no fish but baiting had become her speciality. Through coffee-times and lunch-breaks she scoured the accommodation columns and worked and reworked sums to make it affordable, complaining of expense account executives whose lunch bills would see her through from one month to the next. He increased her salary and she moved out, promising to continue contributions. Little Shazia announced she was getting a Saturday job and they could manage so who needed her.

Her little flatlet made it easier but it didn't make it better; loneliness increased her need of him. Having ruptured herself away from home the niggling fears she'd hidden away erupted into nightmarish giants. He drew away, repulsed at this parody of home from home, a most graphic rebuke.

K Versus K

Persuading the baby that it's ready for sleep turns into a session of tickle and giggle. The doorbell cuts through their squealing, and wondering at this unexpected caller Kurshid lifts up the baby and goes down to answer.

It takes some time but not too long before she recognises the inhabitant of the dank, dingy dressage. Kurshid's face fades pale and drains Kuli of her own audacity.

Nothing to stop us being friends she had said to herself and realised the mistake as she stepped in. The past was a wedge: guilt edged on both. There shouldn't be any blame she wanted to say, can't we reach through to each other? You're here because of my past and my present is because of you. Kurshid's face is a stony mask and Kulwant knows she should turn and go, but the effort of deciding and finally arriving prompts her to persevere. Kulwant thinks in irrelevance, both our names begin with K. Indians would surely read something fateful into such an alphabetical coincidence. Why can't we reach each other? Cut away the layers of imagined wrongs. It may not be as you think. Don't misconstrue my motives.

Who has the right to say how people should live and whom they should meet? Life was not always like this: there were jungles and deserts and glaciers of ice: ancestors who hunted and wore the skins of their spoils, to whom life and death were but an instant apart; and they say there was a time when women ruled and men obeyed, if that was so do you think they would think my visit so wrong? I won't ask to hold the baby for you fear I will steal it. Not carry it away, body and blanket, but those stories of wicked step-mothers and wives scorned adorn your mind with intimations of fear. Her look could steal the baby's soul, you think, for half of the father is in half of the child and she in her body has borne three that were his, don't that confer a territorial right?

'You're scared of being alone,' says Kurshid.

'I'm not empty yet.'

Ammi had never been the same after Diana, was Kulwant staggering to the crazy house too? This recalling of Diana makes Kurshid recoil as Kulwant sits opposite. Kurshid tells herself this is her house and she is in power and can ask her to leave whenever she wants, specially now she's coming out with weird talk about jungles and glaciers and women who ruled. She hugs the baby close to herself and repeats a line to erase all that Kulwant is saying: 'if you can't hold on to what you've got, you've got to mourn what you've lost . . . if you can't hold on . . .'

Good. She was picking up her stick. She must be ready to go. What's she saying about being friends? Why? She wants to come and spy!

Kulwant left, knowing she had failed, wondering if she would try again. Couldn't they learn from each other? Two women linked to the same man. If women could change, they'd change the world. Her stick-leg-shuffle-leg-shuffle fades away down the street.

Kurshid takes the baby upstairs and puts him in his cot. Her hands lingering over the soft woolly blankets covering him as much as over his body. She tucks him in and sitting on her bed watches him sleeping, groping for the contentment that was hers before Kulwant's visit. She couldn't have done different she knew; how could she take Kulwant's fine and noble words at their bald face value. She wasn't born yesterday was she. She'd fight for her home like Ammi never did, she wouldn't be the woman left behind like Kulwant now was.

Slumberland Samosas

Big Sister was busy, getting ready for a meeting. Maya sidled in, unseen, slunk into a chair.

The room was small, barely big enough for the desk and cabinet and an ancient vase of dust-coated plastic flowers. However, Big Sister's name was on the door. Big Sister was going places. Big Sister looked up. She didn't look pleased.

'Come to do some more research?'

'Sort of.' Maya wanted to absolve herself, wanted to Lay the Blame on him, but kept quiet, for whatever she said in explanation would only sound like a string of excuses and Big Sister's face would only twist to a greater degree of disgust. The tool cannot always blame the workman.

They had first, and last, met when Maya had gone to a factory, gathering material for the play, giving assurances of non-exploitation and fidelity to the truth. Big Sister was forewoman and had been helpful, accommodating and interested. Any which way to further the cause of workers, especially Asian women workers. And Asian women writers. As time progressed Big Sister asked friendly questions. Maya hinted at a team effort, letting Big Sister assume the female gender of the other. Big Sister asked to meet this shadowy collaborator. Maya circumnavigated. Big Sister found out on the gossip grapevine. Big Sister said she wasn't angry. Disappointed, more. What was wrong with Maya's legs that she needed to be his crutch? Maya defended. Then found her hands empty as the play found a theatre. The theatre wanted changes.

He obliged. She raged. He took possession and was accepted into the profession, going out of her life in a glare of publicity.

'Some learn their lessons the hard way,' remarked Big Sister, gathering her papers into a pile in front of her. 'I don't have much time. What can I do for you?' Unthinking even of the 'what can I do you for?' that others would have trilled out with, greatly pleasing themselves with this most amusing redistribution of words. Maya was hesitant, thinking Big Sister would chuck her away like yesterday's papers.

'Madness in the Asian community?' Big Sister rolled it round her tongue. 'Isn't madness everywhere?' Maya agreed. 'Being another man's lackey?' Maya pointed out that she was on a salary. 'No self-respecting prostitute would agree,' retorted Big Sister. Maya gave up and prepared to say goodbye. 'You're in an awful hurry. Come and see me at home.'

How could she decline Big Sister's invitation, though some might think it was more akin to a royal command. Strictly following the precise directions, Maya arrived at a neat terraced house, with a tidy garden, and flower baskets hanging over the door. Maya didn't have X-ray eyes into the past, so how could she know of what this place had been underneath what it was now.

The door was opened by younger sister Shazia, Indi-pop blaring out behind her. Shazia led Maya into the kitchen and invited her to join the samosa-making session. Maya had expected tea and stilted conversation; so she was more than grateful for this conversion of her expectations.

'Destination Greenham women,' explained Shazia. 'If we don't do something about Ammi's dreams they carry on. Her shouting keeps me and Big Sis awake. I've got my exams coming up and Big Sis needs to rest for her working day.' Ammi was busy at the table, filling and folding, contentment in her hands and face. 'The latest dream was a nightmare, not to say they're ever nice . . . that's why we're making these . . . listen, will you do the frying and I'll roll out some more circles . . . nightmare to figure out . . . my friend should be coming any minute. Another pair of helpful hands . . . You ever done this before?'

Maya shook her head and said in explanation that her mother had never let her; in those days Maya had been smug and snide

74

that she was one girl who didn't have to spend her evenings in domestic drudgery. Only when she had to cook for herself, to satisfy her body's craving for Indian food, only when she was faced with having to eat her botched efforts, did she come to a dawning realisation of her mother's revenge.

Shazia was hardly listening to the story, her eyes on Maya's hands, handling the pooni like a fishing net, frantically chasing samosas through the boiling oil. 'Look, how about you do the rolling and I'll do the frying. Don't want you branded with burning oil do we? Don't get neurotic about getting the dough into perfect round pieces; just roll out a big piece and use this saucer to cut around.'

Shazia turned down the flame under the karhai, and as Maya hung rather nonplussed over the table, came back and showed her what to do. She either felt no irritation with Maya's ineptitude or hid it extremely well. 'Put enough flour under it so's it doesn't stick to the table.' Before rushing back to the cooker, to lift out the brown cooked samosas. 'We can have two each, when they're all cooked. That's what Ammi says. If we have more it's like snatching samosas out of the mouths of freedom fighters . . . that's what Ammi reckons the Greenham women are. Right, I was telling you about the dream, the one that led up to this culinary consummation . . . it's okay to use consummation like that isn't it . . . I mean you get the meaning. I'm a journalist by the way, or I will be when I've done with what other people think I should learn. To return to the point: Ammi's latest dream was a problem, a b-i-g conundrum. Usually Big Sis and I can work it out – this one really had us foxed, and then when we'd sussed it out, how to cater for it? That's a pun, you're free to laugh. She described the dreams. Horrible, they were.'

'Nightmares usually are, aren't they,' interrupted Maya.

'Ammi's are different!' replied Shazia, voice like reinforced steel. 'If you're bored I won't carry on. We can always talk about the weather.'

Eat humble pie Maya and beg for more.

'A lot of it was emptiness, silence, nothing. Doesn't sound up to much does it, but, you think about it, how'd you like to have a dream like that? Scare the wits out of me! Another part was people exploding into fire, bodies pressed flat into the ground, so that if you walked, you had to walk on them, not an inch of earth left bare . . . voices in the air, crying for help, mercy, and there wasn't any help. No one could help them after what had happened to them. And menace from the sky. Something dreadful in the sky was gonna come and get you. And you couldn't hide anywhere. Wherever it was it would get you . . . etc . . . etc . . . What would you reckon it was?'

'Hiroshima?'

'Not bad,' Shazia obviously gave credit where it was due. 'That was it. But what to do? 'Ere, these samosas aren't meant to be lobbed at the bombs, you've got to roll the dough thinner. That's Angie,' as the doorbell rang and she scooted out to answer, coming back in a few minutes, followed by her friend.

Angie was black. Maya was surprised. Younger sister did the introductions, as Angie washed her hands at the sink, and then settled down by Ammi to do the filling, first giving Ammi a kiss.

Angie was an expert. Maya was surprised. Younger sister returned to her boiling oil.

'I dropped in on Mrs Ghosh,' said Angie, 'they've done a hundred. Not much if you ask me. Mrs Gill and her gang at the Gurudwara have promised stuffed parathas. Poonum says she's got her area to organise the clothes collection, specially quilts. I don't know if quilts are a good idea. Keep them warm I suppose, though sleeping bags would be more suitable. I'll check on the others at school. Mum said her church group were still considering. Considering most of them are men she's going to have to do a lot of talking. That's okay. Mum's got the gift of the gab and she loves using it. That's my report so far. I'll check up on the rest at school. Tell Ammi.' Shazia translated and Ammi nodded her head in approval. Maya picked up the saucer to cut out the circles, and watched in horror as it slipped through her fingers, fell to the floor, spun on its back and came to a rest. Intact.

'Clumsy,' said Shazia, scooping it up and putting it in the sink, giving her another one. 'Ammi likes that saucer.'

'You were telling me about the dream,' prompted Maya, desperate to divert attention.

'Where did I get to . . . Hiroshima. Not exactly. I mean, we explained, to Ammi about Hiroshima, and what happened, and that it was long ago. Ammi said she understood, but such a terrible thing wouldn't happen again would it? she asked us. We couldn't lie. We tried not to answer at all. The dreams carried on. We hadn't told her about nuclear bombs and everything. We thought it would only upset her. I'm getting low on supplies, you lot speed up your work.

'Do you know what it's like explaining nuclear power to someone who's never heard about it before. Ammi doesn't speak English, so how is she to know? And you hardly get Radio Karachi here to tell you all about it. Newspapers? Her parents never sent her to school. Never did like those grandparents. Big Sis and I put in a joint effort but Ammi just couldn't understand, I mean she couldn't accept it, didn't want to understand it. She said it was madness. We agreed. Who wouldn't, right? I mean those who're sane. Right. So Big Sis told her about the Greenham women. Once she heard, Ammi wanted to go and see them. Once she got there she wanted to stay with them. Well Big Sis and I would have been worried sick, we persuaded her to come back. We wondered why she was so quiet on the way back. Saving her talking for when she got back, wasn't she. She saturated the local Asian women with her propaganda. The dreams stopped.

'They all thought she was bonkers. They think that anyway. No one was listening to her. And she was getting harrassed and worried again, and we thought oh oh here we go, back to square one. So I took her off to the doctor. Wonderful, Dr Gupta is. I like her a lot. Not only 'cos she turned the tide. Important person is Dr Gupta. Married to that guy who teaches at the university. She and Ammi chatted away like they were long lost sisters. Forgetting about everybody else waiting in the surgery. That's how they cooked up – laugh everyone, I always have to cue people for my jokes – cooked up this idea of taking food to the Greenham women. With Dr G's support the wheels started rolling. As everyone said, she's got degrees, this Dr Gupta, that proves she ain't bonkers. I reckon that proves how bonkers some people are, but that's the world innit. The gurudwara women's lot even invited two of the speakers from the Greenham women to come down and talk to them.

'More supplies needed. How are you getting on Maya? Not bad, but work on it, the pastry's still not thin enough. Look that's how Ammi taught me to make them, I'm only passing it on. I'll make tea when Big Sis comes. It got like an epidemic. Everywhere you went, women, Asian women were talking about the Greenham women, about nuclear bombs, about mad politicians . . . I'm just glad Ammi's dreams haven't come back.'

'Will the effect last?' asked Maya not sure what to make of it all.

'Dunno.'

'She's had dreams like this before?'

'Not like this, exactly. You see, she's got to do something about them to make them go away. 'Ere, what d'you think would happen if everyone had Ammi's dreams and had to do something about them? Angie you're not listening.'

'I'm concentrating. You wanted more supplies. The effect? Given half a chance half the women I've met would camp out at Greenham. Anything to get away from their families. I don't know. You live locally?' to Maya. 'Haven't seen you before?' Maya explained that she lived at the other end of town. 'Where do you work?' Maya didn't know what to say, so settled for telling them she was a writer.

'Oh,' said younger sister, 'now I know who you are. You took those women's stories and put them into a play, after giving them the *News of the World* treatment. That's what Big Sis said.'

'It was out of my control,' Maya defended herself, knowing how weak it sounded.

'Sounded pretty interesting to me. I'll see it when it's on again Big Sis can be a prude. That doesn't mean I don't love her. And there she is,' as the front door bangs, 'talk of the devil.'

Big Sis came in, briefcase in hand, water droplets sparkling like diamonds in her short hair. 'Managed to miss most of the rain. How's this going? Get what you wanted Maya?' Big Sis getting straight to the point. 'I've got two minibuses organised.' Angie said she didn't think two would be enough. 'Well Angie, get me a list of those who want to go, and I'll get Mr Patel to donate a coach. I'll help you in a minute,' going out and up the stairs.

Maya picked up another ball of dough, flattened it and starting rolling. Ammi asked Maya about her family, and whether she was married. For once Maya didn't prevaricate and answered Ammi in all the detail she wanted followed by the inevitable question about marriage.

Ammi shook her head in sadness. 'No one should live alone all their lives,' she said, 'and how are any of you going to have children?'

Younger sis was pouring out the tea as Big Sis entered, having changed her clothes and looking fresh and clean. Shooed Maya to a chair for a rest and took over the rolling. 'There's a women's meeting on tonight – Want to come? Organised by the workers at the Asian Centre. More material for your project.' Did Maya detect a sneer? The other two said they wanted to go too.

'What about your schoolwork?' asked Big Sis sternly. Both replied they'd done it, younger sis sticking out her tongue at Big Sis's back.

A foursome huddling under two umbrellas, splashing through the rain, debating whether to wait for the bus, deciding they'd get as wet waiting as walking. Big Sis whiled away the travelling time by recounting tales of the office to Maya. 'Forget fiction. Real life is where the drama lies. Enough of it to curl your hair white and send you running to the nearest nut house for a dose of sanity. Take me. Some of them can't give me enough of the red-carpet treatment, every word I utter is a pristine pearl of wisdom; others think I should go back to the zoo. There was a suicide in the office. Nearly. Richard and Dolly, the sixties multi-relationship couple. Apparently she had a secondary relationship with another bloke, ended up ditching Richard and moving in with number two. Bound to happen at some point. If she hadn't done it first, Richard would have. Richard took an overdose. In the office, during lunch. I ask you. I'm not giving you a morality lesson. Seems to me people are experts, out and out professionals at piling up their own problems. Hmm. Your look says you don't agree. You do agree? Perhaps. Problems are part of living with people? Hmm. Here we are. Out of the rain, into the warm.'

Rebel With a Cause

Rosalind is kicking at the surgery door, not with any aim of forcing it open, but when time hangs heavy on your hands, you gotta do something to fill the passing minutes. Standing back she surveys the row of half-moons kicked into the paintwork. So what! The shoulders shrug. Dr Gupta's got enough money to have it repainted a hundred times without feeling the pinch. So what! Money's got nothing to do with her, Rosalind, and vice versa. Sitting down on the top step, Rosalind plucks a rose and detaching the leaves one by one, pops them into her mouth, chewing slowly, savouring the flavour, swallowing and reaching for another one.

Stick-leg-shuffle-leg-shuffle. Stick-leg-shuffle-leg-shuffle. Strip of sunlight falling across the pavement, its triangle of light a slice of fallen gold. 'What's the matter sun?' she shouted, face uplifted to the sky, 'Remembered your job description suddenly.'

Pavan Gupta is sitting at a table by the window, watching Kulwant shaking her stick at the sky. Kulwant had kept her waiting. Pavan wondered whether it was deliberate, a ploy to teach the daughter-in-law her place; unlikely, she decided. Petty power politics had never been her style, I'll bet she's thrown away her watch, she could hardly have retained that expensive wristpiece with her new ensemble.

The waiter rushed to say the restaurant was closed as the old bag and old clothes bundle pushed the door open, and Pavan as quickly rushed to the rescue. Parrying curious looks, as she escorted Kulwant to her table, who wondered out loud why Pavan had to choose an expensive restaurant in which to meet. Pavan replied, while settling her in, that it was near her surgery. Kuli queried the purpose of the meeting, not that she objected to having a decent meal, hating to cook for herself. Pavan concentrated on pouring the wine, her plans for a warm-up, a slow lead-in, dashed on Kuli's sandpaper moodiness. Pavan suggested Kuli come to live with them, with her and Anup, coolly sponging up droplets with her serviette as Kulwant spluttered on her wine, spattering her chin and the table.

'You need a cheap baby-minder? Take a look at what I've produced, I wouldn't recommend me to go near shouting distance of a baby.'

'You could have your own flat in the house. There's enough room. And I can't have children.'

Too much food for two. Long silences in between. Pavan throwing lines to Kulwant, who abandons them to litter the table. 'I wanted to adopt two children from India but Anup won't agree.'

'So you'll adopt a mother-in-law?'

Pavan looked at her watch and said whenever you want, come to stay. 'We're all cut off from each other. Shirley and A/A hate us. Because of you, they think. It isn't impossible to reach each other. You tried with Kurshid.'

'All secrets are common knowledge!'

'She phoned. Complaining. This is a country of terrified people. All hoarding their love to take to the grave. Are you coming to Greenham for the feeding of the women?'

Time for work. Pavan paid the bill and rushed off. Kulwant half dozy with warmth and stomach satiation, ambles aimlessly behind her tapping stick, not wanting to be reminded of that little sentence about Shirley and A/A containing that four-letter word, hate. Because of her, Pavan had said. Hate in the family because of the mother! Not the first time in history a mother had been the object of filial hate. What had she done? What hadn't she done?

Rosalind is waiting, first in the queue. Rosalind hates this doctor. Hates the Indian beauty in a sari, gold bangles jangling on her wrist, the crisp authority in her voice, the sindoor in her hair and the red dot on her forehead. Hates the Hindi words that are casually, automatically, thrown in to enhance nuance and underline emphasis where English fails.

Don't you give me your Indian greeting, I was born on English soil you know. So what if my colour's different? It's an even sun-tan.

Who wants that mumbo-jumbo of languages, identity, saving for the future, work and respectability strung around their neck? Pay your bills on time, don't buy on hire purchase; don't they know life is a hire purchase. 'Love child', my mother used to say of me, don't get it wrong. You couldn't if you knew her. And we all live in coffins. Some are velvet-lined. Some don't have a lid. You play your good Indian wife role. I tore my way through the net.

Rosalind's nihilism is a brick wall for Pavan. Rosalind smiles sweetly, as Pavan talks of her family left behind in India, a way of life that nostalgia brings so near she could reach out and touch. Everything she had meant to tell Kulwant pouring out into unlistening ears. Pavan's changed her tack this time, no pep talk of groups, therapy or changing life-style. Just give me what I need and let me go, where there's no life there's no change.

On the way back Rosalind passes a skip and looks to see if anything useful can be rescued. Salvages a saucepan and old blanket, covered with dirt. What's wrong with that when we are dust ourselves. Michael's waiting outside the house, huddled by the entrance, the entrance being the sheet of corrugated iron they levered open one night. A camp stove between his feet, the blankets under his bum and their tin mugs and frying pan in his arms. She knows immediately what's happened. At least she thinks, smiling sarky, they had to wait for me to be out of the way before they did it, didn't they. Michael's faded blue eyes look up from under the dirty blond hair, pleading. She hands him the package and, abandoning everything, he scrambles behind the iron fencing. She picks up their possessions and follows him.

Leaving Michael behind, whose smile shows he's drifting towards his magic carpet of contentment, Rosalind wades through the overgrown garden to the unhinged back door.

Rosco has placed an iron bar across it. He'll be waiting inside. Running her fingers along the cold metal she struggles to decide. Lift the bar and she may lose, become his possession for he would have more than power over her. Turn back and he would pursue through the tongues of others, news of her weakness spreading from one mouth to another, till their paths crossed again and she would have to surrender. Having once turned her back on him she gives herself into his hands. She can't run away from running away. Her fingers clasp tight and lift. He may have strength but she has fire. She's stepping inside, into the cluttered unsafe dark, nervous fear pumping through her.

When Rosco's Magdalena left him, he had turned to her, expecting to cash in a favour, the favour of allowing them to stay when the others had vetoed. Not enough room were the excuses, which was a laugh echoing in the empty rooms; no strangers into the group, which was no laugh 'cos winter was coming on. Rosco had been holding himself on the outside, waiting for the others to decide. When they went negative he turned positive; fear and unpredictability can aid and abet each other, accessories in any act of intimidation. His hand appropriated the warm sleeping bag under her arm. 'Corner up top. It'll do you.'

'Where you from?' he asks one day.

'Argentina,' brushing away his hand.

The days were spent in foraging from pockets and shops, only taking what was needed, not out of any political conviction or compromise with her conscience, merely that she'd long ago turned away from the clutter of possessions. Michael spent his days in a haze, having relinquished himself into her hands, knowing they were capable, expecting her to do everything for him, knowing she would. And she did. Michael had long ago inveigled her into obligation and she didn't recognise the pattern till it was too far set, and then didn't mind because she thought, as long as she was with him she could pass for one of them.

Something happened one day, when they were gathered around the newly acquired television set, rescued by Rosco, he wouldn't say from what captivity. The picture didn't last all the time, blanking out to leave the sound. One day Michael started quoting poetry to the soppy music. Magdalena knelt down by him and said how beautiful it was. Michael inflated with pleasure. A long while since appreciation had come his way. Getting tired of Shakespeare he announced he was going international and holding up his hand commanded attention. They all obeyed. To hear Michael even talking was a novelty, to hear Michael spouting poetry was truly unexpected entertainment.

'This is called,' holding up his hand palm outwards, '"How".

'How she missed the banana boat is a mystery to me,
How she kissed is history to me
How she gave me emotional dysentry, is plain to see
How she fucked was fantastic to me
How she sucked was news to me

How she ran to her wig-wam was bad to me
How she turned her back was sad to me
How much a wog she was, was clear to me.'

Much clapping and cheering, Michael was a hit. Encore upon encore followed, voices joining in at each repetition, arms around shoulders, joining in a circle, stomping into a dance. Rani has sent a message from the limbo-land where Rosalind has banished her to tell Rosalind to get out. They crouch out in the hall, in the darkest corner, fearing what discovery would do, a fear fed by each wave of laughter.

Why not pick up a blanket and go, the tube will whizz you round and deposit you in the middle of your nowhere, because everywhere in London is nowhere to you; you've wiped out geography and you use it as an erasure across Greenwich Mean Time: time has no meaning, why count the hours and days when you're not selling and you're not buying.

But you're tired of moving on: moving from job to job, always downwards because everyone else is scrabbling upwards; when you've stepped off the bottom rung it goes against the grain to have to get back on. And it's not a very attractive prospect to look back up at the millions of two-legged ants running ruin on each other's heads.

Michael's voice rises above the din in the room,

'I'll give you all my history,
You'll not need no dictionary
The kiss of a wogess is addictory,
Begin at the beginning with Kuli
Zig-zag A to Z and pick up Julie.
She pretended very coolly
She hailed from upper Colindale
I didn't see her peeling in the heatwave
In fact I couldn't see at all,
Her blackness was my blindfold
She turned every midday into
Deepest darkest midnight.'

Rani and Rosalind listen to the chanting, clapping, stamping and dancing. Rani and Rosalind take out the last shreds of an expectation, and tearing it into smithereens, they roll it into a ball and push it through the floorboards. When you don't belong, you don't belong.

That was weeks ago? Days ago? She didn't know.

The house is empty of its usual human sounds. A few had left with Magdalena, others must be taking a discreet day's outing: sometimes it don't do to know it all. She's stealthy, one foot placed carefully in front of the other, hoping to surprise him, gain an advantage.

A push from behind and she falls to the floor, the iron bar hitting her chest. Rosco laughs and claps his hands, saying, 'Give in now and we'll have fun.' A crouching animal she backs away, one hand clutching the bar the other scraping on the floor, eyes riveted on him as he strolls leisurely towards her. She'll only have one chance, if that. The wall is behind her and she straightens up against it: wary, watching; wondering if she's already his cornered prey? He stops a few paces away, talking of how it will be, and how when he's bored with her he'll hire her out, never have to worry about bread no more. He's never had a Brownbird before, his mouth's been watering ever since Michael read his poetry.

'Don't believe everything he says. He's never had me. He's old and wasted.' Rosco laughing, disbelieving. Waiting for her to come to him. Shaking her head she slides away, her hand cutting on a nail.

'Don't give me no bargy, you fake Argy. Ashamed of it yourself, aren't you.'

Stall for time, it's life or slavery. Behind her back she's levering the nail out of the wall. He's coming near, too near for safety. Nail in her fist she slides away again. He's following, getting bored, he's going to pounce. She drops the bar, he leans over, reaching for her mouth, knee jerks up and the nail plunges into the neck. His fist sends her flying. In pain they're both scrabbling for the bar. Don't think, fight for life, this pain's nothing to the agony you'll get. Teeth and nails and feet and arms. Use the weapons biology gave you. The bar has rolled away and he's reaching for it. You're done. Fly towards his neck and dig the nail in deeper. Agony twists him round and his hands clamp around your throat. The world is a red haze, don't hesitate. Claw at his eyes, tear them till the blood gushes out to free you. Split second of a chance in which you reach for the bar, which without volition or thought swings through the air and into his head.

Michael is blowing bubbles and doesn't see you as you collapse beside him.

Bonnie and Clyde

Bonnie and Clyde across the racist divide. Arvind/
Arnold and Shirley. He forgets time, forgets about going home,
in fact home doesn't even enter his thoughts. She sneaks out,
evening turns to night, and they kip out in a stolen car.

It's a Saturday night and they're leaving the pub. He says he's
got to see her home, 'cos a woman in the dark is a target for
attack. His words are all wrong, for the four who block their
path want a wog not a woman. They tell her to run and save
more than her skin. She thinks that four against one isn't much
of a contest, and as their fists and boots pound into his flesh, she
attacks from the back, at least her nails are sharp and their hair
is a handle to pain, jerking the neck back she gets a punch in the
stomach. Her eyes open on the ground and she sees the crowd
looking on, cheering at the fun. Melting away like snow in the
sun as the cops screech in.

'Arvind, Arvind,' she's screaming for Arvind as they bundle
him up, and chuck him in a van, his blood and teeth dropping
like confetti. Her Dad's a cop, else it would be much worse, and
they let her off but keep him in. She refuses to go, and Dad's
face goes red with rage as someone snickers about nigger lovers.

That wasn't the first time, and her Dad says it can't go on for
ever, he's lost his patience and she's got to go. Her home doors
close fast and it's no use knocking for no one's going to hear.

We're alone now.

They're huddling by the Thames, hands curving and covering
around each other's, the flesh of one can keep the cold away

from the other. They walk in amnesia, till the Embankment gives way to stairs leading up, and brick-eyed streets watch their bleak and bare meanderings. She won't give in to tears and huddles in a doorway as he goes off to beg from the Indian Take-away.

They give but can't resist the temptation to interrogation. 'Why's a nice Indian boy like you going begging like this?' He mumbles something about passports and no right to work, and they invite him to stay and eat where it's warm and dry. Murmuring thanks he back-walks towards the door, breaking into a run as soon as he's out and panic, panic as he can't find her, each doorway a Shirley-less black hole, each black hole a step into madness. Hot curry sauce spilling over his hands, throat locked tight with fear, unable even to shout her name to spread a net of sound to pull her near. Eyes feverishly combing the surrounding dark darkness. Had he come out by a different entrance? Had he lost his way and was in streets miles away? Had he lost her for ever? Food slides out of shaking hands, horror-filled eyes fade-out to blankness.

Tentative hand exploring in question, voice whispering, quivering in suspension; like thread and needle, her touch and tones drag him back, eyes clearing, focusing on face appearing. She's here. Wrong turns can be quicksands to disaster and if she hadn't given up waiting, they could have gone through life amputated of each other.

Stick-leg-shuffle-leg-shuffle. Stick-leg-shuffle-leg-shuffle.

Arvind/Arnold lifted his head from under the car bonnet and wiping his hands was about to go into the office when he noticed the three-legged, long-coated creature turning in at the IN entrance. Shrugging off a suspicion of something familiar he told the cashier to give her a couple of fags and shoo her off, 'This is no rest home for the retired.' The cashier looked sceptic and suggested they may as well open a soup kitchen. A/A smiled and said, 'It's no skin off your nose,' and walked off into the back for his tea.

The cashier was shocked because she was unmistakably Asian and she was a she; they had a regular clientele of old dossers passing through for fags and drinks: all recepients of A/A's generosity. The beginning had been two elderly Asian men, cold walking in shivers, their beards desolate in freezing temperatures, perching for a regular rest on the low wall round the garage. Rain or shine they came every day, around the same time: their turbans dipping towards each other as they talked, their hands deep in coat pockets, noses shining like polished wood.

Once, on a particularly cold day, A/A sent out tea for them. They drank and coming back with their empty cups asked if there was anywhere they could warm up their rotis. A/A took them to the back where there was a little kitchenette and so taken was he by their vagabond air he stayed around to hear their talking.

Both widowers, their sons had brought them over so that they could spend their last few years in comfort. Thawing out they laughed and told of a topsy-turvy life where grandchildren couldn't understand them and they in turn couldn't understand what went on in their families any more. Gap-toothed mouths grinning widely: the children wanting to use their homes as hotels, the girls wanting to do everything the boys did, the daughters-in-law running between jobs and home chores, the grandfathers left lonely and alone. To escape homes that became like morgues during the day the grandfathers took to walking the streets. Made each other's acquaintance in the park and each gained a companion for the day's travelling. The rotis were their lunch, cooked in the morning and carried around till hunger got too much. Not that cold rotis could fill anyone up. A/A handed them plates as the rotis and the sabji that had been stuffed in the middle sizzled into life, releasing the combined aromas of onion, garlic, ginger, vegetable and masalas. His own taste-buds salivated, ready for action, but he refused the offers to share, saying that his wife was cooking lunch anyway. They looked at each other, and said he wouldn't get Indian food as good as this. A/A smiled and said Shirley's food was ten times tastier than his mother's. If the mother had heard she would have agreed.

Thus had started the trek: they came each day for their tea and hot rotis, and like the pricklings of an underground movement, slowly, solitary and singly, others followed in their

wake; mostly English. And no one knew how they could have
known. In the end A/A had a hot drinks machine installed from
which they could be served, and a few packets of cigarettes set
aside each day. His workers thought he'd gone mad in the head,
his wife defended him vocally and ably, and he asked in tones of
pretend puzzlement, 'Doesn't charity begin at home – isn't that
an old English saying.' They weren't in agreement, for you can't
live your life on a proverb, and they didn't see the need, but why
should they say anything, after all it was his money. He knew he
was no philanthropist, he didn't even know the word, but he
liked the element of quirky eccentricity these derelicts added to
his days.

He was stirring a third spoonful of sugar into his tea when the
stick-leg-shuffle-leg-shuffle sounded behind him and a quavering voice asked for a light. The kitchenette was out of bounds!
Turning round sharply. Accidentally knocking her with his
elbow, and spilling tea over them both. Staring at each other:
him in consternation, her smiling ruefully.

'Did I hurt you? Are you all right?'

'If you're going to make another cup I'll have one too. I didn't
fancy one from the machine.'

Turning round to switch on the kettle, and bending down to
mop up the tea, eyes hiding as they looked her over. 'Why don't
you go into the house. Shirley's there, she makes better tea and
I'll join you in a few minutes.' Shirley did everything better.

'I thought I'd watch you work for a while, and here are your
cigarettes, I haven't taken to smoking. Yet.'

'Mother!' Throwing the rag into the sink. 'You look like a . . .
I don't know what!'

'Oh dear son. Sorry son. I suppose if I carry on like this, you'll
be forced to disown me.'

''Ere guvnor,' Harry shoving his grey head round the door,
'that chap with the Datsun's here agin. Still complaining.' Harry
avoided looking at her. Did he recognise her?

A/A looked harassed, said these Patels were particular, said
to mother to please go into the house, said he wouldn't be long,
and bolted out behind Harry.

He didn't notice the stick till she was half-way across the yard,
looking up from the Datsun he stared at her retreating back.

If Shirley was surprised she didn't show it, after all who was she to comment on her mother-in-law's assemblage, and got on with making tea, in between sending someone off to fetch samosas.

'Why don't you leave the tea till Arnold comes,' suggested Kulwant.

'Arvind,' corrected Shirley stiffly, pouring water into the teapot.

'I'll make it fresh for him. Never know how long he's going to take,' voice tight and remote.

Kulwant told herself not to let it affect her. That four-letter word from Pavan's lunch had been burning in her brain. No amount of paracetomol or aspirin could rub it away. In the end the only way was to tip-tap over and see what she could see. Of course she had felt Shirley's hostility before; difficulties she had expected with an English daughter-in-law, but not this wall-like dislike, and God knows anyone could see she wasn't the typical mother-in-law. And having married young herself the age gap between her daugher-in-law and her was minimal. They were all wives and all at each other's throats. Except perhaps for Pavan who seemed to be drifting off-course entirely.

Shirley arranged the paraphernalia of tea on the table and a sudden occurring thought made her look up, eyes wide in self-blame: 'Did you want Indian style? I'll make some. We can throw this away.' Kulwant waved her objections aside and tapping with extra emphasis on the tiled floor sat down at the kitchen table. Telephone ringing through the dark arc of water as it transferred from teapot to cup. As if released, Shirley pounced on the phone and, one arm folded under the other, body leaning against the wall, got comfortable to make this call last and last.

Kulwant stared at the spacious high-tech kitchen, and the lounge leading off: decorated in pastel shades, blending into each other, a harmony of colour underscoring and emphasising the luxury. No Punjabi daughter-in-law would have chosen these colour schemes, her eyes would have needed something stronger to feed on. Arvind or Arnold as Kulwant loved to call him had chosen Shirley, not because he wanted to be English but because he hated to be Indian, especially the kind of Indian his family approved of. Anup and Malkit, the older brothers, had once congratulated him on being a social phenomenon, 'Most people move up from the working class to the middle class – you must be the vanguard of a reverse trend.'

Kulwant wondered if he was happier now. Had he found peace among his profit margins? Had his serrated anger disappeared now he had his garage and bank balance to parade against the degrees and doctorates of the other two. A real working-class Black-Englishman hero, with his white wife at his side. A/A and Shirley were well suited to each other, both street-wise smart and sharp as knives. Shirley had helped to make him what he was: her greed for affluence and influence channelling his restless energy into a business he created and bossed. She knew A/A would never have survived the subordination of working for another; Shirley stood ever-ready behind her man, helping and supporting him, her loyalty contracted to him for life.

The wall phone was being replaced back on its hook.

'The lounge looks lovely,' said Kulwant trying to thaw the freeze. 'When did you redecorate?'

'John's an awful long time with those samosas,' complained Shirley. 'We had the whole house done. Arvind chose the colours.'

'After all, he chose you.'

'Or I chose him.'

'A wog?'

'A wog who's got guts. That's him. Not like the rest of your cardboard cut-outs. Like that Patel over there, sitting on his accountant's arse all day, or like his brothers. Oh, don't drink that, it's stone cold. I'll pour you another,' going over to the sink and emptying the cup. 'He needed guts to survive that place you brought him up in. I suppose you called it home.' Coming back, the cup grating dangerously on the saucer. 'We were in school together.' Smiling harshly. 'Didn't know that, did you. Did you ever bother to talk to him.'

How to tell her, of the efforts to shield him, protect him, reach him? How one day he had turned on her and demanded to know why she didn't despise him like the rest. Why? Because she was a misfit too? The accusing child's voice had said it all, how had he guessed? Perhaps because he was the child of her will, born of her stubborness. After two sons she had wanted a daughter, had wanted to bring up a girl and give her all the choices and chances she hadn't had; had wanted to create a new woman who would, by her example, inspire many others. Idealistic ideas straight out of Cloud-cuckoo-land. She'd gone ahead, gotten pregnant and delivered a bouncing healthy boy. Her husband hadn't been able to hide his smirks.

A/A had started badly and declined dangerously: schoolwork degenerating, police record accelerating. Not that his schoolwork had ever won him gold stars; was it instinctive rebellion against the core values of a family, and an extended family at that, which set absolute store on academic success? His rebellion being dynamic, not static, he had poured his energy into school fights, stealing cars, and what he called anti-racist retribution. 'The ARRs,' as said in a gutteral way in the throat.

Shirley knew him inside out and she whose insides had nurtured him had been shut out; as if with the severance of the umbilical cord all symbiosis of blood and care disappeared. His physical needs nurtured for as long as he had allowed, till that too became superfluous. Long after the door had shut she had hammered for admittance at his mind's door and who could know of the jealousy swallowed when he ushered Shirley into the family home: blond hair falling over his shoulder, white hand clasped tight in his own.

'I gave up the Archangel and you've brought home his witch sister.' The unsaid hissing in her mind.

Who wandered through the house on his nights of no return? Who became the laughing-stock of the local cop-shop as anguished phone calls of his disappearance established the pattern of a regular laugh-in? And she knew well enough they would see no dividing line between destruction and what he called his anti-racist retribution. Another joke for the cop-shop-station!

'Where are the children?' asked Kulwant. More small talk!

'Hindi lesson,' putting too much emphasis on the 'd'. Shirley sat down, opening a packet of chocolate biscuits. Kulwant's stick fell to the floor in surprise; getting her sons to Hindi or Punjabi classes had been a weekly nightmare till she'd given up.

Their biggest complaint being that Mummy didn't know 'Indian' either so why should they learn. 'Been going for six months,' continued Shirley 'and I make them practise when they're at home. Picking up a few things myself.'

'Arvind was never interested . . .'

'I decided. It'll be good for business. Knowing the lingo,' chocolate biscuit staining her lips, 'besides I won't have them being ashamed of anything. Not their Dad, not me. They've got to be proud of what they are. In spite of you.'

Knockout number two! Kulwant decided she'd fall off her chair. It wasn't a funny fall, more an undignified slide over the edge, landing with a thump, body jarring. Opening her eyes, straight into Shirley's blue ones.

'Thought you were all right. A stranger might say that you fell off deliberately.' The doorbell rang. John with the samosas?

Kulwant could hear Shirley's voice. 'About time. Did you start making them yourself?'

'My Tops course didn't say nothing about buying samosas.'

'More's the pity.' Slamming the door and Shirley's staccato steps marching back. 'I mean, what am I to tell the children?' Kulwant got up, settling herself back on Shirley's chair. 'They look at the photographs of the others: all those saris-jewels-food-flowers-booze-people-dancing. The brides decked out in everything they could lay their hands on, looking like tinsel town on two legs. They're going to ask, what happened to you Mummy? Aren't they? Stone cold!' Unwrapping the samosas. 'Bet they just took them out of the freezer and slung them at him.' Kulwant was feeling stone cold herself, but she didn't fancy being put in the oven like the samosas. 'Should have told John to tell them they were for me – they think they can pass any old muck on to English people. Drown it in curry powder and no one will know the difference. The children are never going to believe we're properly married.' Shirley was marching over to the phone, Kulwant shrank back as she passed her, though what was the point, she was already on the firing line. 'Tell Arvind his tea is ready and his Mum's waiting. Yes. A-r-v-i-n-d is Arnold but he's really Arvind so why don't you learn it. Nothing in your Tops course about strange names? It's actually a very common

London name, becoming commoner by the day. Go and tell him. Now!'

A/A hadn't asked if he could marry Shirley. He'd announced. The others had sniggered when they heard. 'That solves the problem. With his record who'd have had him – unless we'd given a dowry. A car to the father and a blindfold to the girl.'

'I suppose you think I wanted to act out *Carry On Up The Khyber Pass*,' Shirley's voice bringing her back. 'You did everything you were supposed to for the others. Didn't you think Arvind deserved the same? Even if he was marrying an uneducated white slag, who didn't have enough nous to hook a honky. You gave your envelope of tenners like you were paying protection money.'

'Something's burning.'

'Yes. Me.'

'The samosas?'

Shirley's sprint to the oven would have done Zola Budd proud. Only a few of them burnt, their peaks smoking like volcanoes. 'Ruined my wedding night. He tore them up. One by one, smaller and smaller pieces. That and the drinking. Twelve months of hell it was. I didn't know he was doing extra hours so's he could buy me the jewellery and things you should have given me. You could have pretended to accept me. If only for his sake.' Arms unfolding and marching over to the phone, where she gave someone an earful about A/A's non-appearance. Marching back, she looked hard at Kulwant. 'Now you know. Happy?'

'I'll wait for Arnold . . .'

'Arvind!'

'. . . then I have to go.'

'Busy social life.'

'Hectic.'

Kulwant had argued with her husband, saying we must let them marry as they choose, why should they be forced to go through our Indian rituals and customs; young people are fighting against them, not perpetuating them. Her present unremembering the past of her own younger self, forgetting what it's like to be hybrid in England and live with the

95

crystallised nostalgia of the exile, an empty womb carrying around another you. Ah, but for England, I would be whole.

'You never said,' she said to Shirley.

'Waited for you to say, didn't we? Fat lot of good it did us.'

A/A arrived and was concerned about the stick; taking her hand and sitting by her side. Another surprise. This was a new A/A. Opening his hand, her fingers trailed the callouses, the nicks of broken skin, permanent black caught in the creases: so different from the soft, well-manicured hands of the other two.

The past was permanent, nothing she could do to change it, the future fluid. Forget seriousness, let her play her games: with A/A and Shirley for an audience she acted like she was playing to the gallery. Head drooping down in sorrow. Ah me! This is the reward of a hard working life: pains, aches, body falling apart, legs giving way under her. Perhaps she should go back to India. A/A's hand moved away to pick up a samosa, not one of the burnt ones, Shirley had moved those away from him. Just like a good Indian wife, thought Kulwant. Like the kind of wife I never was.

India would be good for her, said he. All that vitamin D in the sunshine, friendship of other women, the luxury of being in one's own country. She would get stronger and healthier and happier. She pretended she hadn't heard the last, incongruous with his history, years ago it would have choked in his throat. No need to worry about money, said he. She tilted her head and looked sideways, new angle gave no clue to any inner change. He who had counted the pennies borrowed and lent, and scorned the family pot of common 'geld'.

Eyes looking far she embroidered the tissue of fantasy, delineating joyous reunions with childhood friends in the village, tucking away the inconvenient fact that most would have been married off years and years ago; over there she would be able to employ a servant girl to do all the work. What about your socialism? She could almost hear the sneer but no sound touched the listening air. 'No more English winters,' he said, 'vegetables fresh from the fields. And you know how you love those V.E.G.s'

Her predilection for vegetables had become a family joke. 'Some people get high on booze, some on hash, Mum on veggies.' Anup amusing the family. She mused further on the advantages of getting away from the dirt and filth of an English city, sleeping under the stars and waking up with the fresh morning sun.

'You could choose a plot of land for us,' said Shirley, joining in the game. 'We want to build a house in India, and of course it should be where Arvind comes from. Somewhere for the children to go to.' No holiday cottage on the Costa Brava for Shirley. Shirley was the true adventuress not her.

Children! But her children were such a comfort. No, no. How could she think of leaving them. Unfinished business she wanted to say, but didn't. Don't give too much away or it'll be remembered and used against you. What was life without one's nearest and dearest around one? How could she go to India if it meant leaving them all behind?

Stick-leg-shuffle-leg-shuffle. Stick-leg-shuffle-leg-shuffle. A/A walked her to the gate and even asked if she wanted to go in a car, he could spare one of the boys. She asked instead if he was happy with Shirley, mind clanging inside, not knowing if this was the thing to say, ask or do.

He didn't answer for a long time, and she thought perhaps he wasn't going to and she'd gone and stepped on his bunions again. Taking her arm he walked alongside her. 'Colour's not everything. She didn't have a home, and neither did I. I mean not a home that we could belong to, so we belong to each other.' Face creasing into a smile. 'Hardly likely I was going to meet an Indian girl, was it?' he continued. 'Not at that time. I was lucky if I came across one once a year. And I got around. I wasn't the one for sitting at home, was I? And even if I had met one . . . I wasn't the right type, was I?' It was an ingratiating smile, but she wasn't ready to respond. 'That's how it is.'

Her stick-leg-shuffle-leg-shuffle faded away. He stood watching her till she was out of sight, her oversized coat swaying around her, buffering the loneliness knocking at its threadbare fabric.

She waved before she turned the corner, and seeing his hand lifting in response wondered about the possibility of parallel lines ever converging towards each other.

Buppie

Stick-leg-shuffle-leg-shuffle.   Stick-leg-shuffle-leg-shuffle.

More flower bushes! Perhaps Pavan was planning to leave medicine and go into the gardening business. A gold plaque shone by the door announcing Anup's residence to the world. 'Hello. I'm University Lecturer/Research Scientist, First Class Honours, Ph.D.- Anup.' That wasn't what the plaque said but if he could with decency that's how Anup would want himself introduced, how he would want to be seen by the world. His Indian name and Indian-ness didn't bother him for he had transformed both into an asset; they added a dash of exoticism to the sophisticated, urbane, intellectual image. The doorbell rang through the house and rang again as no one answered.

Wasted journey? Anyway what was she doing going from son to son today? What could she possibly hope to find?

Her hands ruffle the wall plants, withdrawing as a few leaves fall out, drifting to the ground. It was autumn after all. Nature going to sleep for the winter. The stick twirled round among them.

'Hello?' aproned body standing at the door. Of course, why answer the door yourself when the home help is around?

Feet and stick too loud on pine-laid floor. Anup is on the phone, wide-open eyes on her as she waddles in. Sitting down, sinking into deep cushions, eyes wandering over the books and pictures, arrested by an arrangement of frames: her and them through the years, Mum, Dad and the brothers; Anup and

Pavan crowning the pyramid, glorious in wedding garb. A little further to the side, line drawings of a family tree? Intrigued, she forgot the stick and walked over to survey. Beginning with her grandparents, Anup's great-grandparents, branches cataloguing names, marriages and children.

'Not very impressive yet,' his voice and him standing behind her. 'I was going to ask your help with it.'

'You haven't got Kurshid on it?' she remarked. In reply he asked if she would like tea or coffee. 'After all you have a half-brother?'

He remembered he had to make an urgent phone call, and as the dialling filled the air her fingers trailed over the books. Mostly science, a few fiction, mainly Booker Prize winners. Anup never had been much for imagination. Phone still held to his ear he passed her a sheaf of typed papers, and newspaper cuttings. *The Invisible Indian.* He started another call. She read his plans for a book charting the Indian contribution to England's economy and society. Scowling Kulwant looked daggers at Anup, he saw and raised a questioning eyebrow.

The door opened and Rita came in with the coffee tray. Kulwant asked after Rita's children and invited her to have coffee with them. Rita was anxious to finish and go home, her husband would be tired after having looked after the children all day. Three years unemployed and still no job in sight for him. 'We've talked about going back to India,' Rita was saying, 'What do you think? Thing is, it frightens us, I mean he hardly remembers India, and I was born here. And our parents didn't make any provision, they thought they were here for life. Not like others who built their houses back in the village and bought land and set up businesses. Our parents "integrated" into the English dream. Perhaps we'll move up north? Though that's the wrong way round, isn't it, I mean people come south for jobs. Try anything once, as they say. Try this cake, I made it.' Generous slice on a tasty plate, then with a smile whizzing off out the door.

Anup was looking sulky as he swivelled his chair around to face her. 'What do you think Mum? Good idea. We're like people without a history and of course one will be accused of doing an Asian *Roots* but a publisher friend suggested it and there's nothing similar on the market at the moment. I think the approach should be, like this cake, a slice of the variety: we have Indian royalty living here, millionaires, professionals who are experts in their fields, the rising Buppie class . . .'

'Buppie? Buppie what?' Kulwant might learn something new after all.

'Black Yuppies, Mother,' explained Anup with great resignation, 'the successful Indians. They are the ones who are invisiblised – to use your rhetoric, Mother. However I'll sprinkle a few stories of the proletariat for contrast. Otherwise you would never speak to me, would you?'

'As if it needs to be said. It's like trying to convince them we're human beings too. And as for your Buppies, life is hardly a bed of thorns for them.'

'Well it's certainly not a bed of roses.'

'At least make it intelligent.'

'I'll do my best,' said he with a suitably earnest expression.

'Have you seen your father recently?'

'He's always welcome here.'

'Kurshid loves him.'

'Which is more than you ever did,' he flashed at her, impatience jerking his body into aimless walking round the room, ripping open a new packet of cigarettes, nervy hands struggling with the lighter. She took it from him and lit his cigarette, taking one for herself, more for effect than satisfaction. Aim achieved she sat back down. 'If you had been more of a wife,' he was saying, face averted, 'more as a woman should be, Dad wouldn't have been attracted elsewhere.' She kept her silence, waiting for it to goad him. Anup, her eldest, child of her body, was a traditionalist with a longing for respectability; prepared to pretend that he was flirting with danger, but never the kind to venture outside society's boundaries. Conscious of his comforts and fearful of the unknown. Anup would never have the courage, would never see the need, to step outside the threshold of the established order; anyway to him it would be like biting the hand that fed him – how could he turn round and kick the system that made him feel successful, an achiever, part of an elite.

'You were always arguing,' sitting back at his desk, putting distance between them. She could see what he was saying: instead of providing a comfortable home she had insisted on bringing arguments and controversies into family life. He puffed out smoke waiting for her to retaliate, in vain. All their lives she had used words to try and break the mould of English/Asian boyhood, to prevent the gelling of their adulthood into too familiar a pattern. Useless. She had succeeded only in alienating them: she became 'silly old Mum', 'you've gone crackers Mum', 'Mum and her weird ideas', 'don't understand you Mum'. This last one was said with the most bitterness and resentment, the others were half mocking, half teasing. They couldn't understand what she was trying to do by trying to make them different from all the other boys that they knew. If she had tried to make them totally Indian or push them into being westernised they would have understood; they would have had something concrete to rebel against. They never had rebelled, no matter how much she provoked them. How early had their male antennae picked up that boys were okay, Boys Rooled, Boys were Tops.

Had her husband been right when he had accused her of driving the children away by not bringing them up properly? As far as she could see most children were brought up improperly. 'They fit into this life,' he had said in exasperation. He was wrong but she herself didn't know how to be right; in the end all her grand ideas had boiled down to who did what in the kitchen, where she insisted they learn everything and do everything. The boys knew that the outside world didn't agree and asked why they should have to listen to her. An unorthodox mother is such an embarrassment.

Anup said come and have a look at my new computer and afterwards we can go out shopping, eyes on her clothes. Space invaders zoom in to zap the humans and Anup got quite narked as her score rose higher than his. Another cup of coffee and she was about to leave when Pavan arrived, looking delighted to see her mother-in-law and inviting her to stay for dinner.

'Another time,' she said gathering up her stick and getting ready to leave this house of connubial bliss when Pavan launched into a description of her harrowing day.

'I don't know how to cope with some of the things that come

into the surgery. I shouldn't be talking about this but I don't know what's happening to our community here, especially the young. If it's not drugs it's violence. I have a patient, an Indian girl, who will insist on calling herself by an English name. She had been badly beaten up. Told me a rather confused story about having an argument with her boyfriend. She needed to go to hospital. Told her I was calling an ambulance. She became abusive, started throwing a tantrum . . . she won't do my reputation any good, everyone in the waiting room must have heard her screaming and shouting. They must wonder what I do to my patients once I get them alone. Cut-throat Gupta will probably be my name from now on. Thankfully I saved on a sedative. She wound herself into such a state of hysteria her body gave up on her and she fainted. I must say I find her very interesting. I did warn the hospital she was likely to get up and walk out at the first opportunity. She lives rough, smells, her clothes are disgusting, she looks like a jumble of rags,' Pavan looked away from looking at Kulwant, in case her words were taken to apply to more than one. 'She refused to give me an address, says that she has no family, no friends. I'm afraid I've been rather unethical, I made up an address for her, for the hospital.'

'Ours?' questioned Anup.

'Seemed to be the most logical thing to do. I was surprised she even came to me, that girl is quite indomitable. She must have been in extreme pain, otherwise I can imagine her carrying on till she dropped. Really. What is it this country does to our young people?'

'Some of these youngsters don't know what's good for them. They have to rebel even when they don't know what they're rebelling against.'

'I'm afraid,' said Pavan looking at Anup, 'I've become her next of kin.' Anup replied that as long as it wasn't him, he didn't much care, but he did think Pavan had missed her vocation, she should have trained for saviour of the world.

102

Maya and the M.A.D.s

Maya remembers the room as she walks up the stairs, aggression gathering within her at each upward step. Perhaps she should chuck it in; madness working for money when the work made her so angry. Think back to the beginning when she'd told herself not to let it affect her, it's a job, that's what it is. And he's never going to get what he thinks he is. Hands folding unconsciously into fists she enters the room.

Martin Andreas Davidson turns to her, surrounded by his greenery, a smile decorating his face, introduces a friend, smoking underneath the cheese plant: 'Maddison Angel Dupont, we call him Madd for short.' Madd turns out to be a well-known director, who will direct the madness once she's done her work.

They listen intently as she verbalises her report, saying the framework of life is so loose people lose their way; they're like Hansel and Gretel without the stones to mark their return route. And when they find they can't make it back, they try to replicate what they've lost. It's not so bad if the jungle is yours and the birds and animals come out of your cultural imagination; you came to know them in the days of infancy when they were outside you, and now they're you and inside you. Witches, giants, ghouls and ghosts lose their power to frighten, over the years they become such familiar friends you pass them on to your children; your monsters and horrors come speaking English or dressed as Banquo in your video screen mind. But what of the immigrant? The sad story of the immigrants, who've moved oceans away from the familiar terrain of their childhood nurturings? They attempt to replicate the frames that informed their lives, but they can't hold on because the frames they make here are constructed of material foreign to them and like anti-climbing paint it repels their grip; there's nothing user-friendly in these frames for them.

When they fall, they flounder in the in between spaces: and this is worse because the doors of reality, which stand guardian to our senses, have fallen away and taken with them the knowledge that this is the other place. The other that you entered on airplane wings and passport propellant. You've lost the guiding stick and won't know of the pot-holes, won't recognise the cat-calls and even lose the history of why you are here. When the monsters and mice are from someone else's mythology, fear and certainty displace each other in musical chairs. Not that you knew about musical chairs for parlour games were never played in sun-baked courtyards; though you learn to smile as the snow rains down, a blanket to cover the cold. When the thaw comes you search for your children's footsteps. That's madness as we all know.

M.A.D. and Madd look at each other, not sure of what they have. One leaves the shelter of the cheese plant, the other swivels in the chair, the circling blurring his name on the designer sweater. Not quite what we wanted they say.

'Never is like that,' she replies.

He, who genesised the idea, fingers his beard and suggests a more realistic approach, handing her a list of psychiatrists, who have all handled Asian patients. She promises to investigate and adds a warning that the unmalleable cannot always be captured in accordance with our receiving aerials. They say that's why we hired you, for you will have a better understanding, culture being important and all that.

'Only if you accept what I suggest.'

They say they want to aim for an objective median, which cannot be beyond the capacity of reasonable human beings. 'For instance' adds he, who was beneath the cheese plant and who now nestles next to the cactus, 'those who are mad here, would they have been mad there? Is it the here that's important or the them that's coming out, which would have come out anyway?'

104

'I don't like the word mad,' she says, too slow to bite her tongue. Bang goes this job and the salary that goes with it. One drums his fingers on the desk and suggests a list of case histories for the next session, 'a framework for a more productive meeting.' He smiles.

'If you promise to go light on the anti-immigrant paint.'

'We're all friends here,' says Madd now half-way between the cactus and the cheese.

Horror in the Asian Centre. Asha looks disgusted and looks away, Farida says some people will do anything to line their pockets, 'don't expect us to collaborate.'

Maya knows she's wrong-stepped yet again and explains at greater length the worthiness of her project, her words coming out mere shadows, floating without conviction, for she has no confidence within herself to underpin them. Perhaps a change of tack inviting them to explore the subject: 'Surely, someone,' she says, 'should be looking at the hidden agony. No one can deny mental problems, illnesses exist in our community, any community. Is it right to let people carry on suffering. How long can we draw a veil, sweep everything under the carpet. There are many who'd rather that we didn't exist, at least not in their country . . .'

'Ours too!' snaps Asha.

'I was speaking from their point of view.'

'Don't bother.'

'We're making ourselves invisible, which is precisely what they want us to be. It's like the old nigger in the book who says, "Please massa, you're right massa, I'm not here massa."' Asha scrapes back her chair, looking ostentatiously at her watch. Warming to her subject Maya is not to be silenced: 'If we have a right to be here, don't we have a right to be human, warts and all!'

'We don't have to give them something else to ridicule us with.'

The door opens and Shanti enters, shivering in a thin sari, her feet bleeding in their chappels. She won't wear a coat or closed shoes, as they would muffle her sensory antennae, knowledge has to be garnered and deciphered in between the split second of

105

its happening and its passing; harder than catching butterflies is catching the fleeting product, thrown up by the transient conjunction of people, time and place; we write upon the environment around us and those whose braille is attuned are able to read the coefficient.

Shanti tells them she has hurt her foot on some glass. Farida fetches dettol and cotton wool and would kneel at Shanti's feet, except that Shanti props them on a chair, to make it easier for the cleansing.

Asha has gathered together her files and slinging on her coat and bag leaves for a meeting with the housing officer, muttering something about families who are homeless, about women who can't bring their husbands into the country, women who are battered and thrown out of their homes, while others muck around for muck to sell to the white media.

'Would you like to come and see the house?' Farida asks Shanti. 'It's almost ready and we'll soon be appointing workers.'

Shanti replies she'll see it with the other members of the management committee and if Maya is ready to leave she'll go with her. How does Shanti know Maya is present, she hasn't spoken a word since Shanti entered because she's busy sulking. Looking at Shanti's feet, Maya says she'll call a taxi, thinking that Shanti will refuse, which she doesn't, saying it's a long time since she's been in a car.

The mini-cab has nylon fur covers and Indian film songs. They have no opportunity to talk, the driver talking above Lata Mangeshkar singing songs of Mukesh; they all fall silent as Geeta Dutt's pearl rounded voice pleads in 'Na Jao Saiyan', pleading for him not to go, not to tear his arm from her clasp, else she will not be able to help her tears.

The music stops as the cab comes to a halt at their destination. Maya shuddering into awareness, surfacing from memories of this same song washing over two entwined bodies, followed by other memories in which she played it in masochistic endlessness, an irrational hope that the singer's pleadings would reach him, as hers, wherever he was. As someone once said, you got to go down before you can go up.

As the driver gives her the change he also hands her a card. 'Please come. It will be a pleasure. My last daughter's wedding.

Five daughters I have, and now she is leaving too. Each time it is harder to see them go. As the poet says, not even the daughters of Kings and Princes can stay in their parents' house,' his eyes misting over, 'and we are only poor labourers.' Leaving the card in Maya's hands he drives away in a blare of music.

'Some people's heart is too soft,' said Shanti, 'it melts even in the English sun, which is nothing. Come, I want to show you something.'

The something was a week-old newspaper. Shanti holding it in her hand, reverentially like a bible, 'Something in this paper for me, I don't know what it is. Read it to me.' Leafing through it Maya asks what she should be looking for. Shanti hasn't a clue. Maya tries to go through the headings of different articles, 'Local politics? Gang rape? Robbery in the launderette? Local flower show? Weddings? Sports? Film-star loses his pants?' Shanti shaking her head till it became a swinging pendulum. Nothing for it, thought Maya ruefully, she would have to read through each item. Associating with eccentricity had its penalties. The lead story was about a prisoner on the run, who had escaped in the middle of the night by disguising himself in a warder's uniform, 'I thought that only happened in films.' Another one about a local computer hero, who had tapped into the local council computer and couldn't get himself out. Weddings: 'Multi-racial wedding. "Sangheeta marries Simon." Looks very much like an arranged marriage to me,' muttered Maya, 'Daddy of Sangheeta owns Golden Video shops and Simple Simon, not so simple, owns Firebird Video Productions. One of the largest video companies in London. Ha. Sangheeta graduated in Business Studies. Who says there's no cultural integration?' Voice tiring, reading each and every printed word. 'The local socialist council, practising socialism, going to war on squatters. Double-securing empty properties. On a recent inspection, for the purpose of updating their lists, they found the body of a young man. He'd died from wounds to his head, probably from an iron bar found near him. The police are examining it for fingerprints. They are hampered in their investigations by the Mafia-like loyalty of these sub-world itinerants, who have opted out of normal life and live like urban gypsies. A man is helping with enquiries.' Maya flicked to the next page, covertly counting the number of pages left. Five more to go. This was the local weekly and jam-packed for a whole week's reading. She hoped Shanti wouldn't want her to read the classified ads too. 'Music section!' glancing at Shanti she wondered if she could get away with skipping pages. How would Shanti know the whole paper hadn't been read to her. Seeing Shanti's closed eyes concentrating on her, she knew she'd never get away with it. 'Film section! Reviews of what's on at the local. Oh, we're on the classified ads now,' looking up pleadingly. Shanti stood up, hobbled out, came back with a glass of mineral water. 'Tap water here tastes disgusting. In a minute I will make you tea. Also have some fruit.' Maya takes a deep breath and continues. Accept the inevitable and shoulder the burden.

It's over, and Maya leans back, massaging her vocal chords, throwing the paper aside, 'No doubt about it. You want to know what life is about: Look no more/Hook your local. Want a slice of real life-LIFE/LIFT it from the local.' Shanti's disappeared. No sight or sound of her. Maya wanders through the flat, checks the bathroom, kitchen. Nothing. Damn! She goes back to the lounge and gathers together the scattered sheets of the paper. Some of Shanti's reverence for it seeping into her, for she smoothes out the creases, fits the pages inside each other and carefully folds it up.

Mea Culpa too, Faust

Stick-leg-shuffle-leg-shuffle. Stick-leg-shuffle-leg-shuffle.

Damn Caroline! She'd tried to call Caroline. Sid had answered. Said Caroline was away with Rachel. Sid sounded grumpy. She didn't ask him why. She didn't want to know. She didn't care.

Blast Caroline's letter! She'd discovered it lying wrinkled and grimy at the bottom of her bag. Caroline had said it was urgent. True or False? She'd decided to deliver it – back to Caroline. No Caroline. Stumped! She'd have to get rid of it. She'd have to go.

Stick scraping, forgotten on the pavement, eyes unseeing, mind a jigsaw of scattered pieces: 'Last night I dreamt I went to Manderley.' It was wrong. She never could remember quotations right. Her Manderley wasn't the Manderley of the nameless heroine: it was Keats' nightingale flinging its soul-song into the frozen caves, emerging into the horror light of Faust and his agony. Faust, who bartered his soul for the beads and trinkets of hell's duplicity, becoming a territorial conquest in the colonialist war between the White God and the White Devil.

No wonder they overran the planet with their marauding armies and marauding merchants. Christians had direct examples from above, the orders transmitted at every Sunday worship, assimilated through generations of congregations.

Mea Culpa too, Faust – I fell for the beads and trinkets too. Should have remembered they've had heavenly examples to teach them the ways of bartering with the natives.

She didn't go in, but loitered outside, hoping to catch someone going in to whom she could pass on Caroline's unveiled attempt to bring her back into contact with the fold. The one unbridgeable divide between them in all the shared years of childhood and adulthood. Caroline was now an integral cell in the body of the party, believing in it, working for it and defending it. She had never been able to reconcile herself to Kulwant's exit. If Kulwant was turning her back on the party, where did that leave her? Both had avoided talking about it. Kulwant never wanting to and Caroline never daring, scared of bringing the rupture into their personal lives, deepening the ripple effect of the fracas. They were both stained by it and a single word could have been spark on dry tinder.

The house had been repainted. Window sills, pipes and door gleaming a bright red. Geoff must have done it, he'd been talking about it for the last seven years. The front garden too had been tidied up: emptied of the debris of years of pamphleting, placard making, thousands of soggy dog-ends from the impromptu meetings on the doorstep, or the quiet smoking of someone slipping away for a cigarette-break. There were times when Kulwant had wished she smoked too and had the excuse of addiction to slip out for a respite from the intensity or banality inside; as it was, too many eyes would follow, too many minds wondering what she was up to. Was there a secret cabal having a secret meeting outside? Much the safer course to risk cancer than incur their suspicions.

Looking at the brightness and newness she couldn't help the bitter thought that her departure seemed to have been taken as a signal to get rid of the rubbish and get on with the renewal and renovation. Jaundiced you are Kuli/Coolie – Caroline's old nickname coming out of the past. You walked out and put it behind you. Now push it back where it belongs, far enough away for it to topple over into oblivion; if only she could find out where oblivion lay, because amnesia never came when invited.

She searched around for something with which to scrawl a message to the world on the wall. Nothing she picked up would write as she wanted it to. In frustration tearing off a flower, crushing its petals, and another, and another . . .

'Now you can graduate to pulling the legs off insects.' It would be him. It would have to be him. Couldn't have been better timed.

'I'd rather torment the human variety of creepy crawlies.'

'And well-practised you are in it too.'

'Flattery?'

'From a long-time admirer.'

She had called him Karm (Mark – turnabout) in retaliation for his massacre of her name. Of course he had added an A and turned a nickname into destiny: 'Never look a Karma in the mouth.' Tall, stringlike, still carrying his ridiculous wispy beard. But no MP initials to stick behind his name, despite his penchant for adding and subtracting letters. She had been sour with pleasure at his failure.

'What happened to your plastic bag?' she asked.

He smiled (the smile that used to make her stomach turn somersaults). 'Unecological. Why the stick?'

'Need it.'

'Like hell. You're just putting it on.'

His presence no longer evoked the rush of desire, no longer hyper-heightened her senses. Even the embers had died long ago, leaving a little mound of ash that sometimes poisoned her tongue, or lay on her eyes, affecting her view of the world. Burnt offerings for a burnt out affair!

She asked him to take in Caroline's letter. He invited her in for tea.

'Tea wasn't what I wanted from this place, but it was all I ever got.'

'Full of self-pity . . .' He could be jeering too.

Why hadn't it been adultery? That's what the world would have called it, the law, her husband, her sons, her parents' contempt. An animal they would have called her, with an animal's appetite. Adultress! Adultress! No matter how many times she said it, it didn't mean anything to her, it didn't stir any sense of guilt or remorse. She had looked it up in the dictionary. It said: 'infidelity through sexual intercourse'. Was that all that counted? The giving over of one's body? The intimacy of one flesh with another? She hadn't felt adulterous and she hadn't felt unfaithful because what she shared with Karm, she hadn't ever shared with her husband. She didn't feel she was taking away from him to give to someone else. Had her husband used the same justification when he was with Kurshid?

In the beginning she had exerted the force of her willpower, to feel what the romantics said should be felt in marriage. Having forgotten the pragmatism on which she had started the marriage, she felt empty and disappointed that passion refused to ignite, and it grew a yearning within her, for this child of the East had Eros running in her veins.

Damn them and their Gods of romantic love! Ruined more lives than they ever made. Would she do it all over again? Her head shakes before the words even reach her lips. Life is a spaghetti junction of possibilities, forever tricking one into side roads and this was one road she would never want to take again.

She should have been content to be a Food Processor, working in her lab towards the great revolution in artificial food. 'Not another white!' had been the self-shocked thought as suspicion became certainty. 'Not falling for that one again. Cut my milk teeth on one didn't I?'

She had been captivated by his quick intelligence; admiring the way he could string together a series of ideas, make an analysis, draw a conclusion, annihilate others' arguments and throw in a few barbed witticisms. 'Isn't that always the way.' mocked a chorus of women in her head. Later, she would transpose 'barbed' for 'vicious'. Theirs was a bitter ending to too sweet a beginning.

His words interlinked, interleaved and answered hers and she was filled with delight to think that two could think like one. Later, she took the blame upon herself: for allowing herself to be deceived, for attempting to transmute fiction into reality. She was older than him, the mother of children, what made her think she was living an up-market Mills and Boon life? People are fragile and fickle; when caught in a knot of circumstance, self-interest will always win. How could she have allowed herself to become intoxicated by those wonderful words tumbling off his tongue like golden molten lava.

Karm/Mark, not Karl Marx, much as he would have given his eye-teeth, arms and legs for to be . . . was a working-class grammar school boy, who was making it up the academic tree, although he swore he was always out on a limb: 'and I don't want to lose my roots. I'll wither and die, won't I?' head drooping, arms outspread, fingers falling lifeless and listless towards the floor, entertaining her in the privacy of his flat. 'My energy comes from my roots, delving deep into the working-class soil of this land, it's rich in minerals. Hundreds of years have drenched it with blood, sweat and tears. I can drink deep from it, draw it up, through my feet, up and up – stop sniggering woman. Into the HQ. The brain. It will flood through every crevice, gurgle through caves, drench the landscape and drown the deserts. I will . . .' head and hands lifting up, feet rising on tiptoe, stretching towards the ceiling, one hand colliding with the paper lantern, sending it swinging in wide circles, making sea waves of the light and shade, turning the room into an underground cave. '. . . I will regenerate.'

'Making up for not having gone to kindergarten?' she laughed, enjoying his childishness.

'The kindergarten of adulthood,' swinging his body to simulate a tree in a storm, 'nasty weather coming. Want to shelter under my branches?'

'In a storm the most dangerous place is under a tree. I ain't stupid.'

'This tree has foliage to protect and shelter. It also bites back when attacked,' teeth bared lunging for her neck.

He was the little star of the local branch, their home-grown intellectual. 'Not difficult,' she'd thought later, in the bitter sour days of afterwards, 'any slave can be king of the gutter.' He'd made it in sociology, when sociology was coming into rebellious adolescence, worried about its non-disappearing pimples. Karm/Mark had written a book called *Tell-tales of the Unexpected*, whose popularity with liberals, softies, lefties and the shopfloor intellectual had shot him to transient fame and into a mauling by the jealous jaws of Academia. *Tell-tales of the Unexpected* became *Tall Tales of the Predictable*, *Fairy Tales of the Expected*, *Nursery Tales of the Inexperienced*. Ridiculed as a 'pop' book and much nasty ado made of its easy 'let's get around the hearth and talk' style: labelled as indulgent, superficial and inaccurate.

She had asked him to sign her copy. He said, hadn't she heard? Handing the book over to him, she said she preferred to decide for herself. 'You've read it!' Surprise showed as he leafed through the stained, thumbed pages. 'So what's a nice oriental girl like you doing in an imperialist den of corruption like this?'

'Getting to know my enemy.' Some words come true long after the saying of them. She knew he was longing to ask her what she'd thought of the book, wondered how long he'd circumvent. He made a big deal of asking her about herself, raising his eyebrows at mention of husband and children and saying wasn't she lucky to have a liberal husband who gave her all this freedom.

'Freedom is taken, not given.'

'Sharp with it too. I bet you don't need to put chillies in your food. Your tongue's got them built in.'

That was how it started. The intimacy of flirtatious bickering, the sense of unity when they found themselves on the same side of an argument, the growing recognition of each other, the frisson of antagonism when they polarised into opposing sides. A bubble of excitement as she says, 'Believe and let believe?' and he scowls disagreement.

It was the custom to repair to the pub after meetings. She never would. They couldn't understand. Each time the tug and pull of pressure and resistance. She'd argued it inside out with them, maintaining that going to the pub didn't constitute a major pillar of her freedom, there were other, far more important issues to fight for, which would be jeopardised by her frequenting a pub and being labelled an out and out scarlet woman. Her stand invariably aroused a storm of counter-arguments, prominent among which was that she couldn't defeat the oppression of tradition by caving in to it; that she was actually perpetuating it and that progress won't come by changing a brick here and a brick there, the whole structure was suspect and should be challenged as a whole. At this point she'd ask with a big grin what they thought they were doing in the party and the most frequent answer would be from someone looking at a watch and saying that if they didn't hurry up, closing time would catch them on the wrong side and couldn't this argument be carried on in the pub and Kuli, why don't you come along for just one tiny orange juice . . . She declined, and went home regretting the missed conversations and camaraderie. He

114

changed it all. Not that he made her change her mind. An alternative venue. Take-away drinks taken to his flat, that way no one need choose between their physical needs and political aspirations.

'Whose physical needs?' asked a voice with a snigger.

She loved his flat: walls lined with books, plants stretching their leaves upwards to the ceiling and outwards to the room, arms that would draw you in and comfort; paintings and prints on the walls: bright splodges of colour against the white walls; ethnic artefacts, strategically scattered. Picking one up she wondered if it had come from her brother's 'Indian Emporium'.

'Come and have your drink.' He was behind her, lifting the statuette from her hands, 'Do you like it? Got it in Madras.'

Taking her wine, and sitting back on the floor cushion, slipping off her shoes and curling up her legs: 'Don't get too comfortable Kuli. Not staying the whole night. That is, we ain't. Don't know about you.' Snigger voice again. Karm called them to order, saying since they were here they may as well do some work, notepad in his hand, sitting across the room from her, directly facing. Kathy jumped in first, regurgitating conversations about the aims of the leaflet, what they hoped to do with it, ending in mid-sentence, running out of steam; typical Kathy, so eager to please, afraid of stepping outside the ranks of the allowable, wanting desperately to be a part of the happy, incestuous clique. Other voices stepped in, throwing in suggestions, some over the top, some plain silly, some intended to be amazingly funny – whereat everyone dutifully belly-laughed.

She didn't participate, her eyes doing a dialogue with the flat. Her own home was an amalgamation of convenience, her husband's taste, hers, practicality for the children: no room in their house, as in this flat, for the conscious manifestation of a self in material goods, all chosen with care to contribute to the creation of an ambience that was cosy, intellectual, subtly colourful. What luxury to be able to have such space to mould around your own sweet self. Could she have had this if she hadn't opted for her arranged marriage? Useless looking back to ifs. She was in the here and now. Half refilling her glass she sensed the laughter directed towards her and, wondering whether she'd suddenly revealed a big hole in her jeans, quickly, if rather inelegantly flopped back on the floor cushion. 'That should keep you two occupied for a while,' it was snigger voice, 'shouldn't take you too long, as long as you don't start indulging in extra-curricular activities.' Having given up on a collective effort they had designated her and him to complete the leaflet.

'Lovely,' she said standing up. 'It'll be easier at my place. Because of the kids. Can't always find someone to look after them.' She must avoid being alone with him, her resolution may not endure.

She made sure he came to see her, in the evening, when her husband would be there, doing his own work or DIYing around the house. The kids were supposed to be in their rooms, if not exactly in bed. She'd given up the fight to make them go to sleep early.

She had made the coffee, they'd gone through the stages of social chit-chat; the various papers were spread out on the dining-room table and she was squinting her eyes trying to decipher his notes, in spite of his warning that she'd find it impossible, when Anup's body slid round the door and perched itself next to her.

'I'm hungry.'

'Should have eaten your dinner.'

'Wasn't hungry then. Please Mum.'

Oh, the embarrassment of having to be a mother. She asked Karm if he would like something to eat too. He would love to. Out came the atta, the tava and the rolling pin. Her hands busy with the rolling and cooking of the rotis she almost burnt one of the sabjis. Seeing that, he left his conversation with Anup and came over to help her. Standing side by side at the cooker, a parody of domestic felicity.

Smelling the food smells, the rest of the family filtered back into the room, ready for a late feast. Through mouthfuls of food, she bemoaned the lack of progress on the leaflet, feeling guilty towards Karm, thinking she'd made him waste an evening and then wished she'd kept her mouth shut as her husband suggested they try to meet elsewhere. The family home was always like this, privacy could never be guaranteed. She answered non-committally, not wanting to be forced towards a choice, preferring to carry on as they were.

116

Nothing that lives can be stalled for ever and as his hand ran through her, he said, 'I can't believe an Asian woman can be like this.'

She said, 'Don't believe all your stereotypes.'

They did the leaflet and it was good. Sounds like God and his handiwork she thought, feeling God-like herself. The Universe was inside her, all its power, its creativity, its badness and its sadness, it canyons and its waterfalls, its forests and its deserts, the music of the hemispheres, the humming of the rain before it fell; living on the crest of a wave, convinced it would never crash.

Everybody said what a good writing team they made, some keeping their tongues free of innuendoes, others wanting them to know they knew though they knew they weren't supposed to know.

Immersed in delight at finding that politics and a relationship could synchronise, that two individuals could think so alike. It wasn't true. It was a travesty and she compounded it by deluding herself into believing that there was nothing wrong. Nothing wrong with him and nothing wrong with the party. Making allowances, which turned into excuses, deliberately ignoring with her brain what her eyes saw for themselves, U-turns hidden under a mountain of verbiage, internal politicking, promises never fulfilled. At least she had kept the symmetry and left him when she left them. The skeleton was one and the same. In both cases the parting hostile, accusation against accusation, anger against anger. His final words had been how are you going to achieve your aims now? Going to join the Workers' Revolutionary Party? Communist Party? Tories?

Back to today, and Karm's lifting his hand to his cheek, just as he had done when the back of her hand had slammed into it and her ring had left a long line beading with blood. As usual, words had exhausted their usefulness; far too genteel to express the holocaust within her.

'We're old now. Let's put the past behind us. You've been sulking for years.' Did he do it deliberately? Dropping little matches on anger that she thought was dead, fanning it back to life again. He probably did believe that all these years she had been doing nothing more serious than indulging in a long-term fit of the sulks. 'Come in. It'll be more comfortable.'

'I've given up tea.' He deserved all the lies she could dish out to him; time was when she'd scrape her insides to give him the truth, wanting the glacial clarity of honesty between them. He'd hoarded it, shaped it into bullets in his mental munitions factory, ready for when the time came to use ammunition. Should have remembered one of the first sentences she'd ever said to him.

'Giving up everything in your old age,' he was saying, 'the true Hindu way.'

'Of course you know all about us. When are you going to write your "Introduction to the Ethnic Asian in Five Easy Stages"?'

'Can't. You skipped out on me before I had enough material. I don't suppose you'd consider another liaison – I meant liaising – on such an important piece of writing?'

Silently, she held out the letter and this time he took it. Gathering her coat around her she walked past him, forgetting to bang her stick on the ground to add emphasis to her departure. The passing years certainly proved that you never stop paying for the mistakes of an earlier time.

Why live? Why life? What for? A sperm becomes a body, becomes a person, becomes a bundle of failures, disillusion, regrets. Had it been so bad? Had all of it been her fault? Her childhood image of herself had been as a gorgeous, multi-coloured bird, soaring through the sky, swooping to the ground, iridescent with each wing shake or bright gaudy in the sunlight, as gaudy as the nail-polish tears on her doll's face; by a cruel twist of fate, this flamboyant rover of the skies had been grounded, its wings clipped; left to fight for survival in the cold climes and grey world of England. No wonder it had lost its colours, shed its feathers, lost its way, become one among the soulless throng.

Stick-leg-shuffle-leg-shuffle. Romantic slush. Shifting responsibility on to someone else: were there hidden players playing chess with the world? No. Her past was hers alone. Stick-leg-shuffle-leg-shuffle. Forward March.

Sole to Soul

Maya waves goodbye to the coach and minibuses, her hands raw from cooking all night, eyes sore from lack of sleep. Ammi had insisted on a last-minute rush to cook more food, frightened that there wouldn't be enough for all, that this minimal gesture of support for the Greenham peace women would turn into a fiasco, and her dreams return to avenge her. For Ammi's nightmares have returned, marking her face with long lines of distress, changing her voice into a splintering sharpness.

Last night's cooking session hadn't been the light-hearted affair of before. Younger sis Shazia's ebullience dampened by Ammi's nights of dread, Big Sis wanting to ignore this new problem, concentrating on organising everyone into an efficient team: they chopped up bags of onions, potatoes, made dough, rolled, stuffed samosas, cooked rotis, washed endless dishes. The kitchen became stuffy and uncomfortable from the heat and cooking smells, everyone's tempers irritated and teetering on the edge of exploding. Angie was the only one occasionally breaking into chirruping talk, as if unaffected or wanting to break through the heaviness weighing everyone down.

Music, balloons, coloured ribbons, excited children, cheerful adults, and most amazing of all, the sun shining down: glinting on the sparkly suits and dupattas, refracting on the tinsel-covered party hats. Someone started a spontaneous song and dance. Passers-by stop to enquire if it's a wedding party.

'No. It's an Expedition to Perdition,' announces Shazia, suddenly having found her headline, quickly scribbling it in her notebook. Seeing the puzzled expressions she relented and explained.

An unexpected pool of goodwill in the gathering crowd and a spontaneous contribution of money started by a man with a dog.

'People just want to be led don't they,' said Big Sis climbing aboard. 'Give a start and they'll follow. Can't think for themselves.'

The dholak woman plays out a final round of big fat chunks of music, before she's overtaken by the revving of the engines, and has to rush to take her seat if she's not to be left behind.

They've gone one dream away and Maya returns to her job in hand and looks up the list of where all the psychiatrists reside, unknowing how far to pursue the game to catch many monies if you can, and serve up Martin A.D. an à la carte dinner he'll never be able to digest. Resisting the impulse to tear it up and throw it away, she checks an address and sets on her way. Why not, when you have nothing else to do? Playing games should at least keep your mind in ticking order, and why not gather the material to play the ethnic arriviste, package it all into the novel that will make your name. The name on the doorbell is Sitwell and as Maya presses it she wonders whether the name denotes the method, and that recently she seems to be pressing doorbells to be admitted into people's mentalscapes; it won't be long, she thinks, before I get pulled in too, losing my footing in Shanti's darkness or swallowed into Ammi's nightmares.

The door creaks open. 'Keep forgetting to oil these hinges,' he says, smiling charming, inviting her upstairs into his flat. 'The name's Karm. That's not what I was christened by my parents, it's a souvenir from a friend. What brings you here?' She explained, he laughed, saying that M.A.D. (for that was what they all called him) had it all wrong. Again! M.A.D. was prone to do that; but then one should also watch out, for M.A.D.'s ways were devious and strange. He could have his own reasons for wanting them two talking to each other?

'Tell me,' she asks 'how many Asian people you know?' He counts and says fifteen and a half; her look queries the half and he explains that some people carry on living with you even when they've left.

'How many of them are mad?' she asks. As if shot, he sits straight up and shaking his head, swears he couldn't have heard right.

'You did.'

'That's no question to ask an anti-racist.'

She giggles appreciatively. 'Give me a run down on the Asians you know.'

'As long as you don't ask me to run them down.' He takes a pad. 'I'll write them down, the names and occupations. Why,' he asks, pen poised, 'you must know enough Asian people yourself.'

'Some of us do, some of us don't and some of us won't, and all of us need to go through the chain of the whites, some of us can only discover ourselves through you. Like M.A.D., colonialism has its devious ways.'

'Ouch,' he winces and proceeds to write.

Locking the door they leave for a visit. Karm has promised to introduce her to Mr Bhatt, saying he didn't know if it was exactly the kind of case history she was looking for, but it wouldn't do her any harm to hear Mr Bhatt's story.

Mr Bhatt isn't at home, but his son is. The son's eyes flicking over Maya, surly to see her with Karm. Small hammer in his hand and nails in the side of his mouth, he won't respond to Karm's chit-chatting conversation, relentlessly repairing the pile of shoes in front of him. Karm says he has to go, Maya says she'll wait a while, watching the hammer strokes joining rubber to heel.

'Hi, I'm Rishi,' he introduces himself, as soon as the door has banged behind Karm. 'You with him?'

'What if I am?'

'My mum was white. She left last year. Talk about mixed blessings. Mixed sulphur and carbon if you ask me. Want to see Rekha's Extravaganza? At Wembley.'

'You got a spare ticket?'

'Me mate's the promoter. Don't flatter yourself. This isn't a pick-up. I'll get you a good seat. 'Ere, give me your shoes.

121

Disgusting.' Turning them round in his hand, bending them backwards and forwards, 'Some people don't think shoes have a limited life. Immortality ain't nowhere you know. Only in yourself and then no one knows about it. Some people will live life as if it's going to go on for eternity, others can never get enough and go dizzy chasing its disappearing tail-lights.'

'You should take up preaching,' she says.

'I could couldn't I? I'd make a lot more dough than mending shoe soles.'

'Why waste your qualifications. Karm told me you've got a degree in theology.'

'Some people's mouths are too big for their brains. Here. That'll do ya. Come back in two months for a check-up. Phone me for the tickets. Here's the number and that'll be two pounds fifty.' Rather nonplussed she handed over the money. 'Sorry, you can't stay. I gotta go to my counselling session. Enough broken hearts round here to make you think we was all made in Hong Kong.'

She walked with him towards the community centre where his counselling sessions were held, accompanied more by his incessant chatter than him. 'You have to make me shut up he said,' he said 'saying goodbye' saying goodbye at the tube station. 'Those shoes could do with some black. Polish.'

Greenham hasn't greened Ammi's nightmares: running endlessly up an escalator going down. She mustn't hit bottom, someone's waiting to catch her in their dead arms, while another someone else blows bubbles to block her way. She decides to struggle through one, they're only transparent soap. Plunging into one she's congealed in white plastic, unable to break through and free herself.

Rani/Rosalind is tired of staring at the white ceiling, but she can't close her eyes because she'll only see the blood rushing out of Rosco's head and hear that unearthly sound as bar hits skull. Her tired lids lower and immediately she jerks them open. Think to keep awake, paint the ceiling with your scenes, look again at the full stop finishing off a paragraph. That full stop is a symbol of what is inside her, protected through all the years of being an urban nomad. She had guarded it not for what it was, nor for what they would think of her if she did. She wouldn't give herself to anyone, for the very reason that they all expected that she would. And she knew they looked at her as if she had.

The men in their wanting and the women in voyeuristic condemnation. Even in England's 'liberal' land a woman is still nothing except her spot of blood, her vaginal passage. Judged by who she's with rather than what she is. In saving it Rosalind had saved herself and Rani despite all her wanting not to. Never giving herself over to another, neither in emotional or sexual bondage, she had kept her inner self protected and secure. That's where her strength, her determination to carry on had come from. Another reason she remained an outsider; all the others in the subterranean had surrendered themselves to one thing or another; whether it was in sexual slavishness, or dependency on drugs or bondage to another. Rani/Rosalind hadn't done that. Rani/Rosalind had reacted. Rani/Rosalind had fought for herself. But she'd run away from all that, the wanting, acquiring, struggling, fighting . . . then why had she . . . Rani/Rosalind's rigidity explodes back upon her, spinning her into a blackness, where she's deaf to the sounds released from her own throat.

Ammi slips into a thankful dreamless sleep.

Tandoori Nights

       Stick-leg-shuffle-leg-shuffle. Stick-leg-shuffle-leg-shuffle.

Fingers trailing across fencing of corrugated iron. Kuli closes her eyes, needing to re-acquaint herself by touch and memory rather than sight. The years had glued grit among the dips and rises of the metal, new patches of rust creeping to join the old ones, creating an intricate lattice work of erosion. Childlike she probed, prodded and pushed, till she'd made a hole big enough to push her hand through to the other side, her wrist scraping against the rough edges. The fingers opened, spreading out in a fan. Nothing to the touch, no wisp of a different air to mark the change from her side to the other. Pushing her hand further in she bent it backwards 'and explored the inner side of the fence. Feeling the brush of a plant? a weed? Easier for them to grow on that side, no exhaust fumes or vandalising humans to contend with.

For years all she had seen was the outside of this fence, the other side a red memory. Withdrawing her hand she bent down and put her eye to the hole. Large enough to give a view in segments, piece them together and build a mind picture of the whole. Twisting her body around to get a view of the far side she felt her behind bumping into something.

''Ere. Look out. Mind where you put yer big bum.' Pulling her face away, Kuli turned round to see what had happened, squinting her eyes to focus more clearly. 'Nearly broke the eggs. All over the pram.' She was young, blonde and angry, a dummy baby, no. No. A baby with a dummy propped up in the pram and another hanging on the handles, snot collecting around his nose. 'I'm not a rich sod like you wogs. Can't afford to throw away my food,' flicking the ash from her cigarette. 'What were you doing anyway? Worshipping at the Temple of Fire? Getting down on your knees and grovelling on the ground. That's all you people know. With your mumbo-jumbo and Hari-Krishnas.' Kulwant was transfixed with fascination. It had been a long time since she'd heard this kind of talk, she'd actually begun to wonder whether racism was on the ebb. Blonde Hair had restored her faith in the brutality of humankind. 'Don't know what you got to grin at,' complained Blondie. 'One day, someone'll make hari-kari curry out of you. Out of my way you old bag, and keep that big bum to yourself. It's an insult to women. Stop staring Rodney. Now come on,' grabbing his hand and dragging him away, his short legs pumping up and down, trying to keep up with her high heels. 'What's the use,' Blondie was still complaining, 'probably doesn't understand a word I've said.'

Rodney!! Kuli was in fits. Taking her stick she did a war dance around it, uncurling her voice in little whoops. Then sinking to the ground, back against the fence, legs stretched out in front, her chest heaving up and down. She was too old for these antics. Closing her eyes she waited for her breathing to return to normal.

'You awlriite?' Why open her eyes and disturb the tranquillity behind them. 'Do you think she's had a stroke? My grand-mother had one. Or a heart attack? Uncle Arnold popped off after he got his. Hello.' What a cheery soul, she thought, trying to imagine a picture of the person from the voice: young office or shop worker, judging from the edge of gentility on his tones. 'You try her. My grandmother became a vegetable after her stroke. You can communicate better.' How could the other communicate better, she was puzzled and waited for revelation. '*Thusi thik hai*? Please *bolou*.' Anglicised Punjabi. How sweet. Her eyes flew open. And snapped shut in instantaneous recoil. When she opened them again 'the vision' had moved back slightly. Was it her bird come home to roost? A multi-coloured, dangly earringed, glitter-painted, Asian punk. Dressed in one of his mother's old kameezs: a velvet garment encrusted in embroidery, beloved by Punjabi women in the early sixties; a flowered shalwar on his legs, the bottoms tucked into heavy boots, leather jacket, belts, studs and chains completing the ensemble. '*Thusi thik hai*?' was that all the Punjabi he knew? '*Koi darrd hai*? Doctor *bulaiye*.' The boy was an accomplished linguist. She smiled gooey-eyed at him.

'Thank you. Would you help me up.' Henna-painted hand came under hers, fingernails painted in stripes of gold and silver, curved over the back of her hand, each finger loaded with rings, some of them the almond- or flower-shaped Indian ones. So he was wearing his mother's gold too! He saw her looking at them.

'Mater won't miss them. The economy of this country could be kept going on her gold, does the proverbial dripping with it bit. '"If you've got it, flaunt it", is her motto. If she could be like that old king, who could turn everything into gold, she would. Instead she makes do with my father. What happened to you?' his voice changing tone, 'Were you done over? Did they take anything? Hurt you?' How admit to her fraudulence in the face of such concern?

'Just an attack of juvenile delinquency. My own. Ouch!' A poodle snapping round her ankles. Him, with the family of medical disasters, picked it up and cuddled it in his arms, all the while apologising. 'His name's Anton, my name's Bahadur. I don't let anyone shorten it. You know what it means don't you. Hero. Warrior. Punjabis will worship machismo. I flunked out after they told me I was a genius. Pater booted me out of the house, Mater lets me in when he's not looking. It was a boarding school, would any natural parents send their one and only to be turned into an English thing?'

'And you're still running away.'

'Dead right. You know you got it sussed out. Why couldn't you be my father?'

'Why couldn't you be my daughter? Did your father make his money here?'

'Yes. We're disgustingly *nouveau riche*. Pater's the A.B.C. guide to the Asian success story. If only he'd been born in the States or a Patel, he'd be twice as rich as he is. As it is he hasn't done badly for a village boy from Jullundur Town, who once

126

thought GT road was centre of the Universe. Hey, you want to come along to the Asian elderly centre. I run it. You look under-age but I'll squeeze you in. You could help to bring other women in.'

'Doubt it. I flunked out of respectability too.'

'I like you – a lot. Here's the address. It's only twice a week. Pater's miserly allowance won't run to holding it more often. Must go. We're taking Anton's poodle for his daily constitutional.', Taking Anton's hand, fingers intertwining, 'Bye. Don't forget.' Their stiff, upright hair undulating with their walk, the colours flowing and merging as the hair swayed.

A smile on her face and delight in her eyes she turned back to the corrugated fence. This time she couldn't go without seeing. Kneeling down she put her eye to the hole again. An empty fireplace, intact but forlorn: no chimney through which to send its smoke, no wall to give it a background and no room to fill with its heat; remnants of walls standing like lonely sentinels, orphans of a catastrophe, dark scraps of wallpaper still clinging to a few bricks. Once that wallpaper had been a roll in a shop, and a family had come to buy it. A sudden sweat, beads of moisture on her face, Kuli stood up, leaning against the fencing, feeling the heat of the furnace fire which had taken them brushing at her, from across the years. She had vowed to remember, and with each succeeding year she forgot that little bit more.

He had bought the house and then sent for them, and today they were going out to buy paper for the front room. Reunited after a seven-year parting: the man and woman, diffidently re-acquainting themselves with each other, the two boys cautious, waiting to find out more about him. No such restraints for the youngest, kittenish in her confidence, full of her own importance, telling the world with those clear brown eyes that she knew she was special, she knew the world's attention, love, deference were her due. Just as it was her right to be Daddy's pet. Holding on to his hand she's walking and skipping by his side while the other three follow a few paces behind, the sons showing that their first allegiance is to the mother.

The father controls his anger, telling himself it's bound to be like this at first, but he longs to burst out at them, unburden himself of all the time pent up inside, unroll all the conversations he'd had in his mind through the lonely years, open the little vials of himself he'd been hoarding. To say what it's been for him, to share all that's been growing and flowering in his mind. Now he couldn't utter a word. Everything that had seemed acute and necessary at the time, now appeared to be weak, self-indulgent or plain irrelevant. No matter how he labelled it to himself and excused his non-saying, it left a dissatisfaction which converted into anger when he saw them so far distant from him. 'I did this for you. Travelled thousands of miles. Took their sneers and jeers, ignored their insults. Worked where the dust choked, the heat burnt, where my back splintered with pain each night.'

They thumbed through all the available wallpaper books, the salesman, retiring to his newspaper, long since despairing of making a sale. Eventually a choice was made for a thick, embossed red, luxurious in its deepness. It was expensive. More than he'd planned to spend, but if they liked it, they could have it. His wife looked at him questioningly. She too was worried about money, had always been worried about money, a cheaper paper would do just as well. Because they had some money now, she whispered, it didn't mean they should squander it. The children like it, he'd answered. He wanted it for himself too, the paper itself didn't matter, what mattered was the act of spending more then he knew, in commonsense, he should; paying double the amount he'd intended fed some hunger in him, satisfied a longing to be able to choose and buy without counting each penny.

His years in England had been harder than any years in India: no land of milk and honey this United Kingdom. You only get what you work for and then only after the boss and taxman have taken their cut; and when you've got to split your money three ways, between your parents, your family and yourself, it doesn't come to very much and you wonder what's the point of living. If it hadn't been for her and the children he would never, ever have stuck it, not for a day. He had a longing to get more out of life than the bare necessities, to taste of things other than the daily grind of work, to have time for the beauty that he knew must exist in life. Instead he shopped at Woolworths, bought

128

second-hand clothes, begged for overtime with all the other Asians, swallowed the sarcastic barbs of the supervisor, 'Mercenary isn't the word to describe you lot. What do you want all this money for anyway? Not that we see any of you splashing it round the bar. Scrooges you are, all of you.' He wasn't to find out who Scrooge was until his daughter took part in a Christmas play.

The three parts of his life, the three needy corners of a triangle, three walls hemming him in, till one day they shifted and changed shape and became the walls of a house; the three corners dissolved and changed into four.

The end of every week bringing the time for reckoning and distribution. He often felt as if he was taking away rather than giving. How to balance the needs of all sufficient to fill them? Impossible on what he earned, no matter that he worked all the hours he could get, denied himself everything apart from the necessities.

Hung with care, the wallpaper added a warmth to the old, cold house. The little one had to be continually scolded. She would run her hands over and over it, loving the feel of the embossed pattern and knowing it was special because they'd paid so much for it. They invited the English neighbours for tea, put out biscuits and cake and he taught his wife how to make tea the English way and she said how can anyone drink this boiled water. Not having the confidence to tackle English etiquette they asked Mrs Randall to pour it out. Mrs Randall said, 'Very nice,' eyes roving over the room, 'you people do like bright colours, don't you.' They sensed the attack rather than knew it for sure. He smiled placatingly, his wife hadn't understood and the children thought she was being friendly. Nothing wrong with bright colours and all Punjabis had to have something red in their house. It was a popular colour.

'You got this house cheap didn't you? Lucky!' picking up a piece of cake and ostentatiously unfolding her handkerchief under it to catch the crumbs. They hadn't put out any side plates, one of the kids was sent hurrying off to the kitchen. 'Mr Banner was ever such a nice man, terrible what happened to him. I blame the woman. Flighty little piece she was,' at mention of piece one of the kids leant forward and offered her more cake. 'Ran away with the family plumber. Broke Mr Banner's heart. She must have thought she was on to a good thing. You know how much plumbers earn and this one had his own company.'

'More tea?' leaning forward and almost pouring it over her. He didn't want her talking about such things in front of the children, wasn't certain how much English they understood yet. 'The garden is very big. We will try to grow some vegetables.'

'Corner houses have lovely gardens. When Mr Banner had to sell up so quick my brother was thinking of buying this. But he didn't have enough money. You people always seem to get it. A person might think you printed it.' He didn't tell her about the amounts borrowed from different friends, the four corners all demanding their due. Bringing his family over hadn't reduced the calls on his earnings. Their corner had been taken by the friends who needed to be repaid as soon as possible, for they would soon be wanting to buy their own houses and send for their families. It would be good for his wife and children to have other Indian families near them.

As it happened, it didn't happen that way. The area became up-market, not many Indians could afford to settle near him. Thinking that for once he'd been lucky, he spent all his spare time renovating, replacing, repairing, repainting. His wife once accused him of caring more for the house than them. 'The house is for you,' he'd replied indignantly. 'What's it to me? Anyway will you bring your daughter-in-law into a house that's falling down around you?'

'Slow down,' she'd laughed at him, 'many years before we have to think of that.'

Kulwant's husband had been the one to tell her and for once had come with her; for once holding hands as they speed-walked towards the rising smoke, the acrid wind hitting them the nearer they got. Red hot flames licked the sky, frolicking in demonic freedom, highlighted by a backdrop of thick grey smoke. It wasn't real. It was someone's idea of charity. Free entertainment for the neighbourhood. Guy Fawkes night brought forward in flamboyant style. Must be Americans, she told herself, they always do things bigger and better. As they rounded the corner, heat and smoke assailed their senses, and self-consoling fabrications scattered to the winds. Joining the crowd, they stood aghast in full sight of the inferno. A red greedily devouring monster, licking its lips and cackling its enjoyment. The crimson heat fell on all the upturned faces; a woman's crying threading through them, her face buried in a handkerchief, being comforted by another. Two heads of perfectly permed hair nestling close to each other. Shaking her own head Kulwant turned back to the house. She must curb this tendency to be flippant in the middle of a crisis. Crash! a wall tumbling down, the rubble indistinguishable from the smoke. Taking her husband's arm she moved closer to him for comfort.

The blue lights of police cars and fire engines rotated their dread flashes over the scene. Giant worms of thick water pipes squiggled across the road and pavement; men in uniforms bustled with their authority. An ambulance hurtled around the corner, slowing down to squeeze between a fire engine and police car, its blue light adding to the circular whirling of the others. 'I'll never see them the same again,' thought Kulwant. The back doors of the ambulance opened, four stretchers were loaded in. 'Oh no. Not the girl. Not the girl too.' It was the woman who'd been sobbing into her handkerchief, her voice now stretched into a scream. Kulwant looked at her coldly. What did it matter if it was the girl too? What was so special about her? The wife and her welcome were gone, the boys and their roughness, gone. Gone the woman who would dart out and grab her, insisting that behanji come in for a drink, something to eat, at least for a taste of whatever special she'd been cooking. If there were pakordas, mathia, sagarparae, barfi, whatever – Kulwant would be sent on her way clutching a paper bag of the latest goodies. Her own kids devoured them in seconds. She never had the time for such culinary treats.

Gone. Oh. God. Gone.

Gone in pain, gone in terror.

They must have been sleeping as the petrol poured in through the letter-box, the new carpet muffling all sound. Were they woken by the whoosh of ignition as the match met the lethal liquid and flames spurted into life. Destruction flowing swift, death following right behind. Who woke first? Who tried to save the others? Who controlled their fear and who let it go? Who tried to shelter who? Who first knew the hopelessness of effort? Who struggled to the end?

Would their deaths have been easier to bear if they had been painless? Her husband wiped away tears she didn't know she was crying. Impatiently she shook her head. What use these tears.

The crowd scrambled on to the pavement as another fire engine's siren announced its arrival before it swung around the corner into view, screeching to a halt near the other. Exclamations, gasps and another moving away as a wall came crashing down, throwing up a thick shower of dust, ashes, embers and flames, darkening the already dark smoke, thickening the acrid air. Two PCs came to move them further away. 'This isn't a show you know,' remarked one. 'Why don't you people go home. Nothing you can do here.'

'Are they all dead?' asked the woman with the handkerchief.

'Bloodthirsty one, aren't you.'

'She's their neighbour,' added the other permed head in great indignation.

'What about the husband?' asked the neighbour, voice wobbling with tears. Pulling some tissues from her bag, Kulwant leaned over and thrust them into her hand. 'He'll be at work. He still does nights. He won't know. He'll come back to this,' voice rising, spinning out of control. The friend put her arms around her, murmuring little words of comfort.

'Your house will be all right. You needn't worry about that.'

The comforter looked up, quite outraged, 'That's not at all what she's worried about officer. She was very fond of the family.'

Kulwant turned to her husband, wanting to go. She'd seen enough. He said perhaps he should go to the factory, in case they didn't know where the husband worked. Perhaps he'd rather an Indian told him. Is that to comfort him, or to comfort yourself, she thought. Didn't know these were the sights in store for you when you came over to marry me, did you? Alternative Tourism.

'You don't know him very well.'

'What does well mean on a night like this? You're thinking like the English.'

She was. And she wasn't. Never could be English. At least one choice had been the right choice. They hastened back home, constantly casting glances backward at the flames and smoke still laying claim to the night sky. He hurried off in the car. She checked on the children. All sleeping peacefully. What had she been afraid of? That they'd been kidnapped? Spirited away? Burnt? Recoiling on her own thoughts she went round the house checking all the doors and windows. She must make a list of all the things they should do in the house to make it racist proof.

Sitting in the kitchen with the cold night around her, unable to write a word on the sheet in front. Outside, the fruit tree swayed against the pane, its leaves sliding on the glass. Soundless. Except that her nervous anxiety heard and she looked up to see her own face on the window's blackness, distorted, floating in space. Getting up she closed the curtains. From now on, they must make a habit of doing that. It was a big window and anyone looking in could see them acting out their life like figures on a lit stage. Something to write on the sheet.

The sentence was nothing to do with him, but his name got written as she finished it. Karm. Karm/Mark. Karma with the a. He wasn't her karma, he was her choice, to be repudiated whenever she wished. She should do it now, it would be like putting another lock on her house. Lock herself in white-tight. The flames made her want to burn him out of her life. For he was white and he shared in their guilt.

'That's right. I do.'

His voice coming out of her mind. If he was here that's what he would say. He would accept the bowl of blame. She wanted to hate him. It wouldn't come. Not this night. The nights when she would burn with hate were yet to come. Startled, she jumped, the pen falling from her hand. The telephone was ringing. Her husband at the other end. 'I'm at the hospital. They're trying to save one of the children.' Only one! She closed her eyes, wanting to go hysterical. 'Their father is here. He'd already left by the time I arrived at the factory. Some of the men he works with are here too.' He paused, waiting for her to say something. She wouldn't. If she spoke it would only be to ask of God why this insanity? And which God? The white one? The 'ethnic' ones? 'I'll bring him home, unless he wants to go with one of the others.' He won't. He'll want to stay near the burnt flesh. It grew from his body. Flesh of my flesh. It's mine, he'll say. We always were dark coloured. He'll want to hold them to him. Close his arms around them, for ever and ever.

The letter-box sealed up, opened only in the mornings, locks on all the windows, a burglar alarm, fire alarm and fire extinguishers. Her husband had suggested she was going over the top. She'd stared at him with hot, hard eyes, 'Your money or your family, which is more important.'

At night, she checked for herself that all the doors and windows were properly locked and the alarms switched on; refused to have a cat flap put into the back door. 'If she stays out late, it's her fault. She'll learn. Cats aren't stupid.' A/A hated her. She was being cruel. Not as cruel as the coffins.

Four of them, laid side by side, smothered in flowers. The flowers are for us. For them it's over. It's we who need the flowers, because we will bear the memories. We need the perfection of the blooms, the glowing gorgeousness of the colours to counterpoint the cutting of the last link. Each year we'll think they would have been this old, in this class, growing taller, growing up, choosing careers, girlfriend problems, arranged marriage problems; she's still wearing the same old clothes, when will she spend some money on herself? Our memories will live out the canvas of their lives. We must carry them with us, in case we forget, knit them into our lives for they now belong to all of us.

Any one of us could have been them.

She didn't know how much to tell the children. The plain story they knew, the motives too. Clear-eyed they said it's because of our colour. How far explain the whys and wherefores? Colonialism? Imperialism? Huge words for their small mouths. Her husband told her not to, 'They won't understand or they'll misunderstand. Let them find out their own way. It won't take them long. We can't move a step in this country without coming up against it.'

'There's more to it than being called Wog, Paki, being burnt down; they need to know how it operates, how to recognise it in all its forms. It's not always scrawled out on the wall. How are they going to fight it?'

She needn't have agonised. They worked out their own strategies for survival and defence, and each settled into his own niche. She then found herself quarrelling with the nature of their solutions; for years she wasted her breath saying they hadn't understood racism and its infrastructure, its sophisticated implantation into minds on a mass scale.

'What?'

'Mother's been hijacked by her rhetoric,' said Anup as sarcastic as he could make it.

'And you've made a pact with racism,' she had wanted to spit out at them. Wouldn't have been accurate. You can only hope to guard yourself against it. Place yourself where it's hard for it to get at you. As far as possible they side-stepped it, and were only prepared to deal with it if it came slap bang in front of them and socked them one on the jaw. Would it have been different if they had been older when the flames danced in the sky and the coffins rolled into the incinerator. Fire to finish what fire had started.

No. They had had enough other atrocities in their growing years to influence them. England didn't lag behind any other nation in racist brutality: the old grandmother roasted to death, slowly, piece by painful piece, the medical student beaten into paralysis, the doctor knifed to death in his own car; the casual beatings on streets, in parks, pubs, anywhere. No dearth of examples. They wanted to live comfortable lives, she wanted them to shoulder a share of the common burden. 'If you don't do it, how can we get white people to do it?'

'Surprised at you Mother. You must be over-exerting yourself. What kind of an argument is that? It comes from them, not us. Their duty to put their house in order. Our duty to defend ourselves, however we choose. You do your picketing, campaigning, demonstrating. We'll do it our way. What's the problem?' spreading his arms and shrugging his shoulders.

'Your way is selfish.'

Withdrawing her eye and lifting her head back, she blinked as if waking up from a long sleep. The corrugations in the fence had left their mark on her hands and coat. Her eye ached from too much looking, both inwards and outwards. Rubbing it with her hand she felt the grains of rusted metal that had stuck to her cheek; brushing them away her hand left lines of dirt across her face. A weird red Indian, unknown to herself, but on show to the world.

Ticket to Hide

Ammi is falling through the black holes of a sieve and every time she tries to hold on she's tossed into the air and, coming back down, falls straight through and into a tunnel darkness where a cry hits and buffets her, evading her thrashing hands each time she reaches out for it. Sickening tumble up and over into the air as the sieve is shaken again, the cry coming closer each time she's shaken through. Ammi knows the crying is seeking for her throat, wanting to wrap itself around the vocal chords, squeeze them tight, annihilate itself by extinguishing the apparatus that can produce it and others like it. Ammi knows it's a cry crying for solace and if she can catch it first, cradle and heal it in the womb of her hands, she can save them both, but the sieve comes to scoop her and shake her yet again.

Would our pains be less if we had no way to express them? We wouldn't have to repress the bitter crying knocking for release in our throat; Rani/Rosalind will not utter a sound as sleepless eyes stare at hospital ceiling, one hand closed around her throat strangling the strugglings inside that wanted life. The nights are hers for mental roaming, the days for evading the hospital staff and sleeping beyond the limits of her need, keeping her eyes closed even as sleep evaporates from her clutching need. They would shake her for mealtimes and coffee times, but had given up on doctor's inspections, wary of her hysterical rejection, eyes expanding into warnings of 'no trespass', body shaking taut into rigidity.

Rani/Rosalind pushes her emotions away, displacing the

immediacy; her throat relaxes and Ammi is saved from the threatening lasso of the cry. She falls into a grateful sleep, knowing it's not the end, only a respite; Rosalind is on the escalator going down, double depth, this is a deep station and she wants to travel to the molten core of the earth. The moving stairs downwards end, and she stands in the middle, a platform on either side. She knows neither one nor the other, but will not let random whim dictate her choice. Pacing up and down the two platforms, grimy in black dust, cigarette ends like amputated worms, flattening under impatient feet; she studies the maps on both: one goes south and the other goes north, both passing through business and pleasure centres, ending in suburbia. Nothing here that interests her. Calmly she sits down and waits. The urgency of departing has been neutralised by entering into the tube's black mouth.

Ticket in her hand boarding an outward bound train. Touch Birmingham, near enough the heart of this country. Exit from the station into darkness, meander through the night, aimless. By dawn light decide to enter, voluntarily, into the mouth of this urban whale. Breathe and live in anonymity. You have abrogated your past and become a blank page, Kora Kagaz but not in the filmy way, let the world do its writing on you; vindicate your worst suspicions.

Rosalind sells clothes on a market stall. Watching women punters come and survey. They finger the material, comment on the colour, judge the style according to their fantasies; which garment will fulfil their determination to outshine the others of their ilk, make them the cynosure of all eyes, be a net to get and keep a man for life. Rosalind watches, never intervening, untouched by their concerns and strivings. Her X-ray eyes ever seeing the flesh falling to dust, the ephemera of their efforts.

Well-settled into a niche, removed from the convoluted family interaction, personality stripped of society's scribblings, passing her days in a contentment of vacuity that could have continued for ever, but Joe said to her one day, Joe who owned the stall, to help herself to whatever she wanted from it, whenever she wanted. Listening to the spoken and hearing the unspoken she picked up her bag and left.

Started working at the other end, the cutting, stitching,

stretching and fitting, all under the roof of a modern-day Victorian workhouse. No questions asked and getting paid by the day. Drowned by the clatter of sewing machines, packing the products into boxes, her back to the women, most of them Asian, all reminding her of her mother. For though the younger ones were only a few years older than her they were replicas of the life left behind: covering the spectrum from waiting to be married. Married. Pregnant. Mothers. When they asked her she said she was Rosalind and no she didn't understand any Indian, and perhaps they were right, she was half and half. England, the angrezi mother. She co-existed as a co-worker, keeping herself on the periphery, refusing to be drawn into the waiting warmth of their Indian bosoms, joining them in their brief lunch-hours and tea-breaks, hogging herself on chips while they tucked into rotis and parathas. An adult among adults, she is now party to tales of children, husbands and parents-in-law. A woman's world glimpsed through anecdotes, boasts, or grievances. Tales of lives revolving around the sweaty intermingling of flesh and genes, heredity and domesticity.

Come the weekend: tired, drab, overall-wearing women chrysalising into bejewelled, sparkly, up-to-the-minute-fashion butterflies, parading the high street and mega-supermarket on Saturday afternoons; fluttering into religious conscientiousness to see and be seen by those who may have missed the sights the day before; willing ears and tongues soaking and hyping other's doings and misdoings into delicious gossip. Rani/Rosalind kept her distance, refusing invitations to homes and happenings, protective of her self-exile.

Preeti lost half her hand one day. A moment's concentration switched to looking up at the clock, and zip, the machine teeth chewed through it, spewing blood on polka-dotted silk blouses, her scream, merely a broken line underneath the frenzied clatter. Preeti is rushed off in the boss's car, the others gathering to each other in sympathy and solidarity, shocked hands trembly at re-starting. In the days following variegated reports swoop and circulate of fingers amputated, hand lost, arm damaged beyond use. If nothing else is certain it's sure that her family are asking for compensation; the company is defending, explaining at length and in detail that as a casual worker she is not entitled.

The lunchtime talk takes a radical turn. Comparisons are made between this factory and others, those who had predicted many such fatalities say so in voices ringing with vindication; the owners have lost the status of invulnerability, criticism is rife, and 'unloyal' thoughts, previously suppressed at birth, now live loud in indignation at uncaring and unjust treatment. Ears aren't always deaf and as the days go by, those who have worked the longest and are the loudest in condemnation are winkled away, and new ones who have no past knowledge come to take their place. However not all stories peter out in a damp fuse, and anger, if suitably fed, will continue to grumble and growl. The ex-workers join forces with Preeti's family, their numbers increased by some who are still in work but brave enough to risk jobs and demonstrate goodwill. They picket outside the door, give interviews to the press and for a short time embarrass the owners into defensive action. Into a scurrying hurry to remedy the best of the worst conditions.

Unsatisfied but mollified, all were ready to go their separate ways in search of other jobs, if Big Sis had not landed like a grounded Concorde in their paths. The dying embers of the anger glowed back into life, given a new lease of life by exhortations to fight for legitimate rights and the promise of support from a union and other workers. Optimism took root, the struggle began and where there had only been the need to earn money the word scab rang out each day, bringing the workers and ex-workers into the fold of mainstream worker-hood. For a while those who would have worked inside came and joined forces with those outside till Rani/Rosalind remained the only Asian going in.

The owners and new workers inside admired her bravado, thinking in spite of her skin she was one of them, while the dispossessed outside hated her for being a traitor to solidarity and race. Rani/Rosalind was beyond being sucked into any maelstrom. The owners used her as a justification and cited her presence as an endorsement of 'things couldn't be so bad as some would want to make out'. Coming face to face with Big Sis at the picket was no jolt to her conscience either for Rani wasn't looking for anything beyond a means of putting food in her mouth. Big Sis's persuasions cut no ice with her and, being blandly stonewalled, Big Sis's frustration boiled over into screeching anger; Rani walked in and Big Sis sat down to recover her breath and pull together her shredded equanimity, determining, for tomorrow, to keep her cool and stick to reasoned argument. Good resolutions all gone to waste; come tomorrow Rani/Rosalind didn't appear.

Party Parting

A ringing through layers of sleep, fling back the quilt and totter over to the phone. Caroline at the other end wanting to know how she is.

'Sleepy.'

'I'm going AWOL from the café. You need company. I've packed a night bag. I'm on my way.' Click!

Not bothering to puzzle over the background to Caroline's visitation, Kulwant went back to bed and her memories. Why bother to get up when there was enough in one's picture-palace mind to keep the mental organs churning over.

The fire had scorched the retina off her daily life; fears and anxieties accompanied the waking and working hours. Her heart ached for going back. India was no utopia of peace and order, freedom and equality, but at the very least their right to live and work wouldn't be questioned, they wouldn't have to guard against racism at every level every day. They might get you for all sorts of other things but not for being a different colour.

The time did come when she could no longer stay, but it was the party she left, not the country, trailing denunciations for being divisive and undemocratic. The woodworm had always been there had she cared to look; however, how could she when she herself had plunged and participated in the politicking rather than the politics.

'Until you saw the Ethnic light of Enlightenment eh,' teased Karm, trying to break her unsmiling stare. 'Can't say you've got lily-white hands,' voice changing to mockery, 'is that a racist insult? Your chance to haul me up in front of the CRE.

142

Sweetie.' And that 'sweetie' was the serrated edge of a saw. Damn his Bombay friends for teaching him that particular endearment. Damn him for being able to say it with the laid back Bombay drawl.

'Love gone bad,' whispered by someone, deliberately audible to all.

Consistent with the form of their relationship their last private struggle was also replicated in a public struggle. She was supporting and wanted the party to support the application of an Asian man to be endorsed as parliamentary candidate. At a time when all were calm waiting for Karm to be rubber stamped.

'How do we know he hasn't confused this with buying another corner shop?' winked the pet wag.

'Jealousy!' He says, flicking it from his tongue like acid. She's zapped into silence, shock streaking through her: she thinks of the distance they've travelled from being two separate individuals, to being one, thinking like one, acting like one, laughing like one, machinating like one. Or so she had believed. More fool her. 'Why do it through a man? Nothing stopping you from applying. Go for it baby. Don't be coy. The first Asian woman MP. Think of it sweetie. Immortalised forever in the history books, not to mention the rewards of the here and now.'

Why are you doing this, she wanted to ask, knowing full well why. He was getting rid of her, clearing the decks: a shiny new MP couldn't have a sordid love affair with a married woman hanging around his neck. Particularly an Asian woman. Wouldn't earn him no kudos with anyone except the woolliest of the woolly liberals. And who needed them, they were way out in the cold. And who could afford to forgo the Asian vote.

'Was I your contribution to anti-racism? Not only can you say "some of my best friends are black," but also "some of my best lovers . . ."'

'Sweetie, it was you who never wanted to go public with me. Wanted to safeguard your home, keep your kiddies and hang on to hubby. I was your bit on the side. Light entertainment to relieve the tedium of suburbia. Nothing like a dose of illicit sex to brighten a housewife's day.' He was dismantling their relationship crudely and brutally. Subtlety can be misunderstood.

143

Everyone fights for their own corner and once Kuli had rocked the boat and stirred the still waters others came along carrying their own oars: 'I'd like to remind everyone of the agreed anti-sexist policy,' enunciated Kate, vowels carefully rounded, a deliberately cultivated incongruity with her hippie appearance. 'It is amazing, though hardly unexpected I suppose, that the first chance you get to put this policy into effect, you all back-pedal so fast, you wonder how you landed back in the middle ages. One battle won can mean victory in war. We've all talked *ad nauseam* about how few women are in parliament, how necessary it is to redistribute power. Here's your chance to put your fine words into practice. Support your Sister. Don't fluff it.' Approval and applause from other women, but not from Kuli who thought there's a new meaning to the cliche 'isolation of the Asian woman'.

Incredulity from the women: 'You're supporting a man against a woman. We know your scene with Mark didn't work out. Is this the replacement?' NO. She thought, I don't deserve that. 'How about some sisterly solidarity? Or is it too early to ask? Still finding your feet after hanging on to Mark's coat tails for so long.' Yes, she thought, I second that, but on second thoughts who needs this brand of snake spit.

She had believed in the mainstream, in working within the system, had wanted other black people to join 'because', she said to them 'this is where the power lies. To get some of it, we have to be part of it; to influence it we have to go in there and change them.' Those were the happy days of faith in her words and words of faith from the party. 'We're never going to go back. We should throw away our pipe dreams of returning home. How many of the children are going to go back? And if the children aren't going to go back how many of the parents will? We're caught whether we like it or not. Whether they like it or not. And because we're here to stay we have to leave a legacy for the future, for the children to whom India will be just another country. Immigration part of their history. They'll be British by birth but never by colour.'

Objections were many. 'All very well to talk about the future,' they said to her, 'what about the present? They've split families, deported so-and-so, made laws against us. They think

144

by giving us the CRE they've given us our guardian angels? Well, the CRE is their invention not ours, and they will do what suits them. Why should they listen to us; we may seem many but we are not enough to make changes. No swamping. Not yet. Perhaps one day? They say our families are too large, don't they. We're an uncivilised people thinking too much of our pleasures.' Followed by a little grin.

If it's possible for a woman to be a misogynist then I seem to be well *en route* thought Kulwant, ditching my white sisters to support a 'representative of Asian patriarchy', as some say. 'You can't leave,' they said, 'have a break and then you'll feel ready to come back. This thing got blown out of proportion; in the heat of the moment people say things they don't mean. You've made us all think very seriously about the issues. We go back a long way. Naresh is a very good candidate and he is bound to get a seat somewhere soon.'

'What've we been given in this country? The hardest, the dirtiest, the filthiest jobs. Second-hand Rose had better hand-me-downs. Look at how many of you have been happy to take more wages than your black 'brothers and sisters' for the same work. Yes. Let's talk about solidarity. You crammed your ships and exported your surplus labour to America, Australia, Canada, Africa, Asia and any other parts of the world you could infest. Talk about population problems. You sent yours overseas. And who did a sweet U-turn? Who happily imported natives from the colonies to keep their factories running and their production high. And lest we become restive, you keep us docile: you promise change, participation, equality . . . beautiful, beautiful words.'

'It's the penalties of the game. Only one person can be chosen.'

She didn't listen. She didn't go back. They called her on the phone, 'bumped' into her on the street, 'dropped' in to see her. The boys started making jokes about Mother's variety of boyfriends. All she could see were pink tongues in pink lips forcing her to think thoughts she wanted to put behind her, forcing her to talk when all she wanted to do was forget, forget, forget. 'Why do they want you back so badly?' wondered her husband, 'you're not indispensable.' She wasn't. But her departure kept the 'disagreement' alive, gave it an importance they would prefer to deny; she had been one with them (or so she had believed), all members of a quasi extended family. And extended families are notorious for never letting go.

Her tongue worn out, brain drained hollow, echoing and re-echoing all that had been said and done. Her body collapsed, sank into passivity and lethargy. Her alarmed family treated her like an invalid, looked after her and sent her off to her Indian in-laws to convalesce. India for an injured mind. The hot heavens for a body missing its backbone. No thinking, no talking, no doing. An unfurling under the sun. Old D. H. Lawrence was right. How had he known about the sun?

'Kuli! Cooeee. Let me in you old ratbag.' Bang! bang! Caroline on the other side of the door. How long had she been knocking. Kulwant hadn't heard a sound.

'What a welcome I must say,' as a bleary-eyed Kulwant opened the door to a breezy bright Caroline, who deposited her bag on the floor, removed her coat and talked non-stop. 'Time to put your life in order my dear. Swimming before breakfast, every morning. Healthy food, and we must organise some fodder for that brain. Now which room shall I take? Never mind, I'll wander upstairs and choose one.' She was at the top of the stairs before Kulwant found her voice and followed her.

'Caroline. What's wrong? Who's looking after the café? Why're you here?'

'Nothing darling. Sid's in the café and God's in his heaven. And since you . . . and what's that thing . . . if Mohammed won't go to the mountain then the mountain will go to Mohammed. That is why *je suis ici*!'

'Don't believe you.'

'That's because you're a wicked doubting woman.'

146

Family Portraits

Shirley accepts Pavan's invitation and takes the children to visit their aunts and uncles. A/A doesn't think it worth the bother, but Shirley's eyes are fixed twenty years from now, when the children will need to know what they are. Anup sees them driving up and comes out to welcome. The ice between him and Shirley would do any freezer proud. Apparently Pavan will be late. He apologises and leads them into the house. The children follow, shivering in the chill. Malkit and Geeta, middle brother and wife (middle-brow, mid-ranking, middle-of-the-roaders, is how Anup describes them) are already settled, eyes fixated on their two-year-old. Anup exits to organise refreshments. Geeta informs with glee that she and Malkit will be moving to the States, he's been offered a very nice job there; while all the while her eyes wander over Shirley's sari: 'So beautiful. Won't it spoil in this dreadful weather?' Shirley shrugs and says she gets her saris cleaned in India. Geeta had promised herself she wouldn't, but Shirley's careless indifference to cost gets her goat and before she knows it she's talking about the six-figure salary, the house with a swimming pool, the sunshine of Los Angeles and . . . they hear a car driving up and all say in various ways it must be Pavan. It is indeed Pavan. Followed by Kurshid and new baby.

The talking suddenly cuts. Malkit gets up in a panic. Geeta retires into herself in high dudgeon. Shirley smiles triumphantly. Her children gaze in puzzlement, staring from one adult face to another. Pavan breezes into speech, voice unnaturally high, says to Kurshid why don't you sit down, and Kurshid does, in Malkit's vacated chair.

Anup comes through pushing a trolley, nearly runs out of control as he sees the new arrival. 'Dear me,' he says, counting the cups with exaggerated gestures, 'I seem to be one cup short. Um, are we expecting anyone else? Like Mummy for instance.' Pavan shakes her head though she's sinking under their censure. Anup nods understandingly, 'She had a prior engagement,' and goes out, back stiff in a huff.

Pavan hurtles into conversation, trying to draw in Shirley, Geeta and Kurshid. None responds to her. Determined not to be despondent, she doles out the coffee cups and raises hers to toast Geeta and Malkit on their new life, 'And don't forget us poor relations left behind.'

Shirley asked Malkit what he was going to be doing.

'Research,' he replied, 'important work.'

'Bombs!' snorted Anup.

'It's a defence project,' Malkit objected, putting his cup back on the trolley, with a clatter.

'Careful. Pavan's Pa gave us those. Family heirlooms. He bought them in Woollies when he was over here studying in the forties. I kid you not. I was about to say, old chap, no need for you to get so defensive about working on a project that could kill us all dead. For instance it could be said A/A's in the same field: cars kill thousands of people every day, you'll kill milllions/billions in one day, in a few seconds of a day to be precise.'

'Interesting,' said Shirley, 'shows what a nice, normal family we are; we've got kids, mixed marriages, broken marriages, and now a couple of mass murderers. My husband being one of them.'

'No no no that wasn't what I meant,' Anup wasn't too keen on the killer gleam in her eye and quickly took refuge in self-denigration. 'Don't get me wrong, I can hardly justify my existence in society. Pavan has to meet the payments of my social-conscious bill.'

'My mother dotes on Pavan,' said Kurshid, making her first contribution. This woke up the baby who started howling. 'Oh dear, I think it's time for his feed, I'm breast-feeding.' Looking round at everyone, in apprehension. Malkit asked Anup about the garden and they both made a quick exit, not before Pavan said something about it only being their brother. Shirley said she would take the children out too and followed them. Geeta was not to be left behind.

'You didn't tell them did you?' Kurshid was accusing Pavan as Geeta rushed back in for her baby. 'It's all right. I wasn't going to steal it.'

'Some habits are hard to change.'

'Some people will never change,' Pavan is sitting against the bedroom radiator, wrapped in a shawl, the day's fiasco still fresh within her, her voice is drowned out by the screams of the TV heroine, who struggles in the slimy grip of a monster, opening his jaws to swallow her whole. Anup presses a button on the remote control and increases the volume.

Geeta turns back from the baby and admonishes her husband for not giving any attention to his youngest brother, gloating syrup in her voice. 'What happened to your brotherly love? Don't know why I ask. Anyone can see there's not much love spilling round in your family. Now I know why you wanted brides from India, you and Anup. We'd be ignorant of what goes on and be grateful to the favour done us by bringing us over. Let me tell you not everyone wants to rush over here. Seems to look like him. But who can tell. Nothing would surprise me in your family any more.' Malkit turns over and falls asleep, to dream of the woman in the Bhavneeta ad, sari slipping away from a bikini top blouse.

In the house beside the garage, two bodies slowly separate and Shirley begins the tale of the day, recounting what it is to be supplanted as the family pariah; not even a question of being invited into the ranks, automatically assumed she was one with them against her who had torpedoed the conventions. 'I'll wait and see,' she finished off, 'I'm not one to be at their beck and call. Why do you think she did it? It's either pure mischievousness or misplaced saintliness. Good job you didn't go. Did you know your mother went to see Kurshid. Living up to her crazy act. Your family is something out of a soap opera. Oh, don't do that,' giggling, her hands wrestling with his.

Kurshid tells him it went very well, naturally bound to be some awkwardness. She herself had felt very shy, but when Pavan had invited she couldn't have refused, could she? He listens, hears the half truths, knows it'll never be more than a shabby patching up business. Can't have a second start without a clear ending of the first. Better perhaps if they could relinquish totally. She rounds at the click of his cigarette lighter and says do you have to, afraid of him dying a day sooner than he should, afraid of being left alone again. He rubs it out in the ash-tray, thinking her concern was an expression of love. Slipping into bed she tells him her mother's message that came in a dream, to cook and cater for the Greenham women. Thank God she left that house and by the way with the baby to look after shouldn't they get someone to help out in the house, 'I'm so exhausted.' Kuli had never needed anyone he thinks. The past gathering a rosy hue around itself, acquiring a perfection in his rememberings, which the reality had never possessed.

Many A Musketeer

Shanti and the local paper appear in Maya's house. Maya sighs, fills a jug, tells herself she doesn't have much else to do anyhow, and commences the reading marathon from front page to back page. Shanti drinks in each word, as concentrated on the reading as the translation. Different faces, different names, same stories. 'This is interesting,' says Maya, 'a follow-up on the squatter story. The council are offering the people, that's us, the chance to get one of these properties if we, that could be me, agree to do the repairs and renovation. I'll find out more about that.' Maya looked at Shanti admiringly; if she got a proper flat out of this the wear and tear on her vocal chords would be more than worth it. 'They've done a follow-up on the murder too. "It is understood", and I quote, "that the man who was helping them with enquiries will be charged with the murder." It all looks very neat.'

Behind her closed eyes Shanti is disappointed. Nothing that tells her much. She says they will read the paper, next week, only. Bringing out a plastic bag she hands it to Maya, 'For you.' Maya doesn't protest, Shanti's closed eyes don't allow it. A long, wide piece of handwoven cloth, embroidered round the edges. Maya drapes it around her shoulders and picking up an edge sees her name woven in. 'Rani's name is on the opposite corner. Next I will make you material for a kurta pyjama. You can tell me what colours you want. And whatever you want I shall make for Rani also.'

A stick-leg-shuffle-leg-shuffle outside the door and Kulwant comes in upon the two enveloped in their silence. Maya speechless in fingering, feeling the shawl around her shoulders, Shanti sitting quietly, her pose indicating she's switched off, the newspaper open between them. Kulwant has come to invite them to the centre for the Asian elderly, because she doesn't want to be the only woman visiting, her words peter out on their silence. Maya drapes the shawl around her head, tucking it in behind her ears, hands making patterns with the fringed ends. Drawn into their stillness Kuli puts down her stick and sits down on the floor, idly drawing the paper towards her. A gasp escapes, puncturing their engrossment, both look alert towards her wanting to know what she's found that they had missed.

Kuli cannot believe it can be the same. The Archangel caught in a prison cell, wings to be burnt on a charge of murder?

'Yes,' says Shanti, 'we will visit with you.'

Younger sister Shazia brings Ammi to see Pavan. Ammi is thin and nervous, body shaking with underground tremors; the sisters and mother have talked and no one knows what to do. Neither does Dr Gupta so she prescribes pills to induce chemical relief for the symptoms. When they leave she picks up the phone and asks for Rishi.

Going away for a coming back was not where Rani had yet reached; withdrawing from all and pinning down her tongue, was the last refuge of her retreat. Every action has its reverse and her eyes opened, remaining open in perpetual looking. The nurses and doctors talked, cajoled, looking for a key to unlock. Pavan visited, left unnerved, the open eyes boring holes in her head. They talked of bringing in the mind-doctors and be-moaned the fact that there were so few ethnic ones. Books, magazines, newspapers appeared regularly on her bed, and they watched trying not to let her see they were looking.

Shazia folds her arms and looks accusingly at Kurshid, who evades and flips through baby books. The cleaner looks in on them and goes out again shaking her head.

'I'll think about it,' Kurshid finally concedes. 'Shouldn't you be busy studying for your exams. Mustn't let those brains go to waste. Not that I had a chance. I had to go out and earn money for us all. Won't Mother be pleased to see one of us making it good. The Asian dream come true in a BA. If nothing else we aim high.'

'Well you're innocent of all that, aren't you? You aim below the flesh. And Ammi's going to go under if we don't find out what's wrong. You'd better turn up and see her. Bring the baby, it might serve a greater purpose than its usual shitting.'

Passing by Karm's place Shazia decides to see if he's in, and as the ringing of the doorbell dies away she can hear feet pattering down the stairs.

'The Three Musketeers,' Maya giggles as they troop out of the police station, not having learnt anything, and been re-directed to the probation service. 'It's too late to go there now. They're probably closed. I'll go there tomorrow and find out where he is. Let's check out this Asian Grandad centre.' Like puppets both Kuli and Shanti follow Maya's lead: Kuli wondering if she's doing the right thing, digging up the past, particularly where there's a grave involved, her nervous system still reverberating from the shock of coming across his name. Shanti is conserving her energies, honing her senses, intimating a change in her search.

An old church, overgrown garden, grass merging with the bushes, bushes merging with trees. Kuli thinks she must have misremembered the address. She and Shanti wait as Maya goes off to scout, 'Remember I wanted to be an explorer, give me a machete and I'll hack through any jungle.'

'You are yourself the machete,' Kuli and Shanti say simultaneously, looking at each other in surprise, Kuli closing her eyes in reflex at Shanti's rounded lids. They sit down on a wall and feel it sway underneath them. Maya disappears, adjusting her shawl to protect her from the clutching branches. The noise of traffic in the high street, beyond the next row of buildings, reaches them as a constant hum; the time-old silence of the church curving to absorb it like blotting paper. A group of truanting schoolkids pass, staring curiously at the two women, one who is sitting in sleep and the other playing with her stick. The kids debate whether to have some fun but pass on in a hurry, if they delay they'll miss precious minutes of Rambo on the Rampage.

'There's life at the back, sounds coming from a shack,' Maya emerging breathless from a bush, dead leaves and twigs decorating hair and clothes and Kuli says she looks like Puck. 'Forget the culture, let's get to the bottom of this business. Follow me.'

Bahadur shifts position from his game of cards and his eyes blink thinking he's seen three faces at the window, one a blank of closed eyes. Anton's stuff must be getting to him. Settling back to concentrating on the game. Bridge was a game he had introduced, but he and his partner were losing badly. A sudden cessation in the hum of chit-chatter. The three faces with three bodies are standing at the rickety door, hesitant in entering. A smile erupts across his goofy teeth. Juvenile aunty's taken him up on his invitation and brought a posse along with her. He's only half-way to the door when Bhasker Bhai ushers in the 'honoured' guests; all the men have abandoned their cards, newspapers, and conversation. They're standing up, making room, offering chairs for them to sit on, ordering Anton to make more tea, utterly delighted at this novel visitation.

A flood of talk and sound overwhelms the three visitors, their eyes jumping from one face to another, unable to answer or talk to a single one, as the questions and conversations mix and intermingle into a blanket of sound over them. Satwant Singh's 'Bole Son-hial' cuts through like a knife. Stunned into silence, all look towards him. He and Anton are setting out a huge pot of tea and an assortment of cups and other utensils that will serve as cups.

The peak of excitement dissipates, most go back to their activities, while a group linger around the visitors. Satwant Singh pours out the last cup of tea and begins to tell them how the club started, thumping Bahadur and Anton on the back in a show of affection and praise; both flex their shoulders back-wards and forwards to ease the blows; some people don't know their own strength. Satwant Singh recounts the story of how they used to meet at a garage, where they got hot drinks and a chance to warm their food. It started off with only him and his friend, but you know how these things happen, soon anyone

154

who wanted a free cup of tea would land up there. The young man who ran the garage was very nice, another one of our youngsters who hadn't forgotten the old ways (more thumps on the back for Bahadur and Anton), but anyone could see that charity and business don't mix. The boy had a garage to run, he shouldn't have had to run a canteen for the daytime vagrants as well. Gradually they made a move away, discouraging others.

Back on the streets, and park benches in the freezing cold. A chance encounter with Bahadur, Anton and the poodle gave birth to the idea of finding a regular meeting place. Bhasker Bhai knew about this hut from his grandson, who had been skipping school and holing up here with his friends. Bhasker Bhai did a deal with his grandson, pushing him back on to the straight and narrow and staking out the hut to check that the bargain was being kept.

Maya joined a game of cards and Shanti sat down with a group indulging in her favourite hobby: listening to someone reading out from a newspaper, this time in Hindi, cutting out the long-winded translations. Satwant Singh was showing Kulwant his notes on the Life and 'British' histories of the men who came to this club. 'Some of these men have lived their lives on three continents, India, Africa and now Europe. They say we are a traditional unchanging people, if that was true we would have been content to sit in our villages under the Indian sun. Some of these stories are very interesting: look at Jalal over there. Falling asleep over the Caram board. He and Mukesh haven't been able to finish one game yet. Jalal has travelled and worked all over this world. Wherever there was work he was there too. He's even lived in South America; all his life he has worked to feed two families, his own and his brother's family. His brother had an accident and couldn't work. How many English people would do that? They even want rent from their children. A great man,' head nodding in admiration. 'Look at Faris bhaya over there,' pointing to one of the men playing cards with Maya, 'self-educated man from a very poor family, all his life he worked for the trade unions, imprisoned by the British, and now in a different way still held by them. As we all are. Ah, here is the young man for whom I have harvested this crop.'

Anup, making a stately progress through the room towards

them, stopping every few seconds to greet those nearest him. Mother and son reunion in unlikely setting, mother smiling, son frowning.

'Come to visit the proletariat?' she asks.

'Wasn't I brought up in a proletarian household?'

'If you were it doesn't show.'

Maya's tongue loosened, talking non-stop in the car as Anup gives them a lift back, 'I never had grandparents, I mean I did. I didn't have them here. Didn't miss them until now. It's like opening a door into an Indian Disneyland, that's not really the right word, but you know what I mean. Like walking into a treasure-trove mansion, or temple, finding history through memory. I never knew all the things they talked about. One of them fought for the British, an Indian World War Two veteran. Sounds like something that should be in a museum, history books anyhow. How come we never learnt about the Indian soldiers who fought with the Brits. Looks like a deliberate suppression of the facts to me. I mean that's what multi-cultural education should be about, not Diwalis and sari parties. Anyhow I've decided to adopt Bhasker Bhai as my grandfather. He said it was okay by him. There's a lot to be said for old age. That other guy, what was his name? I didn't get to know his name, the one who was wearing the balaclava, he was a real wheeze, a born mimic. He's got you down to a T, Anup, that is your name isn't it? And the stories they came up with! Better than *Dallas*, better than *Dynasty*. You wouldn't believe their family soap operas if they were dressed up in technicolour and plugged into the silver screen. Not even if they were in a Bombay movie and that's saying something, isn't it. I hope you're going to treat them right,' thumping the back of the driver's seat. 'They're precious gems, those guys are, don't go and pawn them.'

'The deprived always romanticise,' said Anup turning a corner.

'Possessors never appreciate.'

'Depreciation is a law of life. Here you are.' The car stops outside Kulwant's house. Anup offers to drop the others at their homes but they refuse. Good thing he says, he has to pick up Pavan from the hospital where she's visiting one of her lost

156

sheep, and her car's not working, if only she'd stick to a straight GP practice life would be easier for everyone concerned. His BMW zooms off in a cloud of exhaust fumes, leaving Shanti coughing and clutching her chest, the coughing turning into a breathless wheezing. Kulwant and Maya hustle her inside, Kuli dropping her stick and rushing back out for it. Not once does Shanti open her eyes as the cough racks her thin body, and Caroline fetches a glass of water. Shanti drains it to the bottom and lies back exhausted, waving away suggestions that a doctor be called, muttering that it won't be long now.

Caroline looks questioningly at Kuli, who shrugs her shoulders, and remembers that she must remember to tell Caroline about the reappearance of the Archangel.

Pavan leaves Rani/Rosalind, of the bloodshot, unblinking eyes; takes a taxi to see Rishi, will miss Anup when he comes to pick her up, will not see the frown as he debates whether to be angry or worried.

Rishi curls up in his chair and calls in the next person waiting to see him, eyes on the Rubik cube in his hands. The swish of a sari makes him look up. Pavan settles into the sofa facing him. A final twist and the cube clicks into place and she says she still can't do it, can't do anything about other people's pain, trained for years and nothing to show for it.

'You're ambitious. We've spent centuries getting into this mess.'

'I've got two cases and they're driving me mad.'

'That's not even the thin end of the wedge. Not even a mere speck off the corner. Listen. No one can live this life and remain sane.' He agrees to visit Ammi with her but insists she plays a game of ludo with him before she leaves.

Ammi jumps up and down, reaching for mangoes that turn rotten in her grasp, the orange pulp staining her hands, a bride waiting for the henna to dry, its corrosive acid eating into her palms. The branches of the tree bending down, inviting her to pluck some more, bending round her, an unwanted lover blocking her escape. Frantically tearing at leaves and fruit, fighting her way out; in her struggle knocking open more fruity

157

pulp, on her head, arms and body, the flesh, shrivelling, falling away, each movement a turn into terror.

Rani/Rosalind is dead. Her needs, strivings, sensations, emotions: all dead. The open eyes staring at the ceiling, the body breathing: inhaling, exhaling, automatic functions servicing biological life. Consciousness contracted to the last pin drop and disappeared.

Disappearing Women

Shacking up with students had seemed to be a good idea. Boxer the Wimp had stumbled across Rani/Rosalind's sleeping body in the dark, in a park. He invited her to the house he shared with other students. Arranged a bed on the floor and a`job in their bar. She was Boxer's proud discovery, but Rishi renamed him, 'Columbus. Because he never found India neither.'

Seven people in a house rented by four: it had taken Rosalind many confusing hours and much affronted pride to sort out who was who.

1. Richard was an original tenant and had smuggled in Carol, true love must never be tested by distance, forget the fact that they halved their payments on rent.

2. Fran had spent a night with Boxer and decided not to go back to her digs, for she hated living without central heating. Fran often hinted that Rishi might like to live somewhere else, specially if he wanted more time to play his 'table' (tabla) drums. By his one exit, easing the congestion in the house, not that she thought he minded it; in fact he must feel lonely, if he wasn't living in the midst of a press of a crowd of people, all rubbing shoulders in the corridors and rooms of one house. Fran didn't like leaving anything to chance. Boxer was malleable, and she had the hands that could mould him, and decided that he would be hers for life, for she knew better than him what was good for them. Her eyes had twisted to a new watchfulness as soon as Rani/Rosalind came following Boxer into the house.

3. Rishi had the nicest room, for he had been the longest in the house, these being his first and only digs since he started his degree. Rishi didn't share with anyone, and the two couples looked with envy at the luxury of space he enjoyed.

4. Stephen the anarchist was the fourth legitimate occupant, long hair flopping round his face when long hair had long gone out of fashion.

Rani/Rosalind allowed herself a creeping interest in Stephen, who appeared to be the articulate mirror-image of her internal vacuum. She was sleeping on their lounge floor, a captive spectator to the endless TV watching, the rambling discussions after the pub, the hash smoking, the coffee and lager evenings. The novelty of her arrival had worn off: she was on a plateau of toleration, on the verge of negation, a non-person around whom the life of the house ebbed and flowed, often nothing more than a fly on the wall watching the unvaried enactments of scenes from their lives.

One night Stephen fell asleep on the floor, and in the middle of the nocturnal clock moved over and under her blankets. Verbal refusal turning into a tussle, escalating into a fight. He was larger and far stronger than her, and she yet unused to such attacks. As a last resort her lungs opening into screams that rang through the sleeping house. A slap of revenge across her face before he pulled away and zipped himself closed as the others burst through the door. 'Frigid virgin got the hots. Scared herself silly.' No one was going to take responsibility for anyone else, and no one stopped him as he left the room and went upstairs to sleep calm in his bed. Boxer comforted and made tea, Fran sniffed, sitting down, waiting for the salacious details, Rishi offered to give her his room. Fran sniffed again, 'Country cousins sticking together!' and as it became clear Rani/Rosalind wasn't going to put out, Fran went back up, telling Boxer not to be long.

Not daring to express his sympathy in physical action Boxer loaded all his feelings into his eyes, blue saucer orbs bombarding her with rays of compassion. Fran came back down to pull him back up.

'How long did you think you could carry on like this?' asked Rishi. 'If you don't live your own life, others will co-opt you, to put it at its nicest. Can't hang on to their toes. It won't be long before they shake you off, if they don't kick you in or kick you away first.'

Rani/Rosalind wouldn't argue with him. Her precious invulnerability had been shaken, she had managed to protect herself only by summoning others. Rishi was suggesting she was only living by living off others, and if she couldn't make it she'd better go back. She put down the cup, her tea unfinished, she wouldn't take any more of what someone else had given her.

Disappearing women captured on polaroid. The stick for the stick-leg-shuffle-leg shuffle leans in its corner as Kuli adjusts the blanket over Shanti and turns to watch Caroline turning the pages of the photo album. Peering over her shoulder is Maya, seeing for the first time the transition of a woman from her early thirties to her middle sixties, to her final exit in smoke. Pauli, her younger brother, had rebuked Kulwant for rushing out with her camera to photograph the plume of smoke. 'Morbid' had been his verdict.

Caroline sees again the girl who first came to school and Maya fills in the gap of Kulwant's story. Pictures of a mother and her two daughters, awkward in huge coats, hiding the new clothes stitched for the new life in England, standing to attention in each snap; photographs were serious business!

They had arrived in England in the middle of winter and her father had taken his re-acquired family to be outfitted in warm coats. A whole day spent wandering and looking at English shops, zig-zagging from the cold of the streets into warm areas of neon light, eyes filled to overflowing with the abundance and variety of goods to see, touch, smell and buy. Loaded with bags, tired and waiting at the station for the train, the father rushes off to the loo; the mother and girls make themselves comfortable on the platform, aching for a rest. Hissed, whispered anger from the father as he returns! No one sits on the ground. Where do they think they are? Back in the fields of the Indian village. The mother complains that they're tired and all the benches are occupied. 'In which case you have to stand.' She couldn't see the logic. He felt degraded.

Kulwant's mother had died five years ago. A village woman

who'd travelled half-way round the world in search of a better future for herself and her children, had died with a cracked heart that no amount of medicines or valium could repair. Kuli had wanted to send the body back to India, 'Mother was never happy in England.' The others had looked at her in amazement.

'She's going to be cremated,' said Pauli, never one for niceties, 'what difference does it make if it's here or in India. Her ashes aren't going to be any different there.' Pauli had become a successful businessman, rich from his 'Indian Emporia', catering to the liberal professional for whom a dash of Third Worldism in their homes was *de rigueur*.

'Her soul will want to be in India.'

'Oh my God,' he groaned, 'Now we have to deal with her hotch-potch mysticism.'

Her mother was cremated at the local cemetery. No fragrant wood, or special oils to fan the flames; Kuli went outside and watched the smoke curling out, being carried away by the wind, till all was dissipated. Sunshine glinted where the smoke had been. That's it, she thought. Finis. The End. So what's all the fuss about. One day she'd go like that. The sooner the better and the less seriously she took herself the easier would be the travelling towards the end.

Caroline puts one album down and picks up another one: photographs of the children, unravelling the past, Kulwant's childhood gifted back to her through them.

'Just like you,' Kuli's mother had said, after having a fight of wills with A/A, 'stubborn. You would hold out and hold out. Rigid to the end. What did you think would happen if you gave in, the sky fall down? The earth cave in?' Kuli would listen, rapt and absorbed. She had had a babyhood like her children and never remembered it, 'You took someone's doll once, and no one could prise it out of your hands. Tiny determined fingers holding on like steel bands. I slapped you, hard, and you punished me by not coming near me for days. I was extra hard on you both, you and your sister. Your father was in England and though it was my married home, I felt under double scrutiny. A woman without a man is a suspect person, as if with the absence of her man the restraining leash of civilised behaviour has been removed.'

'Isn't it the same story for all oppressed groups?' asks Kulwant of her mother. 'If woman is the victim of power she is also the object of fear.'

'I don't understand that,' says her mother, 'all I know is that I had to be twice as good a mother and twice as good a daughter-in-law. These immigration people keep our families apart for years on end. You tell me how many of their marriages would survive even five, eight, ten years of separation?'

'Tell me more. Tell me so I can tell my children,' begged Kulwant. 'They think our history only started when we came to England, that we didn't exist before.'

'Come back!' Maya laughing, clicking her fingers in front of Kuli's face. 'Where did you go?'

'Nowhere.'

'But not here.'

'Definitely here. But a few years ago. I don't need fodder for the brain Caroline. I've got harvests of years that need winnowing.'

'They're capital,' warns Caroline, 'you should live off the interest, but not the actual sum.'

'A true banker's daughter.'

Kuli had bought a freezer, in the days when they were considered a luxury or regarded with suspicion. Her mother came to help her with a marathon cooking session to fill this empty, new acquisition; as well as to cook the dishes she didn't know how to. 'I was too ambitious for you,' her mother was complaining, 'spoilt you. Now you're not one thing or the other.'

'And if I'd become a hot-shot career woman you wouldn't have approved either. Look how you talk about Darshana.' Darshana was the local success story, the only one in her family to get into higher studies, qualifying in pharmacy and three years later opening her own chemist's shop. Five years later she was the proud owner of four; her arranged marriage had been to an accountant. Gossip-mongers sniping that she had been more interested in getting hitched to the right profession than worrying about the right personality; even if he wasn't right,

163

Darshana would soon fix him. 'That woman doesn't have a heart,' said her mother once, 'she has a cash till to keep her going.'

Over the onions, garlic, ginger and chillies the mother starts talking about her own wedding: her voice going back to a rainy day years before Kulwant's birth, and the arrival of the baraat to take away the bride.

The daughter disappears, transforms into the eldest daughter-in-law, functionary of the mother-in-law who rules a sprawling household of family, relatives, workers and spongers: the mother-in-law dispenses authority and judgements over a queendom ranging from the kitchen to the family finances, to property and people. 'England's knocked the stuffing out of you girls,' says her mother, briskly slicing vegetables. 'It's not us who've made you weak. England's taught you all how to behave like ladies, too dainty to say boo to a goose and scared silly of a mouse. The first time I returned to India I took that picture, you know the one of the English woman, standing on a chair, skirt hitched up, mouth open in a scream . . .'

'So it was you who tore it out of my book,' Kuli exclaimed, 'and I always blamed Pauli. Fancy doing a sneaky thing like that!'

'I was embarrassed to own up. Your aunt,' shaking the wooden spoon at her, 'your second aunt, led your uncle a good old song and dance before she agreed to marry him. She had a will of iron your aunt did. We used to laugh because it was said he, your uncle, had to run all the way over to America to escape her domination. That was after we left West Punjab. After the partition.' Partition! In among the cooking, the mother tells her their story of the Partition.

Partition: a people torn apart, families ravaged, homes destroyed, enemies where there was friendship, hate come to stay. The powerful ones, the politicians, the Angrezi and the Indian, intones the mother as if counting off beads: they made the Partition. They made Pakistan. They made the killings. They made the sorrow. They made the pain. The Partition was theirs, not ours. The sacrifice was ours, not theirs. The new country was theirs, not ours. The homelessness was ours, not

164

theirs. The new wealth was theirs, not ours. The rootlessness was ours, not theirs.

Frantic decisions: what to take and what to abandon? The wishing to take each and every brick, every item that's filled with time-enriched memory. Arguments among the household, beggings, pleading, chiding, crying, resignation. A tangle of emotions tying the last desperate days into gordian knots of logic, need, necessity and sentiment.

What are you? asks the mother of herself. Are you your material possessions? The big bits and little bits that you accumulate: the utilitarian items, the luxury items, the decorative, the sentimental? After all no one can take you away from yourself: you are yourself; your voice, legs, face, the different strands that make you up. Are you a shell that has to be filled by material things which will perish in their own time anyway? If you stand naked are you any less than when surrounded by this paraphernalia? Yes. The answer is yes, that's why the choosing and the abandoning is a cutting into oneself. Some are singers and they are their songs, some are artists and they are their art, some are carpenters and they are what they create. I am a homemaker, she replies to her own question. I am my home. Each working day was for the home: from looking after the bricks and stones, to planting that little tree, to choosing that corner for sitting in. This house is as it is because of me, each item is here because it was chosen. I am these things.

In the end we could only take what we could carry in our hands, jolting in one salvaged cart, crossing a frontier that existed only on paper, travelling through a miasma of terror. As if there had been an astronomical happening in which decency was eclipsed and violence freed upon the world. Whole families were butchered, many left bereft of all relatives. We were considered lucky. We only lost one. Your aunt, little Shambu, hardly of marriageable age. And it was not even much of an attack, a little skirmish. If only we had found a body, we would have been at peace. Men were killed and thrown away, women were – disappeared.

Everyone's Paradise Lost

Withdrawal of what he was used to had made Michael even less than what he was. Peering at Kulwant, birdlike neck thrust forward, eyes roving, focusing from Maya to Shanti to Kulwant. 'Did she send you?' he asked. 'She's coming back isn't she? I waited where she told me to wait. Then they came and took me away.' Long silence, his eyes caught by Shanti's closed lids. Shanti touches Kulwant, edging her to speak. Kulwant can't. Horrified by what she sees. Would he want her to know that it's him, desperate like this. What will it achieve? She shouldn't have come this far. She could have sent Caroline. Hands balling into fists. Why hadn't she thought of Caroline. Shanti nudges her again. Shanti knows she's getting near, she mustn't lose this chance.

'Remember me?'

'Give me all your history,' he recites, 'Zig-zag A to Z and pick up Kuli.' Repeating in a monotone under his voice.

Kulwant leans forward, 'Kuli. Do you remember her?'

'How she ran to her wig-wam was bad, bad, bad. Sad sad sad. How she ran to her wig-wam . . .'

'Michael, remember the ring? The one you gave Kuli.'

'. . . how much a wog she was, was clear to me, the kiss of a woggess is addict . . . addi . . . addictor. . .'

'Michael. Remember Him-him? Studying with Caroline.'

'Caroline's party had a garden, the garden had a ring . . .' He's looked at her and he's recognised her, and he wants to go, he wants to run from her. He has his back towards them and he's gone.

166

Rishi has kept his promise to come and see Ammi. Ammi has gone upstairs to fetch something or the other, she was mumbling, so they didn't catch what exactly she was saying. They sit downstairs in the front room and Pavan is telling Rishi about the disastrous day when she tried to bring the family together and they fell even further apart.

'The time was still cacha. But catch it while you can, was my philosophy, with Geeta and Malkit winging off to the States I was afraid I didn't have much time, afraid of things solidifying into separatism if left too late. We're a family for God's sake, why can't we be together even if we are different. People are far too precious about their pride, or what they think is their pride, about wanting their lives to be like other people's lives. As if everyone is perfect. Why can't we start building bridges instead of walking away all the time. Don't ever fall for that line, 'blessed be the peacemakers'. Blamed will be the peacemakers is more like it.

The outside door hangs and Big Sis looks in on them, briefcase in her hand and harassment on her face. Slinging the briefcase on to a chair she sits cross-legged on the floor. Big Sis has had a hard day and is heading for an even harder evening. 'Do you believe in separate organising?' she asks, 'I never used to, but I do now. I think I'm going to chuck up my job. The Asian workers in Dovecote, they make duvets, right. Wanted to join the union. Cause for congratulations one would have thought. What actually happens? This bastard official, I offer no excuses for my language, though why I should blame his mother I don't know, has been putting them off, making excuses not to collect their subscriptions. A sackable offence if ever there was one. What do you think the union, big brother of the workers, is going to do? They're going to send him on a racism awareness course. As if he doesn't know he's being racist. Never mind. I'll make it my business to keep an eye on him. He won't get away with anything from now on. What I need are eyes in the back of my head, talons for a tongue and a footballer's kick to kick them out of sight.'

Rishi wants to look at her shoes and as she takes them off and hands them over, Pavan can't help laughing. Rishi twiddles the elegant court shoes in his hands and tells Big Sis to buy a new pair, with thick rubber soles, that way the unevenness in streets and in buildings won't get to her. He explains the importance of wearing the right kind of sole, 'You're someone,' he says 'who stands squarely on her two feet, but you need something under those feet to take the weight, and leave the mind free to think, without worrying what's getting under its tootsies. Mark my words. It'll do you a power of good.' Ammi enters, bringing them a plate of sliced mangoes, Kurshid following in behind her.

'I always seem to be bringing up the rear,' remarks Kurshid, covering up shock at the sight of Pavan, the baby cradled in her arms. Pavan knows that the baby is a shield against attack and begs to be allowed to hold him. Kurshid hesitates and Ammi tells her not to deny her daughter-in-law. For once united in emotion Pavan and Kurshid stare at each other in consternation, Pavan's arms falling away as Kurshid holds out the baby.

'Rishi to the rescue,' says Rishi, leaning forward and taking him.

Big Sis picks up her shoes and bag and marches out, turning back at the door, 'As I said, I didn't used to believe in separatism, but some people push you to it.' The door bangs shut behind her.

Ammi watched their mouths staining as they bite into the slices of mango, wincing as she sees the pulp eating into their flesh; leaning forward and lifting the plate towards them, insisting they have more.

Conversation is jerky and sporadic. On the premise that if you don't give you don't receive, Rishi launches into a story about himself, from his earliest memories to his mother leaving, how he was never one with anyone, neither the whites nor the Asians. He had to decide for himself what he was. Advantageous that Urdu and Hindi aren't difficult languages to learn, so it was easy to make a choice. Anyway it was the most logical decision because he could pass for Asian but he could never have passed for white could he? His fluency in Hindi and Urdu earned him permanent residency as president of the Asian Society. 'What greater acceptance could anyone desire?' Opening his hands wide in question. 'And those were fun years, you bet! Not like a girl I met when I was a student. Didn't want to be Indian. Insisted that she was South American. Give her credit for being an Internationalist. A genuine 100% rebel she was. Her eyes looked at the world and found nothing pleasing, nowhere. Who can blame her. What does anyone find pleasing in the world, but we make do, we compromise, we are grateful for the little that comes our way, and we make sure we don't open our eyes too wide, don't look too far beyond our feet. If we did, we'd go her way. There's no logical reason for living is there? And she never, ever gave her Indian name. Left after an incident in the house, not that she was a member of the household anyway, but there was a boy called Boxer who was captive to the romantic idea of the oriental woman. Boxer thought he was being protective, Fran his girlfriend thought he was straying where he shouldn't be. Instead of reining in his leash, woman kicked out woman. Rosalind should have heeded my warnings and not believed that paying her way would smooth the path.'

'Rosalind. Rosalind,' echoes Pavan to herself.

'That's what she started doing. At first she was just shacking up, then she started paying a share of the rent, bills, whatnot. Couldn't work, could it? No matter how much she paid? She wasn't legit in the household, outsiders can never buy their way in. Unless she moved in with one of the blokes, that gives automatic entree. If she wanted she only had to lift her little finger to take Boxer away from Fran. One day she was there and the next day she wasn't.'

'I've got to go,' said Kurshid, taking the baby from Rishi, her voice tight and upset, she'd had enough of sitting opposite her 'daughter-in-law'. Pavan offered to give her a lift, but Kurshid said she'd get a taxi. The outside door banged again and this time Shazia came into the room, bringing a whiff of the sweet, outside fresh air with her.

'Where've you been all this time?' Kurshid attacked her, 'Don't tell me school goes on as late as this?'

Ignoring her, Shazia went to her mother, gave her a kiss and a hug and sat down by her. 'Things not going your way, huh?' she asked, looking up at Kurshid. 'Never mind. What would you have done at home? Asked the cleaner to hoover the grass?' The baby wakes up and starts yelling, Shazia smiles with satisfaction.

Kurshid dumps the baby in Pavan's lap. 'Have your brother-in-law. I've got to warm his milk.'

The smile flies from Shazia's face as she looks from one to the other, and realises who's who.

Pavan soothes the baby and wonders aloud if these Rosalinds are one and the same and 'how could Rosalind get into Ammi's head'. She tells them what she knows.

'If there's any chance of this Rosalind stopping my Ammi's nightmares I want to go check her out now,' stated Shazia, standing up. Pavan isn't sure, Pavan is debating, and says she'll talk to the hospital doctor first. 'Nothing doing. Ammi's not going to have another bad night if it can be helped.'

'I'll phone them. Hold your nephew. Look he's a baby. He's not about to bite you.'

Stick-leg-shuffle-leg-shuffle. Kulwant returns and tells Caroline about Him-him's reappearance. Caroline's reaction is interested but subdued and Kuli carries on talking wondering what's wrong, hoping the flow of words will draw it from her. Eventually she asks her outright and waits through the long silence, thinking Caroline's going to put her off again.

'Complications darling. Sid wants to marry a grandmother.'

'Does the grandmother want to marry?'

Caroline's voice failed at attempting to be light. Nothing ever remains static and if it does we have to do something to shake it up. Caroline was happy to leave the relationship where it was because she'd already been where he wanted to go. Coming to this crux would either lead to a parting of the ways or a compromise from one or the other. 'Darling I'm too old to deal with these adolescent emotional problems. I should be repenting my sins and preparing my soul for the life hereafter. I don't believe it can work. First it was curiosity, then needing each other. Now it's marriage and afterwards it'll be children. I can't give him children at my age. But I can't be near him and carry on saying no. Don't look so concerned. I'll visit Michael.'

Maya throws away her notebook, and lies back, eyes closed thinking, thinking that people should close their eyes more; take time out from the blanket bombardment of visual stimulation, listen to the blood churning round their bodies, let budding thoughts not wither unnoticed, thus unwatered, nurture them into the fullness of their flowerhood. Maharishi Maya's canned philosophy! Her eyes itch and she remembers she hasn't removed her contact lenses.

Picking up her notebook, she flips through it again, some interviews, some hearsay from 'professionals', some jottings of her own; all pieces of a puzzle that would never fit together. Our lives collide against each other, bruising, hurting, hurtling past. And we all mould our different shapes of protectiveness, some sad, some pathetic, some hard as stone, and some there are who never manage to mould a protective shape for themselves: their vulnerability raw and exposed to the world, and naturally the world will trample where it can, especially when it's a majority against a minority, whether it be two against one or a thousand against a hundred and she must shake him out of her system, out of her body.

Draw pictures of all those seen and imagined: she draws her own face, to get to know it better. Instead of her face the lines keep moving to someone sleeping with open eyes. Someone's hand, Michael's hand, though Maya didn't know it, reached out and covered the sleeping/awake face; fingers splaying from forehead to chin.

Shaking her head, Maya gave up and went back to her notes, concocting a jigsaw for the producer and director, chainmail linked, making impossible piecemeal extrapolation. If they took one they'd have to take the others and if they took all they'd have to look under the surface. Not that she trusted their eyesight any more than they now trusted her. But what were worms to one could be flowers to another; her sanity their madness, their reason her objections.

Time to go. Meet Shanti at the address in the notebook; which is a tall Edwardian house, behind the backrows of select semi-detacheds, not that Maya knows for sure what an Edwardian house is but she reckons if it's large and old, and still standing, it might fit the label. Walking down the street, diary in hand, ticking off the numbers every few yards. Just her luck! It would have to be the house right at the top of the road, set away behind bushes and trees. On entering, she licked her lips and thought this is a tasty bit of all right, wouldn't mind living here myself. Funny how obsessive the mind can get when it don't like where it's at and escape seems to beckon at the whiff of every possibility. Three months ago she would never have said her flat is as bad, cramped, damp, dilapidated as it seems now.

Entering a carpeted hall, into an institutional homeliness, she followed the sound of voices to the back. She was late and the last to arrive, disturbing the organised pattern of a meeting in progress. Facing the assault of ten faces and one pair of closed eyes; the open ones questioning, probing the reason for her presence. Trying to minimise the obtrusion of her entry, Maya quietly drew up a chair and sat behind Shanti. Farida and Asha looked fireworks at her, but Shanti spoke and shielded her, wanting her accepted.

'As long as it's understood this meeting is confidential and not fodder for the white square screen.'

Maya closed her eyes and then as quickly opened them, hearing someone giggle. Asha brought the meeting back to order, detailing the arrangements for the running of this shelter for Asian girls who wanted to leave home.

'It's not for "Runaway Asian Girls". We don't believe in that headline. It's a transition place for young women who want somewhere that is safe and secure, a place where they have the help and counselling they need, where they will have time to think and explore the possibilities open to them, away from pressures of every sort. That includes not only parents but all those concerned white people who think running away for an Asian girl is some kind of promotion in life. It's our community and it's up to us to deal with the problems in it. But we have to be careful this place doesn't become a dumping ground for any Asian woman the authorities can't be bothered to take care of. For instance, I was visiting a client at the hospital today, and while talking to the sister, she started telling me about an Asian girl who is a patient there. This girl has become totally withdrawn, is refusing to talk to them or take their treatment. And keeps her eyes open all the time. Apparently they're all spooked out by her. Good for her I thought. What the sister, the ward sister, was really after was to pass her on to us. As if we're equipped to deal with that kind of a case.' Asha carried on talking but Maya now knew where that face on her paper had come from.

As the meeting disbanded and the members were being shown around the house, Maya asked Shanti to find out more from Asha about the open-eyed girl in the hospital.

'I have already done so,' said Shanti. 'I will not visit her first. You will do that.'

As it was, Maya was not the first. The police were the first. Michael had talked and told. Tongue loosened by Kulwant's appearace from the past, activated by Caroline's insistence on his remembering, forcing him to pull at the loose strands of his thought and knit them together into a coherent whole. The police didn't believe him at first, and would never have listened if Magdalena hadn't done a corroboration. Magdalena tells them all that Rosalind took Rosco from her, and if it hadn't been for Rani/Rosalind doing a Praying Mantis on him, he'd still be there now when she wanted him again.

Like urchins scaling over a town wall to watch the execution of one of their number, Magdalena and the cohorts of which she was one had been watching with peeled eyes and upturned ears the drama of Michael's captivity and the slow but sure progress towards a prison sentence. They clambered into the court gallery and all joined in a singsong as Michael recited his great works of art, adding a few new lines:

> 'Black bird come to see me do,
> Do the bird in the jailhouse crock.
> Oh me cocks, she ain't worth a crow.
> I got her out, I turned her around,
> I booted her away, her black-ass behind.
>
> Go find your sister, do I said,
> She with the iron and the blood,
> And the teeth and the nails,
> She with the English voice and British ways,
> Pretending hard at hiding her colour
> It won't won't stay, and I won't pay.
> It's Rosco's day. And Michael say.
> Say Rosalind, say Rani,

She ran, she murderess.
She left the body. She eat the soul
Michael say She Rosalind She Rani
She Kali. Kali, Kali, K-A-L-I.

Who hasn't heard of Kali after Indiana Jones. Uproar.
Entertainment. Riot in the court. Michael taken away. Singing,
swinging between four arms. 'Kali had ten arms,' he says, 'Rani
had an iron bar.' Magdalena and her troupe are singing
Michael's songs in the police house, putting it all on blackbird
Rani. Signing sheets to say she did it.

Singsong Extravaganza

Thousands of people streaming in one direction, rows of cars driving round in useless circles, hunting for a parking space. Huge hoardings outside the conference centre announce in sky-high letters and gaudy pictures that this is the night of nights, this is the night of Rekha's Extravaganza! Ticket touts don't bother to be discreet as they buy and sell outside the doors, the price increasing with every passing minute.

'She's only a film star,' protests Shàzia as she and Maya exchange rueful glances.

'Only!' Maya protests. 'What blasphemy! You're talking of the mega mega star of the Bombay screen.' Maya feels like doing a Shanti, so dazzled is she by the glitter, glamour, shine and sparks from jewellery, dupattas, saris and make-up. Angie, looking fine in borrowed feathers, is the only one able to take on the competition: her beaded hair tinkling round her face, one of Ammi's embroidered saris glistening over her long lean body, gold earrings twinkling against her black skin. The speculative object of many an interested stare, she becomes the stalked prey of a gang of machismoes, loudly articulating their admiration in masala lines filched from Hindi movies. Shazia offers to shoo them away. 'Spoil sport,' accuses Angie in a hiss. Rather taken aback, Shazia offers her services as translator instead.

'Huh,' snorted Angie, 'they can admire from a distance. I no tango wid dem. What are they saying? Don't look their way!'

Maya struggles through the queue to buy drinks for the three of them, nearly choking as Producer and Director suddenly appear at either hand. The evil genius and bad angel she thinks. They were here to pick up the flavour they said, both dressed in kurta pyjamas. The producer going one better than the director, flaunting ethnic eclat in a shawl slung under one arm and over the other shoulder. Shazia and Angie were impressed while Maya wished they would disappear in the puff of smoke from the producer's cigarette. M.A.D. and Madd said deadlines are looming ahead and perhaps they'd better have a meeting tomorrow.

'. . . and why haven't you included this case of the girl in hospital with ever-open eyes in your report. A purported murderess at that. What an amazing, multi-faceted conjunction of rebellion, protest, anger.'

'And this weird partnership with a drug addict,' adds the other, 'randy random poet who has a chip on his shoulder about Asian women.'

Maya murmured quickly that she was working on the story and soon planned to visit the girl, not in order to placate them but to cover up her movements to hustle the other two away. However escape is never easy, especially when you turn around and come face to face with the one who left you for himself and her.

He is all tender greeting and special smiley eyes, giving her a throwback feeling to the time when they first met. Maya tells herself to hold on to her dignity and sanity and puncture the bubble he's drawing around them. She turns round and introduces him to the others, bringing them in to dilute the memories threatening to spark a dangerous regeneration of what had used to be between them two. Shazia bristles with anger and is about to scour him with a metal brush denunciation, for she had seen his play and hadn't liked it one little bit, and he should hear from his Asian 'sister', but her beginning words are drowned out by the director's effusiveness, who introduces him to the producer; the three clinch into a conversation, heads bowed towards each other, and Maya could never afterwards work out how it had happened, that she and the others were eased out and left hanging behind. Straining her eyes, she catches tattered glimpses of the three in a huddle, limpets clinging to each other among the moving mass of people. Shazia is still trailing smoke signals of fulmination against him, and turns to ask Maya what he was to her. Maya deflects and points to Angie who's playing verbal ping-pong with two of the machismo gang, watched by the rest who stand in a stringed semi-circle around them, keeping score and forming an appreciative audience.

Maya hooks her arm through Angie's and drags her away, leaving behind a barrage of indignant protest, heart-breaking pleading and terrible recriminations. Shazia is hopping up and down with impatience, the third bell has sounded and they'd better hurry up and find their seats. Angie points out, in a sharp, piqued voice, that the crowd around the door is as jam-packed as ten minutes ago and it'll take that long again for it to clear, and if they hold on a moment she'll be back in a minute, looking longingly at someone behind her. Maya and Shazia flank her on either side and push and shove her through to the inside.

Rishi has done them proud, their seats are near the front, in the VIP rows, and to Maya's consternation, in front of him and her. Maya feels a touch on her shoulder and turning round to the seat behind her, stares at the fluttering green fringe of hair and dress waving like palm fronds in front of her. Maya blinks, thinking she must be having a bad hallucination. Samantha, for that's her name, the one he went to, after her, invites her to tea and he endorses it.

'We're going to meet at the meeting with M.A.D. and Madd.' Maya didn't know that. 'Come round afterwards. Come back with me. And we can have a chat about the research you've done so far. No point in duplicating is there.' Maya stretches her lips into a permanent smile as she makes non-committal noises. Shazia shushes them loudly as the house lights dim and the stage bursts into a profusion of music and multi-coloured lights heralding the mega star who's carried in like rose in a bouquet by her entourage of singers and dancers.

Maya hustles the others into a quick slip-out during the interval to avoid those sitting behind. They bump into Anup and Pavan at the chaat stall and Maya's tension relaxes and she laughs with them as Anup wonders who's come to see and who's come to be seen. A girl with hennaed hair passes by distributing leaflets, pressing one into each of their hands, and urging them to attend the demonstration in support of a group of young Asians charged with grievous bodily harm of a policeman. Anup questions and Soni, that's how she introduces herself, lingers to argue, gesticulating her arms in frustration as he mischievously misunderstands or turns her points upside down; her energetic gestures displace her bag from her shoulder, scattering leaflets all around them. Everyone leans forward to help, forgetting the drinks and food in their hands. Soni shoos them all off, grabs a couple of the machismoes who're hanging hungrily on the periphery, eyes leech-like on Angie, orders them to collect the leaflets, hitches her bag back on to her shoulder, tells the machismoes to follow her, the ring of authority in her voice cowing them into obedience, and disappears into the crowd leaving a trail of leaflets behind her.

Scheherazades over a Sleeper

She's lying still between white hospital sheets, won't and can't say a word of what's in her head. They move her to a room on her own, put a lock on her door. Ammi and Rishi come to visit, meet Maya and Shanti wandering a corridor. Pavan gathers them together and explains the police happenings and Michael's accusations. Shanti is shaking, complaining her feet are bleeding, sitting down holding them between her hands, though Pavan can see nothing wrong. Shanti is terrified to the core. Having come so far, fear of being wrong overtakes her, fear for this girl fills her with dread. The finely attuned senses of her endurance and search desert her. She will not go in. Let Maya and her shawl be Shanti's delegation.

Rani is away in the black hole and Ammi takes her hands tight between her own. Ammi will stay the night because that's when the doors will open for them to travel together. Rishi sits at the foot of her bed, watching those eyes that stare all around and never see. Maya places the shawl under Rani's head, bringing the ends over her shoulders, still warm from having been around her body, her hands smoothing the forehead backwards and forwards, backwards and forwards. There for the grace of something, thinks Maya, go I and many others. Our defences of want, greed and need protected us from the fall where Rani disappeared; Pavan feels redundant and goes out.

Vigils through the nights and days. Ammi no longer has nightmares. She can't sleep till the first light of dawn pales the electric lights in the room. Rani is left more alone than ever.

179

The physical contact of Ammi's hand on her hand breaking their nocturnal thread. Rishi comes and goes, massaging the soles of Rani's feet. Maya comes and gazes, helpless to help; but feeling the beginnings of a change within herself, her past is relaxing its pincer grip and day by day falling away. She brings her papers and sits by Rani's bedside, either drawing or writing. Rani's living death, her withdrawal from life, reflect back to Maya her own obsessive myopia, if life is as useless and wicked as Maya has often claimed then why is she trying to coax Rani back into it, with a murder charge hanging on her head at that.

Kulwant and Caroline arrive each day bringing food and thermoses of tea. Caroline dead certain that what it did for her it will do for Rani. Fennel and cardamom smells change the air in the room, stirring the deepest recesses of memory, releasing thoughts, feelings, stories; they exchange and interchange, talking over Rani's bed, the different voices toning and tailing into each other. Often forgetting whether it was a story that happened or a story told, or something dreamt, and time tricked memory into believing it a real happening.

'Happiness,' began Ammi, who seldom spoke, now speaking of a story, 'is making the best of what you've got. Envy is the devil that drags you down and Plenty the pillow that suffocates. I had a sister whose measure of both was insufficient to her needs. Brought up in poverty and educated to elementary standard, she nevertheless married a man rich in wealth. Neither manificently beautiful, nor terribly ugly, none could believe why he would want to marry her. She would not be dissuaded. The parents were torn between doubt and joy. She had her way and went away. A long time of silence passed. Happiness replaced worry and messengers were sent to find out news of her. They came back bringing reports of sumptuous wealth: a magnificent house, servants and a devoted husband. Joy returned. And so did my sister. She had come, she said, for a holiday. Her clothes and jewels put to shame our house, the shame turned us into her servants, running to anticipate her wishes, cooking and serving choice dishes, such as we would never in our lives have thought of having for ourselves. We thought our sister's stomach is now accustomed to better fare and we should cater accordingly. As her holiday continued beyond the bounds of hospitality, even for a married daughter, doubt again took over from joy. Sensing the change she talked to the mother, asked to be allowed back home, volunteered to surrender her worldly goods. No one could understand and each time she attempted to explain, laying layers of reasons on reasons, the greater confusion she created in the minds of all: one day saying this, another day saying that. She no longer cared for wealth and riches, she was out of place amidst those born to a higher way of life, the servants despised her, riches didn't mean that people were happy, was life only about wearing good clothes and living in a big house? She missed the people she had known before, she couldn't reach out and touch the dirt that we were all made of, her house was insulated against the cries of others, death is a door closing us from life, why live in a fortress that separates us before our time, diamonds are only coals we wear around our necks, food never tastes as good when you've never touched its peeling, cutting and cooking. However she went back and then came back, making endless return journeys between us and him, wanting more than she had, not having the courage to walk away from either, wearing out the patience of all. Our sister didn't have the courage to walk out of the open door. Not like this one,' pressing Rani's hand. Did Ammi imagine a returned pressure?

On the way home Caroline talks to Kuli about Sid, how she can't decide yes or no. Wants both, doesn't want to risk catching pain and unhappiness again. Although that sounds so cowardly. Should she say yes and hope for the best? Or opt for pragmatism and the lessons of experience?

Rishi's hand massages and soothes, he says, 'I'll tell you a story of a man in no man's land. It was the break between two wars, he was strolling in the no man's land between two sides, peace plain to hear in the silence sprouting between the grass,' Rishi's finger's smoothing the cracked flesh, the repeated movements trying to heal it together again, '. . . strolling peacefully, he suddenly fell through a big black hole, down and down he went, till he landed smack in the lap of the Snow Queen. Frozen he was. Poor man. The Snow Queen smiled and said "I have tropical isles, but as you can see I am in no state to go and overrule." She pressed a hand to his feet and he landed up as Governor General of Aidni. Pretty place it was, full of sunshine (of course), seas, mountains, fruits, vegetables, folklore, legends, poetry and people. But he could see the people weren't happy, for they had chains around the insides of their stomachs, everything they made, grew and thought had to be handed over to him, and he in turn had to pass it on to the Snow Queen. He thought this most unfair, and decided he would not be the imperial broker and broke off the connection. The people were very happy. And he was glad knowing he had done right. But in the burning heat his feet started freezing, no matter how he covered them, they got colder and colder, till he could hardly walk, could hardly think, for the shivering in his feet sent a cold chill through his body to his head. No amount of wool or fur or fires was sufficient to stop the cold running into his very bones. He gritted his teeth, struggled and resisted, determined not to surrender, waiting for death. The days and months went by and he realised she would never let him go, would keep him in the no man's land between living and dying. His freedom was an instant away, the moment he agreed to obey. He consoled himself with the knowledge of his deed and the gratitude of the people. Gratitude is a grain in the rain, as many of us know, which is as it should be, and as the years went by, the business of administering, organising and governing the country took priority and the people had less and less time to think of him. New generations grew up and replaced the old. They remembered him as a story, and commemorated once a year. In his no man's land of living/dying the man had many bitter thoughts, and even came to the edge of surrender. As he teetered on the brink he realised that what he had done had been for himself, not the people. It was not self-sacrifice but self-affirmation. This knowledge broke the Snow Queen's power over him and he found himself back on his stroll in no man's land, walking between the trenches of old enemies. His feet were freezing because his shoes had become drenched, so he went home.' Rishi looked down at the feet he was massaging. Had there been the slightest quiver of a movement?

Kulwant calls Shirley and says she'll baby-sit the kids if Shirley and A/A want an evening to themselves. Shirley is non-commital and Kulwant puts down the phone knowing that broken bridges take a lot of preparation and labour to repair. Going down to number two on her list of jobs to do she rings Pavan and asks if the offer of the flat is still open. A silence at the other end and Pavan says she's rented it out, she'd decided renting was better than leaving it empty. Kulwant wants to say that she'd like to meet up again but Pavan sounds in a hurry and she leaves it.

Maya is massaging Rani's forehead and says, 'There are tales of a third eye in the forehead, aren't there. Some people would say that's madness. I tried to capture madness in my notes, banknotes that is. Who doesn't need them. Madness or sanity is an elusive creature, a pregnant mind that never delivers, we see the bulge but can't look at what's inside. The producer won't ever be pleased. I thought I'd offer to water his plants, and then I thought I wouldn't 'cos I didn't want the director pouncing out on me. I never could be directed.

'Let me tell you the story of zig-zag woman, that's how she was born, with zig-zag eyes, and that's how she saw the world, in zig-zag ways. Now if she had been alone in the world, it would have been okay, but she wasn't and it caused misunderstanding, problems and pain. She couldn't see as they saw and they couldn't see why she couldn't see as they saw. They sent her to the best doctors, the greatest psychologists, but no one could do nothing, 'cos if they didn't believe in zig-zag sight, they couldn't cure zig-zag sight. Not that it needed a cure, but that's another story. This woman became puzzled and bewildered; if she couldn't trust her eyesight, what could she trust? She decided she would listen to other people and do as they said and perhaps it would all get better, and she'd be the same as everyone else. Needless to say, it got worse. You can't have others telling you what you're seeing, therefore what you're thinking, therefore what you should be doing, therefore what decisions you should be taking. She tried it, it was a bit like drawing by numbers. No taste, no feel, no self, no her. She became passive, depressed, convinced she was useless. In the depths of her dejection she decided that instead of listening to other people telling her what to do, she'd watch people, learn and imitate. That way it'd be a kind of DIY way of sorting out her problems. So she forgot about herself, observed, noted, and discovered something very interesting. Once she shifted the spotlight on to them, the differences between them shone out like daylight in a dark room. Some covered up their differences, others pretended they didn't exist, others 'persuaded' others to see their way, others looked the other way. Knock me down with a feather, she thought, I'm going right back to my zig-zag sight and just let them try telling me it's wrong. She lived happily ever after. Well, almost. You know what this world is like, it ain't happy till it's got your arms pinned behind your back. However, she was much happier than she had been before and she regretted all those lost years when she listened to other people, instead of trusting herself. Yeh, on the whole it's a happy ending.' Maya's hand sweeping upwards and downwards across the forehead. Was it the accidental brushing of her fingers that made those eyelashes tremble?

Maya is wondering how she's going to extricate herself from her predicament. The meeting with the producer and director had come and gone this afternoon (she'd declined afternoon tea with him and her). Unsaid though clearly revealed was their intention that she hand everything over to him, and he would work on it from here on. 'Not on yer nelly' was her reaction, 'Not again!' Damn. Just when she was going to chuck it in, he had to pop up like a bad penny and force her to hang on to it. In the end they had suggested a collaboration and she had hedged and evaded. 'Not again,' she thought, 'Collaborate so's he can run off with the loot.' They'd probably sensed she wasn't committed to their project, her inertia would swing it his way as good as handing it to him on a plate. So why linger? Why not recognise she couldn't force herself to do what she didn't want to? Why not walk out with dignity instead of plunging back into the old cycle of anger and grievance. She smiled. She would. It was a load off her mind. But no need to tell them right now. Let them wait. She knew what she was doing.

Caroline poured out the last dregs of the tea, and said she'd be back the following day, after visiting Michael. Michael was falling down to the wrong end of a telescope too. Kulwant wondered if it might help to get some other people to visit Rani, a variety of faces and voices might help her. Outside they bumped into Shanti, pacing the corridor, saying it's not time to go in yet.

Subversion among the Vegetables

Stick-leg-shuffle-leg-shuffle.   Stick-leg-shuffle-leg-shuffle.

Feasting her eyes on green, purple, yellow, orange, and all the other in-between shades that nature made; long, fat, rounded and plump with smugness, sheltered by leaves or dimpled all over. Mere vegetables: aubergines, lady fingers, green peppers, cauliflowers, carrots, keralas, broccoli; oranges, bananas, grapes, and even fresh dates nestling in their shiny skins. Gorgeousness for gorging on.

'Hello Aunty. What's it going to be today? Got fresh dhania, them lady fingers came in this morning. Nice and juicy, snap them up before the hungry hordes find out and descend like Genghis Khan on the rampage,' said Soni of the leaflets, reclining in her deckchair.

'I want . . . everything.'

'Tut. Tut. Aunty. Greed. One of the deadly sins. Only to each what each deserves. Or what each can grab. Hey, when did you get that stick? Bet you don't need it.'

'It's essential. Some adopt a cat or dog, I adopted . . . this.' Tapping it on the ground, 'See, it talks to me.'

'Hey, look out, those were my toes those were, I ain't a lump of concrete you know, though some people wouldn't know would they? Guess what, I met your son, Anuppie boy, at Rekha's Extravaganza. Becoming a real smoothie ain't he. He didn't recognise me and I didn't remind him. I thought that's life.'

'He hasn't seen you since before your teenage years. Haven't you got a job yet?'

'Working here ain't I?' she said, outraged. 'Just 'cos its my Dad's people think it ain't work. Not doing this for entertainment. Look at me hands, see those bruises, blisters. Feel the muscles,' flexing her upper arm, 'didn't get those by lounging around, watching the world pass by through mascara eyes. I unload the van, lug boxes around,' ticking the items off on her fingers, 'do the ordering, deal with the reps . . . I tell you I'm an essential pillar of this here establishment . . . It's me who runs the place and others who get the glory. I mean if I didn't remind Dad about the tax, VAT . . . Dad still thinks VAT is something you drink . . . we'd be carted off in a tumbril . . . Black Maria anyhow . . . see how my shoulders sag under this heavy responsibility,' fashionably encased in the latest Indian outfit. 'It's got to the stage where I'm seriously thinking of demanding a place on the board of directors. Or getting this place unionised . . .'

'I like your streaks,' Kuli said, interrupting the litany of grievances. Eyes opening wide, firework sparklers. 'Do you? You're the only one. The moans and groans I get about it from them both. Not as if he can talk. Me old Daddy-o. You should see his old photographs. Hair combed into a quiff the size of Everest, pierced ears.' Head nodding in affirmation, the short hair flopping up and down. 'It's true. He used to wear earrings! A real dandy was me Daddy. I said to him, henna is part of our culture, when he was moaning about my streaks. He just snorted, said there were other things in the culture which were more important and why didn't I follow those things. Like what, I asked,' hands on hips in indignation. 'He said: Respect. Obedience. Hard Work. The three penances for being born Indian you know!

'Well I was really cut up. I mean I do all those things don't I? No appreciation. He's sulking 'cos I put my foot down. Said I wouldn't go to university. The world is my university, I said. No appreciation. Like I said before. I'm polite to everyone, they're all uncle or aunty, the whole world's my family. Except the whites, 'cos they'd flip if I started doing that business on them. Though it could raise some interesting gossip. Might do that one day when I get bored like. Said to the old codger, me Dad that is, like I'd like to get married. Yeh I got that look from him too.

Shock. Horror. Women do do it you know.

'I asked him, all respect and obedience, to arrange it for me. Now what's wrong with that. Thought he'd be pleased – doing everything the right and proper way. He turned round and asked me who the bloke was.' She paused, waiting for the expression of astonishment on her face to make its mark. 'I was hurt. I really was. Look Dad, I said to him, I'm not that kind of a girl. What kind do you mean? he asked. I thought oh, oh, hold your horses, he's in one of his silly moods. But I persisted. I always do against adversity. Challenge a challenge, that's my motto. I was patient. I explained it to him. Spelled it out – that's your job Dad. You're supposed to find me someone. That man's wicked I tell you, even though he's me own Dad. Laughed at me. Said he'd never forgive himself, he couldn't ruin someone else's life by palming me off to them. I tell you, they drive one to do it . . .!'

'. . . do what?' Kuli prompted into the unexpected silence, her stick tippering on the ground. 'How long are you going to weigh up vegetables and onions?'

She, Soni, turned round to give them a proprietorial look-over, 'Nothing rotten here, all good quality stuff. I'll get my hair permed. The Afro-look. What do you reckon? 'Ang on. I knew I had something to give you.' Darting inside towards the back of the shop, where Kuli could hear her rummaging around, hear also the annoyed 'shits' and 'fucks' as whatever it was she was searching for remained unfindable. 'I've got to go upstairs,' she shouted back, 'mind the shop a minnit please.' Feet clattering wildly up some backstairs.

Kuli sat down on the stool by the cash till, next to the spice rack, an epicentre of aromatic aromas. If you closed your eyes, your memories would take you back: back to hot baking sun, the clamour of voices, the press of bodies and all these smells would drop into place: the signature tune of an Indian Mandi: grains and dals on handscales, eyes capable of measuring to the last grain, tasty whiffs from food stalls starting an avalanche of desire in the taste buds. 'Don't ever eat from the food stalls,' she'd been warned on her convalescent trip to India, 'those people mix all kinds of muck with their food. Very very unhygienic.' She hadn't heeded and had indulged in illicit gormandising, ably aided and abetted by Sunny the eldest grandson and Kami-Kazi, the eldest granddaughter of the Indian part of the family. After having stuffed herself in the market she had to eat at home, too, else they would worry and that was how she had come back from India, plump, rounded and oozing health. 'Enjoy life yaar,' Kami-Kazi used to say, taking her off to town. Sunny would bunk his classes and meet up with them: they would go to midday film shows, have long cool drinks, spend hours in endless chatter-banter.

'I want a motor bike.' Kami-Kazi said.

'She's mad for anything on two wheels,' Sunny explained, 'that's why the nickname. Went off on Chacha's scooter when she could hardly reach the pedals. Chacha and Dhadi chased after her, shouting like mad, their dupattas falling off behind them; Chacha ran round the other way, hoping to intercept K.K. Yelling furiously about what he would do if she even scratched his scooter. What fun yaar! None of them caught her. Everyone came out to see the fun and joined in the chase. This silly idiot was doing okay till she decided to do acrobatics and take a flying leap over a hole in the road.'

Kami-Kazi should have her motor bike, Kuli had decided and the three cooked up a plan whereby Kuli would send the money when she got back to England and the bike would be bought in her name. 'And I'll have to "test" it out for you,' announced Kami-Kazi, 'keep it in good running order. Celebration! We shall celebrate with kulfi. Double helpings. But not here. Anwar does the best kulfi in town. It's just around the corner.' Just around the corner turned out to be half-way around the town. 'Every yard yaar, will be worth every spoonful.'

On her return to England Kuli had taken a part-time job. She called it Kami-Kazi's motor-bike job. 'Enjoy life yaar,' she said to Kami-Kazi from her perch on the shop stool, imagining her tearing through the village streets.

Soni and her hennaed hair hurtled down the stairs. 'Here we are. Dad had hidden them, the old sod. He's devious. But not as devious as me. Can you give them out.' A red leaflet, advertising a demonstration in support of eight young Asians, accused of various charges by the police. At first she couldn't help grinning about the colour. Punjabis still hooked on to red! 'I'm going to have paper bags made of them. Won't that be nice and neat. Subversion among the vegetables! Printer says he can't do them till next week. How many people can you bring to this?' Kulwant didn't answer, busy reading the leaflet.

'Hi Pam Pudding,' this dubious greeting being given to a pregnant woman, who had just walked into the shop. 'The usual? Potatoes, carrots and greens. How's the new bloke? I saw him passing by here yesterday. Honestly, love, I don't think he's good enough for you. How are the kids? Why aren't they with you?' Kuli looked up as the other woman murmured a reply. Had Soni actually stopped long enough for someone else to get a word in? Sure enough it wasn't long before her voice took over again.

Kuli switched on the kettle and went back to the leaflet in her hand. The youths had been arrested for attacking police officers, causing an affray, breach of the peace, carrying offensive weapons and causing grievous bodily harm. She shook her head, not believing the charges could be so serious. The leaflet countercharged, accusing the police officers themselves, who had been in plain clothes and in an unmarked car, of provoking a fight. It said the youngsters had been outside a school escorting younger children home, because of racist attacks on them. Switching off the kettle Kuli placed tea bags into mugs and poured the hot water over them, splashing it over the cups and her hand, hardly aware of the pain, her mind turned inwards on herself. Children were being attacked and other 'children' not much older were risking themselves and their futures to protect them. Where had she been all this time? Cooped up in her misery and feeding off her memories. That's where!

Sick and dishonest. That's what she felt! It's all right to play games, to pretend you're something other than what you are when you've got nothing else to do. She had used pretence to cover up her disintegrating world. Every day she had made it her job of work to re-live and reassess her past with Ifs, Buts, Shoulds, Shouldn'ts.

Learning lessons from the past is all very well. Not much good if you cop out of putting them into practice. Had gone into hiding from the future in play-acting; had tried to cheat the future by pretending she was old and past it.

And so smugly lecturing Maya that freedom is endless stepping-stones across the river, 'It doesn't happen in one beautiful bang, you have to make it happen step after step.'

'Hey, the tea's stewed.' Soni, back by her, poking at the mugs. 'You didn't take out the tea bags. Yuck. I'll make some more. We were at school together, Pam Pudding and me. Wouldn't think it, would you. She's already got two kids. Number three on the way. Had a bun in the oven as she swanned down the aisle in shining white. Had to be a white wedding. Nothing else would do. Princess for a day. You know I think that's the real reason she got married. Wanted a taste of all that glitter and glamour. Where else are we to get it from. Not all of us can be mega stars of stage and screen. Flaunted her engagement ring like it was the Koh-i-Noor. I mean you couldn't see the damned diamond 'less you held a magnifying glass over it. He didn't stay. No staying power these white men, have they? And now it's preggers by the boyfriend. Loneliness will drive women into the arms of the shadiest characters. Here ye are,' handing her a mug of tea. 'What do you reckon?' Nodding towards the leaflet. 'Us girls' group is going. You know. The one I asked you to come to. We meet at Sujata's house. Dad is dead pleased about it. Thinks I'll learn to become ladylike and live up to my name – Soni the beautiful. With him adding his fifty per cent to the ingredients, not surprising I turned out the way I did. Hi Tony,' as a little boy walked into the shop. Scalp showing through the skinhead hair, an earring dangling from one ear.

'I'm gonna scrap with you. You grassed on me,' round face screwed up, little hands balled into fists, his whole body taut and threatening.

'Shouldn't have tried it on,' replied Soni. 'You forgot I've known you since before you were in nappies. Used to pat your mum's stomach and tell you to hurry up and come out. Should have saved my breath shouldn't I?'

'You don't know what me mum done to me. Here,' turning and lifting his T-shirt. A couple of red marks if one peered very closely with searching eyes.

Soni sympathised suitably, 'Tough woman your mum. Wow she really went to town. Here how about this tube of Smarties to make up. All right? Two tubes.' Backing out, clutching his Smarties, still threatening dire consequences he turned, and ran off down the street. Soni reached into a corner and brought out another deckchair. Unfolding it, she sat down and stretched out her legs. 'He came in to buy cigarettes. Had a note saying they were for his grandmother. Dad fell for it and sold him a packet. Next time he tried it on me. Known his mum for years. If he's got a grandmother they must have had her hidden in Siberia. Wouldn't have fallen for it anyway, tried all that myself when I was younger, in my long-lost youth. I tell you, sometimes running a shop is like running the social welfare department. Had a battered woman here the other day. Susie-sacrifice I used to call her. Swore for years she wasn't battered. Just accident prone. One day he went too far, started in on their little girl and she finally, finally, finally asked for help. Tony worries me,' suddenly changing tack. 'Lots of kids like him you know. Let him get a little bigger and he'll want to flex his muscles, prove his "bottle",' Kuli winced and Soni looked up at her, checking to see if she had got the meaning. 'It's not among strangers any more you know. They leave school – get whiter, want to be fighters, serve their Queen and country – reclaim the land for white. Ignorance is no excuse you know. No one can say there's racism only because they don't know enough about these 'coloured' folks. No fucking hell,' looking up at Kuli, ''scuse the language. No strangers, not when you've eaten the same yucky food at school. Talk too much don't I? The floor is yours ma'am. I'll make another tea.' Kuli said she would do what she could for the campaign, and that meant her utmost and asked for a favour from Soni, a promise to visit Rani/Rosalind. 'Sure, but you gotta sit down and have some more tannin. You know I'm surprised the racists are so stupid. Every time they attack they antagonise, some would say politicise. They push people over the sidelines into the action area. Some Asians think it's never going to happen to them. Especially the middle class. And when it does – zap go their illusions about England's fair and free land. 'Ere take some of these. On the house.' Throwing some vegetables into a bag for Kuli.

Sisters? and Sisters?

Silence. The home help has gone, he is out at work and the baby is sleeping. Kurshid wanders the house from top to bottom and back again, tracking, trying to catch up with thoughts that seem merely a step away. What do you do when you have everything that you've ever wanted? You tell yourself you are content. Then why the eruptions of emptiness? Why the desolation in knowing that if you stretch your arms out none will come and take your hand. People are out there, on the horizon, where you pushed them in the days of your self-obsessed, single-minded drive to get what you wanted. Why hanker for them now?

Had she always had these needs but never recognised them? Stopping near the hanging plant and picking off the dead leaves. Other people can't reach inside you, fill all your needs. And they are self-obsessed too. Shrugging her shoulders, as she fills her hand with crinkly brown. People are more interested in taking than giving, they'll take your time, your energy, your emotions: invite people into your life and you lay yourself open to all sorts of pitfalls. She didn't need to be bad/sad. Didn't need more than she had. Didn't even know what more it was that she wanted. Opening her hand, throwing the dead leaves into the bin. What happens to time, energy, emotions if they are left untapped?

Going up for another circumambulation she passes the phone and on a whim picks it up and, telling herself she's not really doing this, dials Kulwant's number, the very same number that had been her illicit line to him. It's engaged. Thankfully she replaces it. Then on second thoughts dials home and Shazia answers. Kurshid asks if anything needs to be done and offers to help. Shazia is suspicious and refuses. Kurshid's new intentions are too raw for her to argue. Insisting would seem like begging and she hangs up.

'Obvious she didn't really want to,' Shazia complained to Big Sis, 'so I'll make her do it.'

Pounding up Karm's stairs, Shazia was saying how she thought Rani's case was a shame but anyhow it didn't matter because Ammi's nightmares had stopped, but she did wish that stupid girl would wake up and live normal and let everyone get on with their lives. As it was, Ammi was getting as exhausted from keeping a vigil at her bedside as when Rani invaded her dreams. Leaning forward she helped herself to one of Karm's cigarettes. He moved the packet away from her and refused to give her a light. She walked into the kitchen and lit it from the gas stove. 'For my political guru you don't much believe in freedom. Anyhow I'm not staying long. Admit it. My interest must give you a thrill.' Karm suggested a game of chess. 'So you won't have to talk to me,' she taunted. 'Don't flatter yourself, you're only a passing sister in my life. Well it's better than saying platonic,' she expostulated, answering his enquiring look. 'You should consider it an honour. What did you think of my article?' Shazia was now writing regularly for the local alternative rag.

'Your writing would improve if you ran around less and did more thinking.' Shazia salaamed him, and said if he was going to slam her she could return it too. Karm raised his eyes heavenwards.

'God ain't there. She's here, in me. I'm not going to waste my precious holidays working in a shop. The next issue, the one after this, is on crime in the neighbourhood and the first people I'm going to write about are the local council, their criminal drive against squatters, and link it up with Rani's story. Some could hold you, Mr Chairperson of housing, responsible for her predicament.'

'Oh, on what premise?'

'Several: number one, not providing night shelters.'

'Would she have used them if we had?'

'Point is, you didn't.'

'We're funding the Asian girls' hostel.'

'Big deal. She's right to reject society. What's it got to offer her except council meetings, fat-arsed bureaucrats . . .'

'. . . amateur journalism from her sisters.'

'Shall I assume this is an interview?' Taking out her notebook.

'Learn to do things properly. Ring my secretary and make an appointment.'

'Goodness. We're not very happy today are we? What's happened?'

'Shouldn't you be out collaring the local capitalists for Shazia's propaganda sheet?'

'It's a collective effort, but you wouldn't know about that. Don't look fazed. I'll ring your secretary. Which nights does he work?' Disappointed in getting no reaction from him, she gets up to go. Karm was in a rotten mood today. She couldn't leave well enough alone and turned round at the door. 'What's the problem? Memories? Did you really have an affair with an Indian woman, the one with the . . .'

'Aspiring to gutter-journalism now?'

'I'm only asking for the truth in order to clarify rumours.'

'You'd like me to give you the dirt on your Asian sister? You don't think she has the right to privacy from your prying pen?'

'I'd only use it to lynch you. However thanks for confirming my suspicions. I reckon she and my sister deserve each other.'

'Pardon?'

'Nothing. Bye.'

Kulwant opens the door and stumbles over Caroline's bags. Caroline comes rushing in from the kitchen, food smells following fast behind her.

'Don't panic. No damage,' Kulwant reassures her. Getting up and brushing herself down. 'Going back?'

'Yes. I wanted us to have dinner together before I left.'

'Wedding bells?' asked Kulwant following her.

'Heavens no. Do you think two chillies or three?' holding them in the palm of her hand. 'They're not very big, but you know what they say: the smallest chillies are the sharpest.'

'Three if you can take it.' Kuli sat down, waiting.

'Anything you can, I can too . . .' trilling out the old song as she stirred them in. Putting the lid on the pan, Caroline came over to the table, a bottle of wine in her hand. 'It's very simple darling. I eventually decided what I wanted, and I think I've got it.' Uncorking it and pouring out the rich red liquid. 'I didn't want to lose Sid, neither could I accept his 'proposal' because once burnt, twice shy as they say. Insanity to put myself in that kind of danger again. My terror of history repeating itself would've thrown it off course from the start. We've agreed on a compromise. No marriage but we'll live together as a couple, openly, shamelessly. And that way I'll never feel secure.'

Helter-skelter to the Beginning

Soni and Maya meet over Rani's bed. Both giggle as they recognise each other. Ammi can't see the joke and tells them there's some tea in the thermos if they want it. Rishi is outside talking to Shanti but looks in on them. They giggle at his floppy hair, though neither could have said what was so funny about it. Soni is guarding herself, only allowing the shock to seep into her degree by degree. The sight of Rani's open unblinking eyes spooking her out of her usual effervescence.

Soni brings a chair to sit by Maya, talking about the extravaganza and the reactions of people to whom she had tried giving the leaflet. 'We's not alone in this world, you know, though judging by what people say you might think we was all on islands. People are so thicko, I do despair sometimes. Even if we linked our little fingers we'd change the world. And what are they all afraid of? Afraid of losing their lonely private lives? Their privacy to be cruel to each other in the four walls of their homes? Don't get me wrong. I'm not saying everyone should go off and live in a commune, or be a hippy or that kind of thing, it's just that we all need each other and we gotta do things for each other. Right? Or am I right! So you're all coming on the demonstration? Good. A few more won't do no harm.'

'I'll stay with Rani/Rosalind,' said Maya, 'and Ammi can go.'

'Nothing doing,' protested Soni, 'I want you all there, bring Rani with you. And I don't know why you people got her cooped up in here. I can see she's too weak to walk. Aren't you love?' leaning forward to pat Rani's hand, 'Never you mind.

197

Every solution has its problem. A wheelchair. That's all it needs. Come to think of it, we could go out for a whiff of the fresh you know whatsit right now. I'll go get it organised.' Exit Soni.

Enter Rishi wheeling in the chair followed by a nurse and a doctor. It should be all right, everyone said. Ammi explained to Rani, Soni standing at her shoulder. No response. Ammi, Maya and Rishi, the three who had been longest with Rani, came together to get her ready. Everyone held their breaths, waiting for a reaction, protest, some signal of life; nothing as they lifted her into the wheelchair, covering her with blankets. Rishi massaging her feet before putting them in a pair of slippers and Maya draping her shawl around Rani's shoulders.

Rani and her entourage proceeded out, Ammi holding Rani's hand, Soni keeping up a running commentary. Shanti was nowhere to be seen as they went down the corridor, around corners and into the hospital grounds. The procession wound its slow way along the footpaths, around the flower beds and out towards the exit. Soni steered the wheelchair, no one contradicting her choice of direction. Maya rummaged in her bag and brought out a camera, hopping in front to take pictures.

'Tomorrow,' said Soni, promising Rani a treat, 'we'll go all the way to my shop, have ice-cream, do a bit for the family coffers, work that is. Then I'll bring you back. But I ain't got too much of this spare time you know, you'd better hurry up and get better. Wouldn't mind some help in the shop come to think of it. 'Ello, 'ello, 'ello, who do we have 'ere?' Kulwant and Caroline coming with the daily provisions. 'Regular party you got going here Rani. Let's go in and see what's in them bags, not that me mouth's watering at what I can smell. No tip-tapping Aunty? Where's the stick?

Was that the flash of a blush that Soni's sharp eyes detected on Kulwant's face? 'I gave it to someone more deserving.'

'She realised it was time she stood on her own two feet,' interjected Caroline, nimbly avoiding Kulwant's kick at her ankle.

The smells, the aromas, invaded every inch, every corner of the room. Soni appropriated the barfi, ''scuse me sweet tooth', offered one to Rani, and not getting a response popped it into her own mouth. Taking another piece, she bit half and offered the other half to Rani, whose mouth opened and swallowed. The talk stopped and everyone stared. Soni was disgusted, told everyone to get on with their own thing and to pass over the pakordas, why should Rishi hog them all to himself. He didn't, because Soni and Rani finished them off, half by half.

The police were delighted to hear of these signs of returning life from the ward sister, and wondered what they could do to accelerate the process. Why not bring in Michael? Face to face confrontation often jolts the most amnesiac memory. The only thing they'd have to watch out for would be Michael's bad poetry.

Several days on and Soni and Ammi are bringing Rani back from the shop, both exhausted by the long walk. Before they lifted Rani back into the bed, they showed off her new shalwar kameez to Maya. 'One of me old ones but Rani took a fancy to it,' explained Soni modestly, 'It's comfortable. She can sleep in it.' Soni dashed off back to the shop and Ammi fell asleep on the folding bed. Rishi hadn't yet arrived and Maya absently sat stroking Rani's forehead, her mind cooking up ways to cook Prakash's goose, and mint sauce out of M.A.D. and Madd, oblivious to the ward sister sliding into the room followed in by Michael and two plain clothes officers.

Rani's high-pitched, unearthly, unending laughter brought her back to reality, to the strange smile on Michael's face, and the grins decorating everyone else. Ammi shot out of her sleep, rushing to Rani to quieten her. Nothing could still those vocal chords at long last released from bondage: jagged stones of sound hurtling and ricocheting off the walls, hitting everyone in the room.

Sister was murmuring sedatives when the door opened and Shanti stood framed in the doorway, her closed eyes on Rani and Rani's opened ones on her, the laughter rising to a higher pitch. Anger in Shanti's steps as she marches over, placing one hand on Rani's head, the other passing over Rani's eyes, closing them as her own open. Albino eyes blanking everyone with their stare. Remnants of laughter tearing out, gradually ceasing, breathing easing, falling back into sleep.

'Random Rani ran away
Ran to white while whitey waited
for Kuli-created sins to pay
Nemesis hurryin' on its way,
Access don't pay on judgement day
Whitey open de mouth,
and Black bats fly in whitey's daylight
Don't know nuttin 'bout cricket or fair play
England was a green and pleasant land –'

'Enough!' Kulwant's voice cuts across him, 'no more of your putrid self-pity.' Closing the door she goes over to Shanti, telling them all to leave. The sternness and authority in her voice brook no argument. The police officers promise to return later for a statement, the sister follows them out grinning like the cat who's got the cream.

'Didn't know you could drive,' says Maya admiringly, as she climbs into Kulwant's car. 'New acquisition?'
    'No, no. Years old. Been sitting in the garage.'
    'And that outfit's rather nifty. Years old I suppose. Been sitting in the wardrobe?'
    'No, no. Brand new.'
    'And your pretending-to-be-an-eccentric-octogenarian regalia?'
    'Cleaned and back on the rails of Oxfam.'
    'What brings on the change?'
    'This and that. Here's your place. Hurry up and hop out. I've got to pick up the kids.'
    'Kids! You've got more kids hidden away?'
    'Grand-kids. A/A-Shirley's. Bye.'
    Maya watched Kuli driving away, a frown furrowing her forehead. What process/happening had changed Kuli's mind to make her change? How permanent was this new persona?
    Maya gulped in shock. M.A.D. and Madd were sitting on her doorstep. Rani had become big news. They wanted her and they knew that Maya was an active participant in the drama. Would Maya consider . . . Maya invites them in, licking her lips in satisfaction. She unearths the notes on their Mad idea and

holding their eyes rips the papers into tiny little pieces, throwing the conflict confetti into the air.

Rani's life is again an embryo, growing into gradual consciousness, each inhalation of oxygen feeding it with the will to live. Her past floating in disparate pieces troubling her new-found tranquillity. Awake, she opens her eyes a fraction, seeing someone new, feeding a baby and talking to Ammi. Kurshid had taken over Shazia's job of bringing a change of clothing for Ammi.

Rani listens to Ammi telling her story to Kurshid, recovering the time lost in her attempt to go away a second time, discovering the people who had cared for her, enabled her to come back. Her stomach rumbles with hunger betraying her eavesdropping. 'There's something about Rosco,' she says, sitting up. 'I have to tell someone.'

'No you don't,' was Soni's answer when she came in, 'Okay, if it'll make you feel better tell us. Captive audience. Nothing like it. Maya sweetie get your notebook. Get this down, straight, then replace their crazy idea, them TV people that is, with this. That all right with you RR? We gotta feed our writers with the blood of our reality. Can't let them go hungry, I do love going gothic. What's the matter? You look like a guppy fish.'

'Does Rani really want her life history splashed all over the little square screen?' asked Maya.

'I've got nothing to hide and a lot to tell.' Mother and daughter may be look-alikes but they parted company at the vocal chords, Shanti's bell-like voice, replaced in Rani by harsher, harder tones.

'It's too early for you to make this decision.'

'I won't be able to talk to you like this in prison, will I?'

'Don't have to sound as if you're looking forward to it,' accused Soni. 'Anyhow it might never happen. That'll scupper your martyr instinct.'

'The Justice people have to do their jobs. Strange just when I was ready to spend some time at home, mother's home.'

'Perhàps it won't be for long,' Maya encouraged.

Rani's smile wasn't one, 'Its not the time, its what I'll be when I come out. I could make a run for it. Joke joke,' seeing everyone's expressions of consternation.

'Maybe,' comments Maya who used to be myopic, 'maybe not.'

'Itchy feet!' complains Soni in disgust. 'And I thought you and me were gonna go into business.'

'She's a baby,' Ammi cuts in across their talking, covering Rani's hand with her own, transmitting skin signals of comfort. 'Give her a chance to grow into herself.' Rani's eyes are opened wide and large and Maya fears she's about to spin off into her internal orbit again.

'Reincarnation?' questions Rani, her voice a scraping saw. 'The difference is, I remember. Maya, take the past and plaster it all over the damn place.'

'Hurray! Yippee,' Maya gets up and does a little dance. 'They already done asked me and I said I'd think about it, 'cos I didn't think you were ready for me to even ask you if you'd even consider it let alone say yes.' Sitting down at last and hugging herself in delight, 'And I've got full control over it. I made them promise that. And more money. Ooh Rani honey, you've done me a power of good.'

'Hmm,' commented Soni sourly. 'If I hadn't said anything you would have sat there mum and let another opportunity go down the drain. Maya baby, Rani here is a lot more together than you give her credit for, and you ain't half as sharp as you should be. If you're gonna get anywhwere Maya baby, you gotta move faster than a blizzard. Honestly Rani I don't blame you for wanting to get away, but you ain't half got a lot of catching up to do. Now, ready to tell us the tale?'

Rani wasn't because Rishi hadn't yet arrived, they'd have to wait.

The police arrived before Rishi ever did, and Rani spilled the beans, the others unable to stop her purging herself.

'Delicate problem,' said the senior officer, who was married to an Asian woman, 'but the law must take its course. She can't provide any witnesses, others have testified against her, and of course we can't discount Michael's statement, much of which this young lady has corroborated. It's inevitable that charges will be preferred.'

Rani was on bail but Shanti refused to have her back home.

Kuli said quickly, 'I've got lots of space at my place and Caroline's left the room all spick and span.'

Maya visited Shanti and asked her why, incredulity vibrating through her words, why after all this time of searching and suffering? Shanti was sitting in the wickerwork chair, her charkha standing idle in a corner, her eyes on the television set, engrossed in the convoluted long spun yarn of a Bombay movie. Shanti pressed the button for pause, freezing the film hero in the middle of a supposedly seductive song, his mouth wide open to the elements.

'She's found, she's safe,' said Shanti, 'she's come back from the dead. That's good. I didn't know her when she was here, I don't know her now.'

'But she's your daughter,' expostulated Maya. 'What's the problem? You're angry? You want her to ask your forgiveness?'

Shanti shot her a look, and Maya squirmed like a worm. 'A child can ask for unconditional love and protection; an adult has to earn it. Would you live with someone who despises you?' Maya opened her mouth, then shut it without saying a word. Shanti gave a little laugh, switching on the video, unfreezing the hero. 'However, I have been to see Soni, to ask her how to organise a campaign of defence . . .'

Everyone was roped in, Shanti pushing them all into overdrive, a terror curling under her calm exterior, fear that she would lose her daughter, not only twice, but thrice. The second time to the law and the third to Rani's own anger. Would Rani take the trouble to go beyond her own emotions? Would Rani understand that she must now meet her mother person to person, justify herself: adult to adult?

Shanti visited the Asian Centre, programmed Asha and Farida into action; they had been reluctant citing all the other cases needing as much attention as Rani's. 'These people are not going to jail. Rani may. You can pick them up afterwards.' None could gainsay those glinting white eyes. Big Sis arranged the legal representation, assuring Shanti that it was the very best firm she could go to. Shazia ran the story in her news sheet, full of satisfaction at this dramatic turn of events: all the separate items coming together in one story, miles and miles of mileage to be had out of it. Kulwant visited her sons and gathered sizeable donations of money from them for the defence campaign, unable to extract promises that they would come and give their time too. 'Mum, back on form!' said Anup with a smile. Kulwant didn't smile back.

'Don't imagine it's just for you!' Rani recoiled in surprise. It was the first time she'd ever heard Maya raise her voice. 'And don't imagine that you're unique. That skin of yours means we all go in the dock with you. Understood? We know you did it. Everyone knows you did it. You've made sure of that, OK I'm not blaming you. But you ought to know by now this country don't take too kindly to darkies hurtin' one of their whities. Even if it was in self defence . . .'

'I can do my own political thinking thanks.'

'Then stop carping and start helping.'

Rani couldn't, for she didn't believe; however Maya's anger placed a gag on her tongue, though her eyes were as X-ray as ever and she saw that the world was still the same ghastly place she'd tried to evade. Kuli agreed.

'You lie, you love it,' said Rani.

'Then why did you, my little Sleeping Beauty, bother to come back? Michael give you the Kiss of Life?'

'No,' she says, 'not Michael. Rosco.' Rosco's eyes had died begging for a little more of life. He'd lost it, she'd come back to it, what was she to do with it? Ammi was right, she'd have to be a baby and consciously grow herself all over again. Into what?

Meanwhile Back at the Reservation

     Pavan offered the Rani campaign a room in their house, and use of the telephone. Anup immediately had a new line installed, and despite his aloofness couldn't help watching and annotating all he saw, seeing a new chapter for his book. Kurshid helped Ammi in all the jobs she took on, taking care to stay in the background, as though her wings would get burnt if she came too near Kulwant. Caroline's café became a meeting place and Maya said she couldn't stand all this collectivism and was off to the Old Blokes' club and had anyone bothered to tell them?

They pounced on her as soon as she entered, Anton's dog yapping at the fringes, left out of the crowd. Rani's story was all on their lips. Desperate for an update they sat her down, shooed Anton off to make tea, then sat in a circle around her, ready for the latest.

Heads shook in commiseration as they talked of her courage in defending herself, how they themselves were better off because they were only attacked for their colour, women were the target of any man with animal desires, and our women were in double danger, because of their colour. They decided unanimously, without discussion, that they would help Rani all they could.

. . . The Day Done Come

Kulwant smiled: Shirley had brought the children, dressed in Rani T-shirts, Karm had come with his old plastic bag, Kurshid and baby mingled with the Old Men's club and Bahadur and Anton had dyed their hair specially: green, white and orange spelling Rani. Shanti giving Asha and Farida Rani-flags to distribute, Shazia hopping round with her note-book, pen busy scribbling, Angie gazing gooey-eyed at Rishi, Soni giving last minute instructions on the slogans, Maya deep in consultation with the Director and Producer, who have come to capture the proceedings on celluloid, waving a hand at Kulwant as she catches her gaze, inviting her over. Kulwant shakes her head. Pavan comes over to say Anup will be joining them later.

'What are you planning?' asks Pavan, tilting her head.

'To live.'

'Doing what?'

'Earning my keep for a start. Isn't that the first principle of life. Feed thy stomach, warm thine body, sleep thou under a roof. Rani must feel something similar. It's frightening, coming back to life.'

'Can I have some comments please, on your role in this case?' Shazia landing up by them, pen poised over paper. 'We don't run to tape recorders yet.'

'I don't think I have anything relevant to say,' mumbled Kuli, quickly moving away and coming face to face with Karm.

'Nice day,' he says, 'no rain.'

'But you can never trust English weather.'

'Get ready everyone, we're going to do some shooting,' Maya rushes over, preparing them. 'Hey, you Soni, get back here. Half an hour before the trial starts.'

'Wanted a good seat,' grumbles Soni.

'This isn't a show and the real work is out here, not sitting in there on your bum.'

'I think I'd rather have the old Maya back who couldn't say boo to a goose.'

'I'll sort you out later. Are we all ready? Ready Kuli?'

'Ready to try.'

The Director shouts ACTION!

Nina Sibal
Yatra

(The Journey)

A hugely exuberant and complex novel from a talented new writer, set against the massive canvas of the Punjab, and a background of political unrest, of India's struggle for independence, Partition and the search of the Sikh people for an identity of their own.

The novel centres upon Krishna, a woman without property who is mysteriously able to assimilate the passionate and bloody histories of her ancestors. As Krishna embarks on a *padyatra*, a pilgrimage for ecology through the Himalayas, she learns the lessons of those ancestors and is able, symbolically, to take possession of the whole world; to realise the importance of the environment to India and so, despite herself, to become a leader.

Nina Sibal has worked for over fourteen years in the Indian Civil Service in India and abroad; she is at present studying law. This is her first published novel.

Fiction   £5.95
ISBN: 0 7043 4019 5
Hardcover   £12.95
ISBN: 7043 5009 2

Rhonda Cobham
& Merle Collins, editors
Watchers and Seekers

Creative Writing by Black Women

Here at last is a major anthology of some of the most
exciting creative writing coming from Black writers living in
Britain. These are poems and short stories by African and
Asian women exploring their identity as Black; common to
all is a glorying in the creative potential of language to
illumine and exhilarate. The collection as a whole casts an
incisive eye on social and political issues affecting Black
women and on racism in Britain today.

Rhonda Cobham teaches English and creative writing at
Amherst College, Massachusetts.

Merle Collins is a poet whose published work includes
Because the Dawn Breaks and poems in the anthologies
Callaloo and *Words Unchained*.

Poetry/Creative Writing   £3.95
ISBN: 0 7043 4024 0

Padma Perera
Birthday Deathday
and Other Stories

'Hers is a gift to treasure' Tillie Olsen

A stubborn old woman vows to stay silent one day a week,
until her death becomes her loudest silence; two dubious
holy men wake a child to the irony of belief; an unjustly
dismissed schoolmaster demonstrates the uselessness of
hindsight . . .

Padma Perera's is a dazzling new talent. She has a faultless
sense of language, and the ability to draw her reader into her
world within a single paragraph. Her stories, most of them
set in India, have been published in the *New Yorker*, *Saturday
Evening Post*, *Horizon*, *Iowa Review* and elsewhere.

Fiction   £3.95
ISBN: 0 7043 3984 6
Hardcover   £8.95
ISBN: 0 7043 2874 7

Joan Riley
Waiting in the Twilight

When Adella, a talented seamstress, moves to Kingston,
Jamaica, life seems to promise much: a respectable career and
the chance of professional status. Instead she falls for a young
policeman who leaves her with two children. She is befriended
and married by Stanton, a carpenter, and sails for England to
join him. But Stanton too deserts her, for Gladys, Adella's
own cousin.

She resolves to buy a home of her own, but is forced into
sub-standard housing; in the end even this is taken from her by
the council.

Now a grandmother crippled by a stroke, Adella waits
patiently for her husband to return. Haunted by memories of
the past, she assesses what has been achieved. Her life,
apparently bleak, is sustained by her own generous love, and
the warmth of her children.

This is the moving story of a woman's struggle for dignity
against a background of urban racism. Riley pulls no punches in
her effort to portray 'the forgotten and unglamorous section
of my people' within a system which 'openly and systematically
discriminates' against them.

Joan Riley's first novel, *The Unbelonging*, was published by The
Women's Press in 1985.

Fiction   £3.95
ISBN: 0 7043 4023 2
Hardcover   £8.95
ISBN: 0 7043 5011 4

Joan Riley
The Unbelonging

Summoned to Britain by a father she has never known, eleven-
year-old Hyacinth exchanges the warmth and exuberance of
the backstreets of Jamaica for the gloom of inner-city London.
She finds herself in a land of strangers, the only black face in a
sea of white.

Faced at school with the hostility of her classmates, and at
home from her father with violence and a threatening sexuality
she does not understand, she seeks refuge in dreams of her
homeland — dreams which she must eventually test against the
truth.

Though academic triumphs help, for Hyacinth the real search is
for identity and a place in the world. In her first book black
novelist Joan Riley paints a vivid portrait of immigrant
experience in Britian, refusing to compromise by romanticising
its harsh reality.

Fiction   £2.95
ISBN: 0 7043 3959 5
Hardcover   £7.95
ISBN: 0 7043 2861 5

Suniti Namjoshi
The Conversations of Cow

Suniti and Bhadravati disagree about almost everything —
which is hardly surprising as Suniti is an average middle of the
road lesbian separatist and Bhadravati is a Brahmin lesbian
cow, goddess of a thousand faces and a thousand
manifestations.

Suniti has been unlucky in love and thinks she is becoming a
misogynist. So it's only natural that when Bhadravati
transforms herself into a woman, Suniti decides to become a
goldfish (or perhaps a poodle or another cow). When
Bhadravati manifests herself as a man, things can only get
worse.

Fiction   £2.95
ISBN: 0 7043 3979 X
Hardcover   £7.95
ISBN: 0 7043 2870 4

Kali for Women (editors)
Truth Tales
Stories by Indian Women

Shubha the doctor, Shakun the dollmaker, Jashoda the wetnurse, and Tiny's Granny, the polished and accomplished beggar 'famed for her sleight of hand', are just a few of the many memorable women to be encountered in these assured and skilful stories.

Here at last is a chance to explore India's *popular* literary tradition – a flourishing tradition which includes a wealth of writing by women and which has hitherto been unavailable in Britain. Translated from Bengali, Urdu, Hindi, Marathi, Gujarati and Tamil, these stories offer a rich mosaic of Indian life (town and country life, young people and old, wealth and poverty) and represent some of the most dynamic trends in Indian writing today.

Fiction   £3.95
ISBN: 0 7043 4001 1
Hardcover   £8.95
ISBN: 0 7043 5000 9

Sharan-Jeet Shan
In My Own Name
An Autobiography

From childhood, Sharan-Jeet had a mind of her own. She chafed against the restrictions of her status as a girl in the Punjab, subject to the authority now of her father, in the future of a husband. So she set out to train as a doctor, but when she fell in love with a Muslim the full wrath of her Sikh family descended upon her. She was taken out of medical school, locked up, beaten, and eventually forced into an arranged marriage...

Even when her marriage carried her to a strange country, she didn't give up. The story of how she struggled to assert her own autonomy and establish a home of her own is one of extraordinary courage, faith and determination.

Autobiography/Black and Third World Women's Studies   £3.95
ISBN: 0 7043 3974 9

Farida Karodia
Daughters of the Twilight

Meena, youngest daughter of an Indian father and 'Coloured'
mother, grows up in a suffocating backwater in South Africa in
the 1950s. These are the years when apartheid is under
construction and Meena, quiet and introspective, watches her
family respond in different ways as the pressure on their lives
rapidly mounts. Yasmin, her sister, escapes to a private school,
imitating the 'white' social world of riding lessons and 'coming-
out' balls, which leaves her ill-prepared for the realities she
must face; her father refuses to believe that 'the law' will really
dispossess him of his home and business; and her mother
desperately juggles the day-to-day needs of the family with
ever-threatening poverty.

Yet even as the family is robbed of its home and livelihood, and
Yasmin's cruel tragedy begins to cause the family to
disintegrate, the overpowering impression is one of the
strength, dignity and indomitable spirit of women in adversity.

Fiction   £3.95
ISBN: 0 7043 4017 8
Hardcover   £7.95
ISBN: 0 7043 5007 6